Parker peered down at the small bundle of pink resting in the crib.

He'd been taken with the little imp since she'd emerged, red as a beet, from her journey into the world. Her face had been wrinkled, her hair plastered down, and Parker had thought her beautiful, a miracle, a veritable princess.

She had grown since then, almost alarmingly so. She was less creature and more person now, a genuine pixie who giggled and flirted and generally enthralled. To Parker she was a fairy child, an angel without wings.

And his now. His alone.

"Oh, princess," he whispered, bowing his head to lay his cheek against her tiny face and hide his tears. "I don't know how we're going to go on, but somehow we will. I promise. Somehow we'll go on—together."

Dear Reader,

Well, it's that loving time of year again! Yes, it's February—
and St. Valentine's Day is just around the corner. But
every day is for lovers at Silhouette **Special Edition,** and
we hope you enjoy this month's six novels dedicated to
romance.

The February selection of our THAT SPECIAL WOMAN!
promotion is *Sally Jane Got Married* by Celeste Hamilton.
You met Sally Jane in Celeste's last Silhouette Special
Edition novel, *Child of Dreams.* Well, Sally Jane is back,
and a wedding is on her mind! Don't miss this warm,
tender tale.

This month also brings more of your favorite authors:
Lisa Jackson presents us with *He's My Soldier Boy,* the
fourth tale in her MAVERICKS series, Tracy Sinclair has
a sparkling tale of love in *Marry Me Kate,* and February
also offers *When Stars Collide* by Patricia Coughlin,
Denver's Lady by Jennifer Mikels and *With Baby in Mind*
by Arlene James. A February bevy of beautiful stories!

At Silhouette **Special Edition,** we're dedicated to
publishing the types of romances that you dream about—
stories that delight as well as bring a tear to the eye. That's
what Silhouette **Special Edition** is all about—special
books by special authors for special readers.

I hope you enjoy this book, and all of the stories to come.

Sincerely,

Tara Gavin
Senior Editor

Please address questions and book requests to:
Reader Service
U.S.: P.O. Box 1325, Buffalo, NY 14269
Canadian: P.O. Box 1050, Niagara Falls, Ont. L2E 7G7

ARLENE JAMES

WITH BABY IN MIND

Silhouette®

SPECIAL EDITION®

Published by Silhouette Books

America's Publisher of Contemporary Romance

SILHOUETTE BOOKS

ISBN 0-373-09869-3

WITH BABY IN MIND

Printed in U.S.A.

ARLENE JAMES

grew up in Oklahoma and has lived all over the South. In 1976, she married "the most romantic man in the world." The author enjoys traveling with her husband, but writing has always been her chief pastime.

Chapter One

Kendra smiled at the five people trying to make themselves comfortable amid the jumble of cardboard boxes that cluttered and crowded her small living room. It was so sweet of them to make this gesture. They had surprised her by showing up on her apartment doorstep nearly an hour earlier, toting bottles of champagne and teasing her about being underdressed for a gala farewell dinner at one of her favorite restaurants. It was meant to be a larger party, but some of "the gang" were running late, as usual. At least it was usual for the Sugarmans; well, Parker, anyway.

Marriage had had a definitely steadying effect on Nathan Sugarman. His wife had proved to be the anchor that his drifting life had needed. Though five years Parker's junior, Nathan had shown every evidence of following in his older brother's footsteps until a saucy young real-estate agent by the name of Candace had snared his heart and put a ring on his finger. In the two years since, Nathan, who at twenty-nine was just a year older than Kendra, had become almost dull in his domestication. In truth, he had always been much more sedate than Parker. It was only after the death of their mother, just before Nathan had graduated from high school, that Nathan had begun to imitate his older brother's carefree life-style. Their father had left the family years before, and as far as Kendra knew, they had never heard from him since, so it was understandable that Nathan had looked to Parker as an example of manhood. Some said that the lack of fatherly influence also accounted for Parker's hedonistic ways, but Kendra was not so sure about that.

In the years since Parker had taken what he called "an active interest" in his brother's life, he had become a big part of the close-knit group of friends of which Nathan had been a member since elementary school. During that time the gang had experienced enormous changes as some had gone to college and others had moved in and out of various jobs in search of careers. Several of the group had married, only to divorce again as often as not, while others had drifted from one relationship to another, each introducing temporary additions to the informal club. Yet, the original membership remained intact, with only Parker—and to a lesser degree, Candace—surviving the many convolutions of the association, and in an odd way, all those changes seemed to have brought the group closer together.

As a consequence, Kendra had come to consider Parker as much a friend as Nathan. She saw and appreciated the many fine qualities Parker possessed, but she saw, too, the inherent wildness in Parker's nature, the impulsiveness, the need for the thrill, the unapologetic tendency to seek his own pleasure. So it was that she sat there, smiling at her friends, absolutely certain that whatever was holding up the Sugarmans could be laid squarely at Parker's feet. Honestly, sometimes that man could be so exasperating!

"Well, I don't know about the rest of you," said Walt Lyons, the tall, slightly balding, high school basketball coach, "but I've developed a mighty thirst."

"Right," agreed Jeanna Crowe, herself a public school teacher. "Are we going to just sit here staring at that bubbly all night, or are we going to toast Kendra's new endeavor?"

"Why not?" put in Dennis Scherer, twice-divorced construction subcontractor. "The Sugarmans are supposed to bring their own bottle, so we can just repeat the toast when they get here."

"But that isn't fair," worried Cheryl Randle, looking to her husband, Bill, for a solution. Sweethearts since seventh grade, theirs was one marriage in which everyone had a stake, the common judgment being that if Bill and Cheryl couldn't make it, no such thing as a happy marriage even existed.

"We'll save them their shares of our two bottles," Bill proposed smoothly. "Besides, knowing Parker, they're liable to be at least one up on us before they even get here."

"True," Cheryl conceded, and everyone laughed.

Kendra got up to locate some plastic cups, her glassware having been packed in storage for several days now. Searching among the boxes and excelsior in her kitchen, she finally came up with seven of the small disposable cups. As they were six people, that left only one cup for the three Sugarmans upon their arrival. Cheryl promptly volunteered to share a drink with her husband, leaving two cups for the latecomers, one of which Candace and Nathan, as the only other married couple in the group, could share, as well.

"Unless Parker prefers his straight from the bottle," Walt quipped.

"Maybe Candace will have a spare rubber nipple to put over its end," Dennis said, an oblique reference to the married Sugarmans' infant daughter and an obvious dig at Parker's tendency to overindulge in alcohol. Everyone laughed, but just then Parker's patented knock sounded at the door—one loud tap, followed by three light, quick ones—and the laughter turned to comical groans.

Kendra let him in to a chorus of, "Wouldn't you know it!"

He pecked Kendra on the cheek. "Sorry I'm late. Hey, all!" True to form, his gaze went instantly to the champagne. "Looks like I'm just in time, actually."

"I swear," Walt commented teasingly, "the man has a built-in sixth sense when it comes to corks about to be popped!"

"Damned right," Parker said over the chuckles, "and a seventh for willing women!"

"Women willing to be dumped, you mean," Jeanna commented cuttingly.

Parker swept back the sides of his nubby, cream silk sports jacket and slid long, graceful hands into the side pockets of pleated slacks the exact shade of dark burgundy as the formfitting turtleneck sweater he wore. At a touch over six feet in height and with shoulders seemingly as broad as the door at his back, he seemed to tower over Jeanna as she sat in the center of Kendra's low couch, and his smile was absolutely deadly.

"I don't dump women, Jeanna," he said smoothly. "I tell them up front that as soon as we've given each other what we both want, I'll be moving on . . . and then I do."

"Which?" Walt asked. "Give them what they want, or move on?"

Parker answered without ever taking his eyes off Jeanna's face. "Both."

Instantly Jeanna's cheeks flamed bright red, and her nostrils flared in a sure signal of suppressed anger. Not for the first time, Kendra wondered if something more personal than the intimacy of good friends had passed between Jeanna and Parker, and not for the first time, she felt a pang of dismay and disappointment at the possibility. The others were wondering, as well; it was on their faces, and suddenly, for reasons she couldn't begin to identify, Kendra couldn't stand it anymore.

She forced a smile, laid a companionable hand on Parker's shoulder and steered the conversation in another direction. "What about Nathan and Candace? Aren't they with you?"

He turned his full attention on her, his milk chocolate eyes like warm velvet. "I thought they'd be here," he said softly, adopting that husky voice that he reserved for the select few who currently rated highest in his affections.

Why she had lately made that short list was a mystery to Kendra, one to which she didn't give much thought out of a murky sense of self-preservation. It could, she supposed, have to do with the fact that she would soon be leaving on a yearlong sabbatical from her job as a pediatric nurse at one of Dallas's most revered children's hospitals to take a position as a volunteer on a medical rescue team sponsored by the United Nations. It wouldn't be the first time one of the group had absented themselves for an extended period, but it was certainly the first in a long while, hence this farewell party. A sudden fear seized her. It wasn't like Nathan to be late for an occasion such as this.

"You don't suppose something's happened, do you?" she asked nervously.

Parker's eyes darkened as he asked himself the same question.

"Naw," Walt declared. "Probably the baby-sitter was late."

"Candace would have called," Cheryl said flatly.

"A flat tire, then," Dennis proposed.

"Nathan's got a phone in the car," Parker reminded them, one long-fingered hand coming up to stroke the cleft in his square chin.

"Maybe they got held up with a client," Dennis suggested helpfully. "It's happened to me often enough."

Kendra instantly relaxed. "That's it." Funny how certain she was, especially when she saw the doubt in Parker's brown eyes. "They'll arrive any minute now," she assured him. "Meanwhile, let's crack that champagne."

"Here, here!" came the cry, and soon they were all laughing again and passing a foaming bottle between them.

When the phone rang, they agreed that it would be one of the missing Sugarmans on the other end of the line, so when Kendra recognized the voice of her father, she felt an unfamiliar rush of regret.

"Oh, hello, Dad," she said loudly enough to inform the others. Then regret turned slowly to disbelief and finally to horror as she listened to Daniel Ballard's emotion-clogged voice inform her that the worst had indeed happened. She was trembling, tears spilling from her eyes, as she lowered the telephone receiver. It was Parker who first seized the significance of her grief.

"It's Nathan!" he declared with awful logic. "Nathan works for Dan Ballard."

Someone else said, "No!" Then another moaned, "Oh, God!"

Kendra nodded and burst into tears, thrusting the phone at Parker even as she threw her arms about him. He shoved her aside as if he could somehow save his brother, get to him through the telephone. She stumbled into Dennis, who had already come up to hug her, and then Jeanna was there, her face pale and drawn, terror in her eyes. Parker was shouting into the telephone, arguing with Dan as if that could change the message Dan had to deliver.

"What?" Walt demanded. "For God's sake, what's happened?"

Kendra looked at them all, tears blurring their shocked worried expressions. Cheryl was already crying softly into Bill's shoulder. They knew. Somehow they all knew, but she had to tell them anyway, had to confirm it with irrevocable words of pain.

"They're dead." Jeanna screamed, but Kendra went on as if she hadn't heard her, the words, first stilted, coming faster and faster as she spoke. "Nathan and Candace. A wreck on 635. They were in a company car. The police took the number from the sign on the door and called Dad at the real-estate office."

Parker was yelling, "No, damn you, no! Not my brother!"

All alone, Kendra thought numbly. Now Parker was all alone. She pulled away from Dennis and went to him again. This time he dropped the phone and threw his arms around her, sobbing brokenly. She bit her lip, wrapped her arms around him and held on tight.

"I still can't believe it." Dan Ballard wiped tears from his pale gray eyes with a big, rough hand, and sighed. "So damned young, and with so much promise. God, how will I run the office without them? You know I wouldn't have retired without Nathan there to take care of things."

Kendra nodded, blinking back her own tears, and smoothed the tablecloth with shaking fingers. "I know, Dad. Nathan was very important to the business, and Candace was a large part of it, too."

"Yes. And I was fond of her, so very fond of her. But that boy... Oh, that boy! I loved him like a son. I had even hoped, you know, that the two of you would—" He broke off, his mouth twisting between a smile and a frown.

Kendra covered his hand with her own much smaller one and squeezed. "I never knew you felt that way, Dad. I always thought of Nathan as a kind of brother, a buddy."

He nodded. "I could see that. Why do you think I never said anything?"

She lifted his hand, surprised, as always, at the weight of it, and pressed it to her cheek. "You know me so well. Sometimes I think you know me better than I know myself."

Dan Ballard turned his hand so that his palm rested against her cheek, and smiled, his eyes soft and shimmering with tears. "My little girl," he said. "I remember so well when you were born. Such a tiny baby. You frightened me, you were so small. I wasn't like Nathan. From the very beginning he's handled that little darling of his with such ease and—" He broke off groaning, his eyes clouded with pain. "Oh, God," he said, "the baby! What in heaven's name is going to happen to that precious little baby?"

Kendra pictured the little face, round and plump and cherubic, a puckered bow of a mouth, narrowed eyes black as night, turned-up nose and a wispy fringe of inky hair topping it all. Darla Gayle Sugarman was a beautiful infant, not wrinkled or red or featureless as some babies were prone to be, but an infant, nonetheless, and all the family Parker had left. She wasn't likely to be much comfort to him, poor little orphan. She was only, what, seventeen, eighteen weeks old? Kendra supposed that Candace's sister, Sandra, would care for the child. She was the only logical choice, really, being a well-known child psychologist with five little ones of her own. It was ironic, really, considering how Nathan and Candace had felt about Sandra's theories on child rearing. Still, she supposed there was no other choice. Kendra wondered if Parker would stay close to the child, be a part of her life. For his own sake, she hoped so, but she doubted that he would put forth the effort. A confirmed bachelor like Parker wouldn't have much dealings with infant children, and he was so broken and hurting that he probably couldn't think beyond his own grief for some time to come.

She wondered again if she should have let him go so soon after receiving the news, but what could she have done, really? After he'd pulled himself together, he had insisted that Edward White be called. He had things to do, arrangements to make, and Edward was not only his friend, but his lawyer.

Walt had made the call. It was understood that Kendra wouldn't want to make it herself. She had ended their engagement nearly six months ago, but no matter how firm her stance, Edward still offered to take her back, still held on to that last shred of hope that she would come to love him. That was one of the chief reasons she had embraced the medical volunteer program's solicitation with such enthusiasm. Maybe during her absence, Edward would find someone else upon whom to pin his hopes. She hoped so. She fervently hoped so. She liked Edward White, had always liked him, but that was all it had ever been, and she should not have tried to make it more. Well, it was too late for regrets of that kind.

Right now she was just thankful that Parker had Edward to look after him. One thing about Edward White, he was a good friend. He was also a good lawyer, but Parker need the friend more just now. Poor Parker. Poor, wild, crazy fascinating Parker. He was even more hurt, more grief-stricken than her father. The only person who had lost more than Parker had, was Darla, the Sugarmans' infant daughter, but she would have no memory of her parents, no true sense of loss. Sandra and Heath Pendleton would undoubtedly take care of her, and Edward would take care of Parker. That left only her father for Kendra to comfort, and even he did not really need her. He had Kate, though it amazed Kendra that anyone could derive any comfort from that cold, self-centered woman.

Speak of the devil. Right on cue, Kate opened the back door of Dan Ballard's house and walked in as if she owned the place. Kendra clamped her teeth together and watched helplessly as Dan got to his feet and went to the tall, blond, handsome woman with whom he had replaced his late wife. Deliberately, Kate set aside her briefcase and opened her arms. Dan stepped into them and closed his own around her.

"I'm so sorry I couldn't get here any sooner," Kate said. "I was taking a deposition in the Pollock case, and it took us forever to track this guy down and convince him to testify. I couldn't risk a postponement."

"I understand," Dan said gently, "but I'm awfully glad you're here."

"So am I," Kate said, and her eyes cut to Kendra. Immediately she adopted that brisk, competent manner which Kendra so hated. "Now, then," she said, patting Dan on the back, "first thing we need to do is get you into a hot tub of water so you can relax. Then I'll pour you a glass of wine, and we'll sit in front of the fire and talk. You can tell me all about it then. But first the tub."

Obediently Dan nodded. "I'd like that," he said.

No, Kendra thought, *he doesn't need me, not now.* She stood and slung the long strap of her purse over her shoulder. Dan lifted his head and turned to face her, an arm wrapped securely about Kate's waist. "You're not going, are you, honey?"

"I really should," Kendra told him. "I still have packing to do."

"Packing!" His voice rang with shock.

Kendra winced inwardly. But why should she stay? He didn't need her. No one did, no one here. But there were children in Africa dying of the most commonplace diseases. *They* needed her. Devon Hoyt, chief of the U.N. volunteer medical team, needed her. One of her professors in nursing school, he had sought her out, offered her this chance to be useful, to be needed.

She took a deep breath. "I've made a commitment, Dad, to a very worthy cause. I see no reason to back down now."

He took a step forward, mouth opening, but Kate clamped a hand down on his forearm, and immediately he closed his mouth and halted. *Of course,* Kendra thought bitterly. He would argue with her, but not with his precious, oh-so-sensible, cold-as-ice Kate. She bit back a complaint, knowing it was useless. As puzzling as Kendra found her hold on him, there was no doubt that Kate Ridley wielded more influence with her own father than she did. So be it. She was tired of fighting this particular fight. She had long ago said all she had to say on the matter, but even knowing how she felt, Dan still fancied himself in love with Kate. Kendra did not understand her father's choice of a girlfriend. Kate Ridley was as unlike her mother as another woman could be. But it was his life, as Edward had so often told her.

Yes, she was going to Africa. No doubt it was for the best. Maybe by the time she got back, she would have this relationship between her father and Kate in better perspective. She hoped so. She honestly hoped so.

Putting on a smile, she walked around the table and into the center of the kitchen. Going up on tiptoe, she placed a kiss on her father's bristly cheek. "I'll be over again tomorrow. Maybe by that time we'll know when the services will be. Try to rest."

He nodded mutely, his arm still about Kate's waist. Kendra tried not to mind. "Good night," she said softly and turned away. By the time she had moved through the dining area and the living room to the front door, tears were spilling down her cheeks again. *Poor Daddy,* she thought. *He's going to miss Nathan and Candace so very much.* More, she feared, than he would miss her. Determinedly, she pushed that thought to the back of her mind. She would be back, and things would be better between them. Meanwhile, they would both miss Nathan and Candace, and so would the others. Poor Daddy. Poor baby. Poor Parker. And poor Kendra... poor unneeded Kendra.

"Are you sure?" Edward asked yet again.

Parker tamped down his irritation and nodded. "She's my niece, and I told you, we discussed this not a month ago, Nathan, Candace and I. It's what they wanted, whether they put it down on paper or not. They wanted *me* to take care of her, and that's what I'm going to do."

"It's not going to be easy, old buddy," Edward pointed out. "You don't know anything about babies."

"Neither did Nathan until he had one," Parker countered stubbornly.

"But you're not Nathan," Edward reminded him gently. "Have you thought of what you'll be giving up if you take an infant? The parties, the women, the freedom..."

"Don't be absurd," Parker said lightly. "So I have to keep more regular hours, be more discreet. You're talking like I'll have to join a monastery and take a vow of chastity! It won't be that bad. Besides, what else can I do? I promised my brother that if anything happened to him, I'd take care of his little girl—and that's exactly what I'm going to do.''

Edward sighed. ''All right, if that's the way you want it.''

''It's not the way I want it,'' Parker said. ''It's just the way it is.''

''I understand, '' Edward told him, ''and I must say, Parker, I admire you for this.''

''Don't,'' Parker said. ''Don't admire me, just help me.''

Edward nodded. ''I'll check on the will tomorrow. Meanwhile, I'd advise you to get in there and take physical custody of the child.''

''Right,'' Parker said, but still he sat there in Edward's car, immobilized by the pain of loss. It seemed to him that he ought to be bleeding, that he ought to have gaping wounds all over his body. He could not quite believe that he was physically whole. With pain like this, he ought to have lost at least a leg or an arm, and yet he felt strangely numb. But he had to go in there. He had to face Mrs. Hoft. He had to face that little baby who didn't even know, who couldn't even grasp the awful fact that her parents were dead. But what terrified him most was facing a life without his brother and sister-in-law, going on alone. Alone, except for Darla. And Edward thought that was the way he wanted it. *Oh, Nathan,* he thought, *how can I do it without you?* But he would. No matter what he had to do, he wouldn't let down his brother, not in this. He took a deep breath and got out of the car.

Mrs. Hoft answered the doorbell on the first ring, dabbing at her eyes with a rumpled tissue. The look on her face, however, announced her disappointment and disapproval quite loudly. Parker squared his shoulders.

''I've come for the baby,'' he said. Then he added, ''My lawyer is waiting in the car.''

Mrs. Hoft raised her sagging chin. ''I told you over the phone, Mr. Sugarman, that I'm not convinced this is the best thing. I've called Mrs. Pendleton, and she agrees with me."

Parker grimaced. Sandra Pendleton was one of the most disagreeable persons he had ever met. Not only was she arrogant and overbearing, she clearly thought herself superior to mere mortals and a genuine intellectual. Even Candace had considered her own sister something of a kook, but somehow she managed to maintain a reputable standing with her colleagues, not to mention quite a following among laymen, thanks to her books on "complete" parenting. Sandra liked to say that her methods were a combination of "intellectual and cultural immersion coupled with the natural evolution of perspective," whatever that meant. To Parker, it was all pretty much a bunch of gobbledygook, and his brother and sister-in-law had shared his opinion wholeheartedly. Sandra Pendleton was going to raise his niece, his sole surviving family member, only over his dead body. He fixed Mrs. Hoft with a baleful glare.

"You had no right to do that, Mrs. Hoft. Nathan and Candace made their wishes in the matter quite clear. They wanted me to care for their daughter, and that's what I'm going to do."

"But, Mr. Sugarman," she cried, "you're a *single man.* You don't know anything about taking care of infants."

"I can learn."

"But in the meantime, that delicate babe's—"

"Going to be where she should be," he insisted flatly. "With me. Now stand aside, Mrs. Hoft, or be prepared to watch from the floor while I collect my niece."

"Sir, I think you should wait until Mrs. Pendleton gets here. Maybe she can make you understnd what you're proposing to undertake!"

He shook his head at that, his patience exhausted. With a sweep of his arm, he moved her safely aside and stepped though the door. The house was small and unsophisticated. He required only a moment to get his bearings. Confidently, he strode across the living room and down a narrow hall. The first door he tried led to a cramped bathroom. The second revealed a sewing room. The third contained a crib in addition to an old-fashioned bookcase bed. He walked softly to the crib and peered down at the small bundle of pink resting on its stomach. She was sleeping, her face turned away from him, and he knew instinctively that he ought to try to move her without waking her up, but the task seemed suddenly beyond his capability, and he felt a moment of genuine panic. Then the bundle moved.

An elbow, clearly distinguishable, lifted upward beneath the soft blanket. A muffled squawking emitted, and the bundle elongated. A tiny yellow stocking appeared from beneath the edge of the pink blanket, then withdrew. Finally, two tiny fists pushed out to flank the dark, silky head on either side and the supple little back arched to lift protruding buttocks upward. She was waking, all on her own. Gently Parker pulled away the blanket and turned the little one over with hands that seemed absurdly large. Darla yawned and stretched her supple body into a curve before settling down once more. She looked around her, fixed her big, dark eyes on his face and blinked a couple of times as if clearing her vision. Instantly, a smile parted her rosebud mouth. She knew him! And well she should.

He'd been taken with the little imp from the moment her proud father had presented her to her uncle clad only in a stocking cap, an undershirt, and an oversize disposable diaper. She'd been red as a beet and freshly bathed from the rigors of her journey into the world. Her face was wrinkled, her hair plastered down, her eyes vacant, her mouth seeking anything at all to latch on to, and Parker had thought her beautiful, a veritable fairy princess to have the whole of creation laid at her feet, a miracle. He'd been afraid to touch her and hungry to do so all at the same time, envious of the easy, proprietary manner in which her father had held her in his cupped hands.

She had changed since then, almost alarmingly so. She was less creature, and more person now, all creamy skin, sparkling eyes and coos. She had grown, too, more than doubling her weight, which wasn't saying much considering she'd weighed in originally at five pounds and five ounces. She was truly beautiful now, a genuine pixie, with silky ink-black hair, enormous dark eyes and a rosebud mouth. She giggled and flirted and generally enthralled all who fell within her sphere and according to her mom, had also developed some other less enchanting habits. But Parker had seen none of those. To him, she was a fairy child, an angel without wings—and his now, his alone.

"Oh, princess," he said, bowing his head to lay his cheek against her tiny face and hide his tears, "I don't know how we're going to go on without them, but somehow we will. I promise. Somehow we'll go on—together."

Chapter Two

Diaper bag, carrier/car seat, toy box, extra clothing, blankets, pacifier, stocking cap... Parker frantically went over the list in his head, terrified he would forget something important as he juggled baby, paraphernalia and mushrooming doubts.

He was halfway across the living room, Mrs. Hoft clucking and fluttering around him like a nervous, doomsaying chicken too fat for the hen yard, when it occurred to him that he didn't have so much as a bottle amongst all his burdens, and time was slipping away, bringing Sandra Pendleton ever closer. He really didn't feel up to taking on Sandra just yet, and who could blame him? His brother and sister-in-law were laid out on slabs in the morgue, bruised and scraped and utterly lifeless, foreign objects, never again to laugh or cry or love. Never again to make him feel as if he were a part of a genuine family, as if he belonged somewhere and to someone. As if he were needed, valued, made with a purpose in mind.

Who were going to be his cohorts in fun now? Who would laugh at his jokes and scold him enviously for his exploits? He had been a big brother for nearly as long as he could remember, but how could he be that now when he no longer had a sibling to be older to? It was not that he felt that the baby could fulfill any of his needs, for he did not. Rather, it seemed to him that the baby herself was all need, which only he could address. Perhaps he was no more next-of-kin than Sandra Pendleton, but he was the one chosen by her parents to care for her. He was the one they had told, not more than a month ago, to love her and care for her as his own if the worst should happen. And the worst had happened, the very worst.

The baby had begun to fuss now, and he clasped her infant seat tighter in an effort not to jostle her as he negotiated the living room. He'd have to forget the bottles for now. Getting her out of here before Sandra Pendleton arrived was more important. God forbid that his fairy princess should be left to that woman's ministrations. He could stop and buy bottles and formula on the way home. Home. Lord, where was he going to put her? He didn't have a nursery. He didn't have a baby bed. He didn't even have a bib! But he wouldn't think of that now. He didn't dare. He was already shaking fit to fall apart, but he wouldn't. He couldn't. Nathan and Candace had depended on him. Baby Darla, whether she knew it or not, depended on him, because he was all that stood between her and the resident kook, because he loved her with a fierceness that had surprised him from the beginning, because he was family, *they* were family and nothing and no one was going to take that away from him.

He didn't think what this would mean to his life-style, to his finances, to his emotions, to his *house*. He only thought of getting Darla safely away, of fulfilling his responsibilities to her and to a dead brother and sister-in-law, of keeping himself intact by centering his attentions and energies on something other than his overwhelming loss. He only thought of salvaging something of his family, of somehow going on, of shielding the innocent, tiny person in his arms from the same pain that was threatening to tear him apart.

He made it out the door and very nearly all the way down the walk before the Pendletons' trademark minibus came puttering around the corner. The contraption slid to a stop, and Sandra Pendleton bailed out, leaving her husband behind the wheel and her brood staring out the windows with avid curiosity. She was wearing a cowl-neck sweater beneath a denim jumper with a dropped waistline and a skirt that ended mere inches above her ankles. A lightweight fringed shawl had been slung about her shoulders, and her brown hair hung down her back in a thick, loose plait. On her feet were heavy sandals and pale blue socks. As an apparent concession to the chilly early October weather, she had tied a triangular scarf over her ears. She approached Parker with an outstretched hand.

"Give me the baby, Parker. You obviously don't know what you're doing just now."

"The hell I don't." He grasped the baby seat tighter, put his head down and kept walking.

Sandra clutched her shawl about her and hurried after him, speaking rapidly in a terribly reasonable tone of voice. "You've had a terrible shock, Parker. You've doubtlessly been up all night long, and you aren't thinking clearly. If you were, you'd see that you're totally unsuitable to play guardian to an infant."

"My brother and your sister didn't seem to think so," he retorted, yanking the back door of Edward's sedan open. "They told me that I was to act as her guardian, Sandra." He stuffed the baby and gear onto the seat and slapped the seat belt around them. "They told me, at all costs, to keep her out of *your* hands."

She smirked at him when he turned around, the door closed firmly behind him. "Oh, I know what they thought of my practice," she said lightly, "but they'd have changed their minds within a year or so. Of course, it might have been too late by then, but they would have seen, eventually, how far superior my patients are to the average child.''

"Patients?'' Parker scoffed. ''What patients? You only practice on your own children.''

"And reach countless thousands of others through my books.''

"Well, count Darla out,'' he said flatly. ''She's not going to be another of your experiments.''

"My methods have been proven quite effective by any number of—''

"Your methods mean nothing to me, '' he interrupted sternly. ''The promises I made my brother and his wife mean something to me. That little girl means something to me. You've got enough trained monkeys of your own. You don't need to incorporate someone else's child into the act. Now if you'll excuse me, I have some shopping to do.'' With that, he got into the car and closed the door, but Sandra Pendleton was not to be put off so easily.

She bent at the waist and thrust her freckled face close to the tinted window, shouting through the glass. ''This isn't the end of this, Parker. I have as much right to that child as you do. What's more, I have all the expertise required to care for her, and you have none!''

"Start the car,'' he told Edward, who obediently did as instructed. Deliberately, Parker depressed the button that lowered the window. ''You may think you're better suited to care for little Darla than I am,'' he said to Sandra Pendleton, ''but I have one thing you can never have. I have my brother's blessing. In fact, it was his *express wish* that *I* care for his child in the event of his death—his wish *and* his wife's.''

"Maybe so,'' Sandra said, ''but I won't believe it until I see it, and even then I'll fight you. I will not abandon that child to such as you, Parker Sugarman, not even on your very best day.''

Parker calmed the pounding of his heart and lifted a hand, palm stretched out flat, to point in Edward's direction. ''Sandra,'' he said smoothly, ''meet my lawyer, Edward White. I think you'll be wanting to get in touch with him."

Edward smiled and dropped the transmission down into Drive. "Anytime, Mrs. Pendleton," he said cheerily. "Anytime."

Sandra narrowed her eyes at both of them as if memorizing their faces so she could identify them in court. Then she nodded curtly and stepped back. The car pulled away from the curb, and Parker put up the window, aware only then that the baby was fussing steadily. Edward's smile had dissolved into a frown of doubt, and Parker felt himself beginning to tremble again, but determination made him look forward.

"Get me to a drugstore," he said, "and for God's sake, Edward, find me a piece of paper with Nathan's name on it and his wishes clearly spelled out for all to see. I won't give her up. I'll never give her up."

Edward opened his mouth as if to comment, then seemed to think better of it and closed it again. Parker pushed away the dozen or so niggling doubts that were plaguing his peace of mind and twisted around in his seat to pat at the baby ineffectually.

By the time they reached the nearest drugstore, Darla was howling. Parker knew she was probably hungry, but he didn't have so much as an empty bottle to offer her. The only thing he could think to do was to plug her up with the pacifier, but his sweet little angel took one good pull, realized she'd been duped and spit that thing right back at him, screeching like a banshee. He was shocked to see it bounce off the bottom of her car seat and tumble onto the floor mat. More shocking still was the obvious anger that twisted that cherubic face into a red mask of outrage. She looked positively murderous, enraged, and Parker was surprised to find that he was hurt, literally wounded. It wasn't rational, of course, and he knew that, but he was doing the best he could, after all, and doing it while holding himself together by the most tenuous of means. And she was a four-month-old baby who had come to expect having her meals delivered on schedule. As the car drew to the curb, Parker reached into the back seat to stroke her distorted face.

"All right, sweetheart. I understand, and I'll hurry."

"You'd better," Ed murmured, "or we'll both be screaming."

Parker gave him a droll look and got out of the car. He all but ran into the store and up to the counter, then practically accosted the teenage girl working there. "Give me everything I need to take care of a baby," he demanded.

She blinked at him and turned away to speak to an older woman stocking vitamins on a low shelf. Groaning, the woman got up off her knees and indicated that he should follow. The array of baby care items was overwhelming. There were eight different brands of formula, twice as many types of diapers, half as many kinds of nipples and pacifiers, not to mention specially designed dishes and flatware, medicine dispensers, toys, clothes, even something called "bumper pads." Did babies have bumpers? he wondered. Upon second thought, he reasoned that Darla undoubtedly had everything she needed at home, at Nathan's. What he really needed now was something to feed her and something to feed her with, but which of the many items offered would be the right ones?

With some none-too-patient prodding, he discovered which formula the clerk felt was best. Faced with a choice of small cans of ready-to-feed, large cans of concentrate and canisters of powder, he grabbed some of each and went on to bottles and nipples. The choices there made his head swim, but a little discussion caused him to remember that Candace had been breast-feeding. The clerk seemed to think that mandated use of a certain type of nipple, which in turn required a certain sort of bottle. Parker squashed the sad feelings engendered by the thought of Candace holding her little one to her breast and gratefully accepted the middle-aged woman's advice. For good measure he snatched up a couple of new pacifiers, a bib, a package of baby wipes and two different sizes of disposable diapers.

After paying cash for his haul, he sprinted back to the car and found Edward in the back seat bouncing a gurgling baby on his knee. Parker felt a stab of resentment. She howled for him; she gurgled for Edward. But just then that pixie face screwed up, and she opened her mouth and screamed through toothless gums. Edward shot Parker a harried look.

"About time! I hope you got diapers because this is a ripe package you've got here."

"I got everything we need. Now will you just trade places with me, or do you want to try your hand at changing her?"

Edward plopped the crying baby down onto the seat and nearly bowled Parker over getting out of there. Parker shoved his packages onto the floorboard and climbed in on top of them. The most appalling odor instantly assailed him, gagging in its intensity. His first impulse was to look at his feet to see if he'd stepped in anything he shouldn't have, but even as he did it, he knew that was not the source. With cold, dead certainty, he looked to his niece, who was again wailing at the top of her lungs.

"Crap!"

"Precisely," Edward said from outside the car.

"And you were bouncing her on your knee!" Parker accused. "What the hell did you think you were doing?"

"I haven't the foggiest idea," Edward announced through the window. "But at least *I* am willing to admit it."

Parker glowered at him, but deep down he knew that Edward was right. Still, it couldn't be all that difficult. He could learn and learn swiftly—though he had no illusions about the process being pleasant. He took a deep breath, which was a big mistake, and spent the next several seconds coughing and clearing his throat, but then it was time to get down to business.

First, he took off his jacket, folded it and draped it over the back of the front seat. Next he pushed up the sleeves of his turtleneck sweater. A quick hands-off examination of the squalling stranger, who was kicking and batting her arms against the leather car seat, revealed suspicious stains near the bends of the tops of her legs on the one-piece pink jumpsuit she wore. It would be wise, he decided, to protect the surface of the seat. Rummaging quickly through the diaper bag, he came up with a lightweight blanket embellished with bunnies wearing pink and blue bows. This he spread across the seat beside her. Then, ever so gingerly, he picked her up beneath the arms and transferred her to the blanket. She quieted for a moment and rammed her fist into her mouth, sucking industriously. Welcoming any reprieve from that ear-splitting wail, Parker set to work divesting her of that soiled jumpsuit. The first parting of a snap ended the respite. Her face curdled, and she began to scream.

"Dar-r-la, give me a break!"

Just the sound of her name seemed to calm her a bit, so he kept talking.

"Just let me clean you up, babe, and we'll get on to dinner. A few more snaps..."

He opened the suit all the way up, then tugged at the foot, one forefinger slipping beneath her small, pudgy knee to ease it out. Gosh, but she was soft, like buttered silk. Her little foot popped out, and she clenched her toes, her wail resuming its former glass-shattering decibels. Suddenly oblivious, Parker ran the tip of one finger down the sole of her foot, marveling as she arched it away from his touch.

"Oh, man," he breathed. "You are something."

The screams abated somewhat.

"Like a doll with working parts," he went on, stripping the other leg free. He grimaced, but kept talking. "How anything so tiny and delicate can stink so bad is beyond me. Is this what's called baptism by fire? Well, if your daddy managed, so can I.'' He wondered if she understood so much as a single word.

Whether she did or not, she seemed to be listening. The crying was on automatic now. Her mouth was open and sound was coming out, but her eyes were on Parker now, somewhat apprehensive but hopeful. He took one look at the diaper and frowned grimly.

''Yuck.''

It was dark and soggy nearly to her waist. He needed something to clean her with. Baby wipes. He dug around in the diaper bag and came up with the foil packet. Pulling open the flap, he extracted four of the moist paper towels and laid them on the seat beside her, then reluctantly began to peel back the tapes on the sides of the diaper.

''No offense, kid,'' he said as jovially as he could manage, ''but this isn't my idea of a good time. What do they call it? Quality time? I wouldn't want to rate this experience. It'd be a definite subzero. How about a little cooperation, hmm? I'm new at this, you know.'' He had gotten the diaper open, nearly shredding the plastic covering in the process, and folded it back. ''Oh, God.'' He thought, for a moment, that he was going to bring up the contents of his stomach, which couldn't be much, but the next moment it passed. He told himself that after what he'd come through in the past few hours, he could face any unpleasantness, and he knew it was true.

Determinedly, he took up the first towelette and went to work. Almost immediately a new problem presented itself. What to do with the soiled towel, not to mention the diaper? He gnawed at his lip, glanced around him and remembered the plastic bag in which he'd carried his purchases. Quickly, using one hand, he dumped the contents of the bag onto the floor beneath his feet. The towelette went into the empty bag, and he employed another, talking as he worked. All four towels were used to clean her front, and then the heavy work began.

Gathering her tiny feet into one hand as he'd seen her mother do, he lifted her puffy little butt off the diaper and took a peek. Two things happened next. She shut up instantly—the sound cut off in mid "waah"—and he dropped a four-letter word completely unfit for a little girl's ears, even one who couldn't understand a syllable of English and was covered in slimy dark green excrement from her legs all the way up her back to her shoulder blades. He let her down and ripped six more towelettes—all that remained—from the package, then lectured her sternly.

"Now see here, Darla Gayle, that's no way for a young lady to act. You're going to have to get over this ugly little habit, and you might as well know it now. From here on out I'll tolerate dainty little doodles deposited circumspectly in the seat of a dry diaper, at least until you're old enough to walk, at which point you'll toddle your little behind off to a potty and do your business there. Got that?"

She stuck her fist in her mouth, slurping loudly. After a second or so she wrinkled up her nose, and Parker recognized the signs of an impending wail. He grabbed her ankles and pulled them up. She whimpered and grunted but otherwise remained silent. He yanked the diaper out from under her and got it into the plastic bag, using only the tips of two fingers, then picked up a fistful of wipes and started wiping. In the end, he had to remove her arms from the sleeves and get the suit out of the way, too. After a moment's consideration, he dropped it into the plastic bag with the diaper and soiled wipes, saying, "I'll buy you another one."

Her only reply was a smacking sound and a grimace. Her fist, apparently, made an unsatisfactory pacifier, and he knew his second reprieve was coming swiftly to an end. He rolled her onto her tummy and completed the cleanup, then picked her up, naked as the day she was born, and folded over the blanket before laying her back down. She started to scream, and he sighed.

Edward tapped on the window. "Aren't you through yet? People are starting to give me strange looks."

"Get in the car!" Parker snapped.

Edward got in and started up the engine. Darla cried, and Parker thought about joining her, but as the adult on the job, he remained determinedly dry-eyed as he wrestled a clean diaper into place and taped it down. It seemed damned unfair, but the past fifteen hours had been one long, hateful lesson in just how unfair life could be. Parker pushed such depressing thoughts out of mind and addressed his unhappy niece.

"Believe me, kid, I know just how you feel." She didn't seem impressed, but he didn't let that bother him. He had to get her dressed.

A resigned investigation of the diaper bag produced a green nightgown, a pair of the tiniest blue jeans he'd ever seen and a pair of delicate, lace-edged socks. He put them all on her while she alternately wailed and sniffled, then placed her in the car seat and belted her in.

"You can get moving now," he told Edward.

"Thank God! I've been expecting the cops to show up for the last fifteen minutes."

"Ha-ha. Very funny."

"Who's joking? Child abuse is a federal offense."

"So is lawyer abuse. Shut up and drive."

"Aye-aye, Cap'n."

"In your eye, shyster."

Edward shook his head, but Parker saw his smile reflected in the rearview mirror. Tying a knot in the top of the plastic bag containing the debris of this poignant experience, he instructed Edward to pull over at the first roadside litter barrel he found. Tying up the bag helped subdue the odor, not that Parker was even aware of it anymore. He felt suddenly weary to the bone and immune even to Darla's cries, which had become pitiful, throbbing wails of despair.

"Okay, okay. Almost there," he told her, scrubbing his hands with a monogrammed handkerchief extracted from his hip pocket. That done, he found a can of ready-to-feed formula, a bottle and a nipple. He punched two holes into the top of the can with the sleek pearl-handled pocket-knife he carried, poured formula into the bottle and screwed on the nipple. When he inserted the nipple into her mouth, she lapsed into silence, shuddered and latched on to it, grumbling even as she took long, hungry pulls. Parker smiled down at her wearily. "You're a real feisty little imp, aren't you? More trouble than a motorcycle gang, greedy as a banker, smelly as a skunk—and I'll fight anybody who tries to take you away from me. Anybody."

He gazed down at her, that sad, weary, loving smile on his face, and completely missed the look Edward bounced off the the rearview mirror at him. It was a look of concern, worry and doubt, the look of a lawyer who knew he could well be on the losing side of his most important case, the look of a man in fear for his best friend.

He had never been so tired in his life. He had missed nights of sleep before, but never had he been so tired. Parker sighed against the surface of the coffee in his cup and took desperate solace in the silence.

Darla had cried all night except for brief snatches of sleep that had seemed merely to fortify her for the next bout of screaming. At about dawn he had cried with her, and not just a trickle of silent tears but an uncontrollable cascade of racking sobs and misery so heavy that he'd bent his head against folded arms braced upon his knees just to bear it. He was drying his eyes, hot with embarrassment, when it occurred to him what it was all about. She was crying because she missed her mommy and her daddy and her home and her bed, and he was crying for the very same reason. They were grieving together, whether she was old enough to realize it or not. He had picked her up then for perhaps the dozenth time and cradled her close against him, talking to her in soft, crooning words about her parents and how fine they had been and how inadequate he felt in trying to replace them.

"But I will," he had said. "Somehow I will, because I love you."

And it was true. He marveled at how deeply he loved that little scrap of humanity now sleeping peacefully in the center of his big bed. Just knowing she was there gave him a feeling of peace and satisfaction. He might even have been happy, despite the weight of grief that he bore, if only he hadn't been so tired.

He heard the door open and peered between two widely spaced columns. Across the clean, open expanse of the living area, Edward stepped down out of the foyer and shrugged free of his rumpled overcoat. Whatever he did, however he dressed, Edward never resembled anything so much as a bear just waking from a winter's hibernation, albeit a rather handsome bear with pale blue eyes and thick brows and mustache fully two shades darker than his shaggy, light golden brown hair. Parker supposed it was his size, for though he stood a touch over six feet himself and weighed in at one hundred and seventy-five pounds, Edward eclipsed him in both height and breadth. Moreover, he was built like an ox, all wide, flat muscle and heavy bone. Edward spied him and lifted a hand in hello. Quickly crossing the living area, he stepped up into the kitchen and accepted the mug of hot brew that Parker filled and thrust at him.

"So how'd it go?" he asked, his voice hushed and cautious.

Parker rubbed his eyes with his fingertips. "How'd what go?"

"Your first night with the baby." His tone added an *of course*

Parker dropped his hand. "Fine," he lied tersely. "What's brought you out so early?"

"Thought you'd want to see this," Edward said, fishing a folded paper from his back pocket.

Parker knew fax paper when he saw it. He set down his cup and took the folded sheet. Opening it, he scanned the contents. A ripple of relief so intense, it was debilitating, skittered through him. He closed his eyes. "Thank God!"

Edward slurped his coffee and nodded at the same time, managing to spill hot liquid over his fingers. He flung it off, spattering the smooth, cool gray cabinets and the gleaming black countertops. "It certainly helps that Nathan named you guardian in his will."

"Helps?" Parker said, snorting at the notion. "It settles it, doesn't it?"

A wary look came over Edward. He canted his head slightly. "Not necessarily. People aren't property, you know. One doesn't just leave a baby to whoever one chooses like he would his car or the family silver. Besides, wills are challenged—and set aside—every day." He shrugged. "But then maybe the Pendletons won't challenge."

Parker put his hands in his hair. "Oh, right! And the wind doesn't blow. Of course they'll challenge! This is an affront to her life's work, to her standing as a doctor. She *has* to challenge. Good God, her own sister chose to leave her baby daughter's care to an inexperienced bachelor, and her a noted child psychologist and experienced mother! She'll challenge. Oh, yes, she'll challenge! And she'll win. Oh, God." He pulled a sleek chrome chair out from beneath the glass table and collapsed upon it, thinking of the long, difficult night that had just passed and how inadequate he had felt to the simple task of putting that child to sleep. But he could learn. Heaven help him, he could learn—given the chance. "What am I going to do?" he asked miserably.

He must have made a more pitiful picture than he knew, for Edward dropped a heavy hand upon his shoulder and squeezed.

"We'll fight them," he said gruffly. "If you want to keep that baby, then we'll fight them for her. But, Parker, you're going to have to bend over backward to convince the court that you can care for her. Fortunately, we can verify your claim that Nathan and Candace wanted you to have her, but all that means, good buddy, is that you don't have to prove you're *better* able to care for her than the Pendletons. If we can satisfy the court that you're *as able* as the Pendletons or, depending on how lucky we are in drawing a judge, at least adequate, then the will should clinch it for you. The bad news is, your reputation is going to work against you. Unless I miss my guess, you haven't much time to get respectable."

Parker clenched and unclenched his hands. "Just tell me what to do," he said.

Edward sighed, pulled out a chair and sat down, stretching his long, thick legs out in front of him. "Well," he said thoughtfully, "for one thing, you're about to get religion. What I'm saying is, join a church, any church, as long as it's mainstream and uncontroversial."

Parker stiffened. "For your information, I already *am* a member of a church."

Edward had the poor grace to look surprised. "No kidding?" He seemed to ponder this new information, then shrugged. "Well, all you've got to do then is start attending—regularly."

Parker nodded grimly. Lord, there were going to be some shocked old biddies soon. Well, he wouldn't think of it. He squared his shoulders. "I'll be in church this Sunday," he said.

"With the baby," Edward added.

Parker looked down at his hands. They were trembling. "With the baby," he repeated. "Now, what else?"

Edward hooked an arm over the back of the chair and sipped his coffee. "The kid needs a room of her own," he said.

"Her name is Darla," Parker snapped testily. "And she's going to sleep in the guest room as soon as I get her things over here."

"You can move into Nathan's house once the will is probated," Edward mused, "but for now the guest room will have to do."

Parker had no intention of moving into Nathan's characterless cracker box of a house, but he didn't bother to tell Edward that. By the time the will was probated, the whole custody issue would undoubtedly be settled, so it was pointless to worry about trying to make that architecturally bankrupt "investment" of Nathan's a livable residence. He concentrated instead on how to make this fine old house of his a "family" place. His mind was buzzing with ideas when Edward called him back to the conversation by leaning forward, elbows on the glass tabletop.

"... might be better to just buy all new stuff," he was saying. "I'll have to check that out, but until I know for sure, you shouldn't remove anything from the house. You might want to just go over and look around to see what you're going to need, though. You be the judge. But until the will's probated, we're going to step carefully, you understand?"

"I understand," Parker said, thinking that he'd rather take a beating than go back into Nathan's house knowing that Nathan would never go there again. "I'll have her settled in by tonight."

Edward nodded, his abstraction a sure sign that he had already moved on to other matters. "You'll have to cancel your social calendar," he said pointedly. "No more loud parties, no more hard drinking, no more bars and nightclubs and no more, er, overnight guests. For that matter, don't be spending nights at anyone else's, either." He sent Parker an apologetic look. "Sorry, pal, but your sex life goes on hiatus as of right now. Agreed?"

Parker grimaced. "I can live without sex." *For a while,* he amended mentally. Then he amended that. *For as long as it takes.* He clenched his fists. "Go on."

Edward shrugged. "Well, you're financially secure, anyway, and professionally, you're right at the top. Congratulations, by the way, on being offered a partnership by your firm. It can't hurt that you're one of the top architects in the state. But have you thought about what you're going to do with the k—ah, Darla, while you're working?"

Parker bit back a curse. No, he hadn't thought about what he was going to do with Darla while he was at the office. Mrs. Hoft was out of the question, of course. She'd made it plain upon which side she stood. No, he'd have to find someone more trustworthy than that. He supposed he could call an agency. He had a few days, after all. Surely no one would expect him in the office for a few days. He had a brother to bury. The thought reminded him rather forcefully that he had arrangements to make. Phone calls and decisions waited for him. He rubbed his hands over his face.

"I'll think of something," he said as much to himself as to Edward.

Ed leaned back in his chair. "While you're doing it," he said, "consider the obvious, will you?"

Parker stretched, working the kinks out of his back. "Which is?"

Edward shook his head. "It's obvious as the nose on your face," he said. "What you need, good buddy, is a wife—and the sooner the better."

Chapter Three

"Well, it was just an idea," Edward said lightly. "Your little black book may list more women's numbers than the telephone directory, but no doubt every one of them has been given to understand that you are not the marrying kind."

"Naturally," Parker murmured. But a voice inside his head asked, *Not even for Darla's sake?* Shaken, Parker stared at Ed and faced the truth inside. Without Darla, he was utterly alone in the world. To prevent that, he would do anything, even marry, and if said marriage had the added benefit of protecting Darla from Sandra Pendleton's psychological experimentation and keeping her where Nathan and Candace had wanted her to be, how could he think of *not* doing it?

But holy cow, marriage! He tried to picture himself married and sitting home nights with the baby and the little woman, but the image just wouldn't coalesce. He could put himself and Darla there, but the woman simply escaped him. Names kept flitting through his head, but he couldn't make himself put the faces into the scene—and then suddenly a face popped into place, the name following a split second afterward. Kendra Ballard.

Excitement seized him, excitement and hope. Kendra Ballard. Of course! Who better? He'd known her forever, and she was a pediatric nurse. Moreover, she was not only his friend but a close friend of Nathan's—or she had been. Surely she would want Nathan's wishes fulfilled. She'd want the best for his baby daughter. And she wasn't indifferent to Parker, either. She had comforted him when the awful news had come, and it had seemed natural that she do so, now that he thought about it. But best of all, she wasn't in love with him or even enamored of him! She knew exactly who and what he was. With her, it could be a straightforward kind of deal, as real or not as they wished to make it, and once the objective was achieved, they could end it quietly and calmly without all the emotional angst that would accompany false expectations. By Jove, it just might work!

He blinked at Edward, her name about to tumble from his lips, when the one serious drawback hit him. Edward. Edward was in love with Kendra Ballard, or what passed for love with him, anyway. True, the two of them had broken up some months ago, but everyone knew that Edward was still carrying the torch. He had thought that *he* was going to marry Kendra. Some of the excitement went out of Parker, a vague sense of disappointment replacing it. But wait. *He* wasn't in love with Kendra. Surely if he made Edward understand that... On the other hand, he couldn't see Edward standing quietly by while he played house with the comely Kendra. No, it would have to be a sham marriage to satisfy Edward, no fun and games involved.

Parker was surprised at how disappointed he felt. He had pondered the possibility before of indulging in a little adult play with the delectable Miss Ballard, but Nathan had warned him away long ago. He had even thought at one time that Nathan and she would get together, but then

Candace had come along, and that had been that. Still, Nathan's affection for Kendra hadn't changed even when Candace had come on the scene, so Parker had kept his distance. Well, maybe not quite so much distance as before, but by then she had been involved with his best friend, so he hadn't done more than simply *entertain* the idea of seducing her. It appeared that was all he was going to do now, too. Who would have thought it? Parker Sugarman considering marriage to the one woman with whom he couldn't, or shouldn't, share his bed. His mother had told him that God would punish him one day.

Or maybe he was going mad. Maybe grief had driven him mad, and he didn't even know it. But then he wouldn't, would he?

Groaning, he bowed his head and pressed the heels of his hands over his eyes. Life had been simple once, gloriously simple, and now suddenly he was drowning in confusion. Edward was speaking, and it was very, very difficult for Parker to attend him, but he tried.

"...take care of her alone, anyway," Ed was saying. "Another pair of hands would come in real handy, don't you think? Of course, marriage would go a long way to proving to the court that you've actually settled down and changed your stripes, but the hiring of the right kind of help would at least prove you have your niece's best interests at heart. I'd recommend a grandmotherly type, someone above reproach."

He went on, but Parker couldn't make himself follow. "I understand," he interrupted forcefully. "You've made your point. Now let me think, will you?"

"Absolutely," Edward said, the ring of triumph in his voice. "It's a big step, not to be taken lightly. Try to come up with someone the court would find acceptable."

Parker actually felt his mouth curving in a smile. "No strippers, huh?"

"No strippers," Edward confirmed. "No topless waitresses. No porn actresses."

"I don't know any porn actresses."

"No bimbos."

"Well, that narrows the field."

"No easy lays whose numbers you've gotten off the bathroom wall."

"Give me a little credit for class, will you? I'll have you know that I only consult walls in the very best bathrooms."

"Ha-ha. I'm serious as a heart attack here, bud. You're cleaning up your act but good, see?"

"Edward," Parker asked smoothly, "were you ever a gangster in a former life?"

"Cute," Edward said, getting to his feet. "Maybe the vernacular is cheesy, but the advice is caviar, chum. See that you take it."

Parker saluted smartly. "Yes, sir."

A thin, wobbly wail drifted upon the air.

"You're being paged," Edward quipped.

"So I hear." Parker sighed, suddenly exhausted again, but he got up nonetheless.

"Jeez, Parker, are you really sure about this?" Edward asked, clearly in awe.

Parker thought of how easy it would be to let the Pendletons take the baby home. No more crying. No more diapers. No more worries. No nothing. Something in him protested violently. He swallowed, wanting to get to her as quickly as possible. "See yourself out, will you?" he said, hurrying away.

"You didn't answer the question," Edward protested.

"Oh, yes, I did," Parker called over his shoulder.

Edward muttered something else, but Parker didn't wait around to hear what it was. He trotted into his bedroom and went directly to the bed. He could see her little arms and legs flailing over the tops of the pillows with which he'd surrounded her. She was merely fussing, impatient but not distressed. He leaned into the bed on one knee and peered down at her.

"I'm here," he said gently. Her gaze fixed on him, and a smile lit her face. Carefully, he slid his hands beneath her and lifted her up against his shoulder, recognizing the warmth and weight of a wet diaper.

She grunted sounds at him, telling him she was pleased by this response, and he nuzzled her cheek with his nose, inhaling the peculiarly clean aroma of baby. Her hand smacked him on the cheek, then her tiny fingers found his earlobe and latched on. He chuckled and hugged her ever so carefully.

"I'm sure," he whispered. "Oh, yes, I'm sure."

Kendra watched with more dismay than she'd believed possible as the movers from the used furniture dealer hoisted her—their—sofa, turned it on its side and carried it unceremoniously out the door. She followed them to the door, inhaled deeply before closing it, then wandered back to the remaining chair and plopped down into it. They would be coming back for it in a few moments, but until then it was hers and she intended to enjoy it. She told herself once more that she had been wise to sell the furniture rather than to store it, but she couldn't help thinking that she'd spent the past four years of her life with that couch, this chair and the three matching tables already carted out. She would be less than human—well, less than female—if she didn't feel a twinge of regret. A twinge. That was funny. What she was feeling was no twinge, it was more like a convulsion.

Someone tapped at her door—the movers, no doubt, come for the chair. She sighed, rose and opened the door. There stood Parker Sugarman with a sleeping baby in his arms, a bottle in hand and a diaper bag slung over one shoulder. His dark ash-brown hair was mussed and his jaws and chin bore the sooty shadows of an unshaved beard. Her mouth dropped open, and he must have thought she was about to shriek or something for he lifted a finger and pressed it to his lips, glancing down at the baby. Kendra felt the sudden urge to giggle. Parker Sugarman with a baby. Who'd have thought it?

She clamped a hand over her mouth and signaled him to enter. He stepped over the threshold with the same care he'd have used if it had been a live snake, and the baby slept peacefully on, cradled in stiff arms. Kendra pushed the door shut, careful to prevent any startling sound, and followed him into the center of the room, where he stood, awkwardly staring around him at the emptiness.

"Is that Darla?" she whispered, and got a nod of his head in return. "Is she all right?"

Another nod.

"Are *you* all right?"

The answer this time was a hand raked through wavy hair, a deeply indrawn breath and a shrug of shoulders accompanied by a dubious nod.

Kendra lifted both brows. She supposed that meant that he was as all right as he could be under the circumstances. His brother and sister-in-law had been dead less than thirty-six hours, after all, and his haggard look coupled with the infant sleeping soundly in his arms indicated that neither of them had gotten much rest during the night. She patted his cheek sympathetically, then dropped the hand to his back and pushed him toward the chair. He went reluctantly, dragging his feet, but settled down into the chair once he got there, the baby held securely against his chest. Kendra sat down on the floor in front of him and folded her legs beneath her.

"Now," she said softly, "want to tell me what you're doing here—with her?"

He eased the baby down until his elbow rested upon the arm of the chair, a look of such love on his face that Kendra caught her breath. He glanced up at her, and his expression changed to one of worry. "I didn't know where else to go," he confided. "I've thought it over very carefully and—"

The boom of a fist upon her door startled them all, jerking the baby awake and turning Parker's carefully modulated words into a growl. Kendra groaned. The movers! She leapt up to her feet just as an ear-piercing wail, pitiful in its misery, filled the empty room. Parker quickly lifted the baby to his shoulder and began to jiggle her and pat her back, crooning comfortingly.

"It's the movers come for the chair," she declared over the baby's crying.

The door opened at that, and the two burly furniture movers stepped inside. Parker shot them a look of displeasure as he got to his feet and stepped aside, balancing the squalling infant. The two men looked at each other, shrugged and seized the chair, lifting it easily. Within moments, they were gone, leaving Kendra with a disgruntled Parker and a screaming Darla.

"Oh, Parker, I'm so sorry. Is there anything I can do to help?"

A wry smile twisted his lips. "Well, now that you mention it," he said, patting the baby frantically, "you could marry me."

Her mouth fell open, but then she told herself that he was joking, and the gape became a giggle. "At least you haven't lost your sense of humor," she said, chuckling, but the look in his eyes didn't alter in the slightest. She cocked her head, studying him. He was serious! "It's not your sense of humor you've lost, it's your mind!" she exclaimed.

"No," he said gently. "What I've lost is my family, all but this one precious piece of it." He spread his hand over the baby's back protectively, his expression softening, but his glittering gaze stayed with Kendra's. "I need you," he told her, and her heart flip-flopped in her chest. "I need you to be my wife."

"It makes perfect sense," he insisted half an hour later. "It's the answer to all my problems."

"I'm not so sure of that," she said, "but putting that aside for now, what about me? Did it escape your notice that I'm in the process of making a life-changing move here? I'm on my way to Africa!"

They were sitting cross-legged on her living room floor. Parker was burping the baby, having quieted her earlier by thrusting the bottle nipple into her mouth, and Kendra found that she was fascinated by the way he handled the infant, as if she might shatter into a thousand pieces with one wrong move. He had cooed, too, and wiggled his eyebrows flirtatiously while gazing down at her. The baby had grinned around the nipple, then industriously suckled again, all her energies bent on draining that bottle, while her eyes had stayed glued to Parker's face. She couldn't blame her, Kendra mused. It was a handsome face, all strong angles and planes with those dark, heavy brows, those milk chocolate eyes, sculpted lips and that tiny cleft in the center of a square chin. But marry that face? It was a measure of Parker's arrogance that he would even come here and ask it of her, and yet despite the fact that it was all for his own convenience, she was flattered.

"Why would you want to go to Africa," he asked, "when a helpless infant right here needs you?"

"That helpless infant has you," Kendra answered calmly, "and failing that, the Pendletons."

"Over my dead body," he rumbled, and Darla burped as if to second that. Parker turned his head and grinned at her. "That's my girl." He dandled her above him, and she promptly threw up on his shirtfront. "Yuck! Darla!"

Kendra couldn't help laughing. "I'll get you a towel." She rose and went into the kitchen, which was separated by the living area only by a short bar. She was trembling, and her stomach was tied in knots, but she vowed not to think of it. She whipped a towel from the oven handle and hurried back to him with it. He had laid Darla in the bend of his leg and was tweaking her toes and talking to her.

"Spit up on your Uncle Parker, will you? And after I gave you all that nice milk, too."

"A little too much milk, perhaps." Kendra offered the towel.

He took it and dabbed at his shirtfront. "You don't think she's sick, then?"

Kendra knelt beside them and laid a hand against the baby's face. No fever. She shook her head. "I don't think so. I think she just got greedy and took too much formula, or maybe the formula's too rich for her."

"See," Parker said, "that's the kind of thing I'm talking about. That's precisely what I need you for—that and keeping her with me."

"Are you so sure you should keep her with you, Parker?" she asked gently.

His face clouded and closed over. "I've already told you that Nathan and Candace wanted *me* to have her," he said coldly. "They thought I would be the best guardian for her, and they didn't agree with Sandra Pendleton's child-rearing methods at all."

Kendra sighed and sat down again. "Yes, well, I always did think they were a bit too rough on Sandra. She's a doctor, after all and though her methods may be somewhat extreme, they're not harmful."

"Not harmful?" Parker echoed incredulously. "Do you know that the last time she was pregnant she taped stereo headphones to her abdomen and talked to the kid through a microphone all day long? In two languages, no less! She claims the kid was born with the ability to count *and* multiply. Now how would she know that? It's a cinch the kid didn't tell her! But do you know what really bugs me? She doesn't let her children go to public school. They don't socialize with other kids their ages at all. She says she doesn't want them corrupted. Corrupted! And last year at Christmastime her oldest told me that Santa was merely—and I quote—'an exploded myth used to blunt the natural, healthy impulses of children in a self-centered society.' Not harmful! Well, let me tell you, she's not going to put her zany ideas into this little one's head! No, sir. This *bambina* is going to have a nice, normal American childhood with all the attendant neuroses!"

Kendra stared at him in wonder. "You're really committed to this, aren't you?"

"Damned straight," he muttered, scooping up the contented infant. He cradled her against his shoulder, his long, powerful hand dwarfing her little round head with its thatch of silky black hair. "I promised my brother," he said huskily. "I promised him that if anything happened, I'd take care of her, and that's what I'm going to do."

Kendra sobered, the weight of grief suddenly descending again. She reached out and closed her hand upon his wrist, receiving a direct look so filled with pain that it cut her to the very heart. "It just doesn't seem possible that he's gone," she said softly. "Nathan's been around all my life. I can't remember when we weren't friends. Dad's so broken up. He depended on Nathan, thought of him as a son. None of us is going to be the same now that he's gone."

Parker turned his arm beneath her hand and closed his fingers around her wrist, just as she had done his, and for a moment they were stronger simply because they touched, because they held on to one another. And then he looked down at the baby nuzzled against his shoulder. "She's all I have," he said. "All I have."

And Kendra knew he was right. His father had skipped out on the family more than twenty years ago. His mother, his grandparents, an aunt and now his brother were dead. There was no other family, none but Darla, and if what he said was true, he stood to lose her, too.

But surely the Pendletons understood how important Darla was to Parker. Surely they would foster the relationship, welcome him into their home, for Darla's sake if not his. Wouldn't that be best? He couldn't hope to care for an infant on his own. The Pendletons were experienced parents, offbeat maybe, but capable. Darla would be better off with them. Wouldn't she?

Kendra looked at him, cradling that baby in his two big hands, and she shook her head. "I don't know, Parker. A baby is an awfully big responsibility."

"You think I don't know that?" he asked, shifting his gaze to her. "The last twenty-four hours have been the toughest in my life, but..." He nestled a drowsy Darla in the curve of his arm. "I love her." He looked up again, pinning Kendra with a determined stare. "And I promised her father, so whether you help me or not, I'm going to fight to keep her."

"Parker, it's not that I wouldn't like to help, but marriage? That's such a big step."

"It doesn't have to be," he said quickly. "I wouldn't hold you to it. I mean, it wouldn't be forever. It'd be legal and all and as far as everyone else is concerned, it'd be the real thing, but we wouldn't have to... That is, I wouldn't expect..."

"Sex," she supplied bluntly, wondering why she was so stung by his willingness to forgo that particular part of marriage with her.

He grinned and shook his head. "There. See? That's why I want you. You're so practical, so levelheaded. I can talk to you, be honest with you. We've never played games with one another, you and I. And I trust you. You don't know what that means to me, Kendra, to know there's still someone I can trust even though Nathan's... gone."

She sighed, well aware that the patented Sugarman charm had just been focused on her, full force. "Parker, this is a screwy idea."

"No, it isn't. Edward says that if I'm married they'll have to give me Darla."

"Edward!" she scoffed. "Why am I not surprised to find his handiwork here?"

"Edward's a good lawyer," Parker argued. "He explained it all to me. It's in the will, see, but the state's obligated to follow certain guidelines when it comes to children, and single men just happen to come after married child psychologists, no matter how weird they are. But if I were married, there'd be no contest because there would be no reason *not* to follow the last wishes of her parents. Look, Kendra, I have a reputation—"

"A well-deserved reputation," she noted.

He inclined his head. "Granted, but that's behind me now. My reputation became my past the moment this little girl became my future. Without her, I have neither. You have to help me, Kendra. Do it for Nathan if not for me or Darla. It's what he wanted. You know it is."

He was right. On many an occasion she'd heard Nathan and Candace disparage Sandra Pendleton and her notions of superior parenthood. What was more, she knew they'd both loved and in a way even admired Parker. She supposed that made him the logical choice. But no one ever seriously expects to need a guardian for their children. No one ever expects to die. Still, Nathan would have given it serious thought before he put it to paper. Oh, Nathan. Once again the despair of loss assailed her.

Grief was a strange thing. You could put it out of mind for whole minutes, and then suddenly it engulfed you, as relentless as the tide and as cold, as biting. If it was like that for her, what must it be like for Parker? She watched him gently rocking from side to side as his niece slept snuggled against his chest in the bend of his arm. He wasn't even aware that he was doing it. It was that automatic thing she saw so often in parents who stood vigil over sick beds, the instinctive action of one who sought to comfort, to protect, to cosset.

Maybe he should have Nathan's daughter. Maybe that miniature female clasped to his heart would be the one to save him from his own excess, to teach him to love. She would like to see that. Oh, yes, she would like to see that. What an extraordinary man he would be if that came to pass. But to marry him!

A chill swept down her spine. Marriage to Parker Sugarman, even a sham marriage, would be undeniably difficult. Just the idea of living with all that charm, looking at that sculpted face over breakfast, saying good-night to it . . . But no sex. He had promised no sex, and she had felt the first real stirrings of disappointment, the first tentacles of pain. There. That was the real problem. They were only friends, and he would never see her as anything else, while she could so easily see him as so much more. No. Marriage, especially a sham marriage, to Parker Sugarman would be an act of extreme folly on her part. Better to stay on the course she'd already chosen.

"Parker, I sympathize with you, really I do, but I've made a commitment to help bring medical relief to the most stricken parts of Africa."

"But you can still go to Africa," he argued. "Africa will still be there in a year...a few months. Six months! Give me six months, Kendra. They'll understand. Things happen. People get married every day. Tragedy brings people together. It magnifies feelings. You're friends one day, spouses the next! That's all they have to know. Then in a few months you're divorced—or annulled—and you want to take your mind off your own troubles, pick up with your life. You go to Africa, after all. What could be more plausible? And when you go, it will be with the knowledge that you and you alone made fulfillment of Nathan's last wish a possibility. Think about it, Kendra. Don't say no now. Just think about it. Please."

She opened her mouth to tell him to forget it, but she just couldn't. She looked at him there with that baby clasped to his chest, his day-old beard and his tired, reddened eyes, and she just couldn't refuse him. She put a hand in her long, thick, rusty brown hair and closed her eyes. They were hazel, with so much yellow in them that sometimes they were almost golden, times like now, when emotions were in conflict, when doubts assailed from every side. She moaned, feeling trapped, feeling threatened, feeling uncertain. Finally she opened her eyes.

"I'll think about it," she said flatly, and the light of hope fairly beamed in his smile.

"I knew you wouldn't let us down," he said, putting back his head in a gesture of relief.

"I only said I'd think about it," she cautioned him, but his smile stayed.

"Thank you. Oh, Kendra, thank you. I know you'll want to help us once you think it through. It makes such splendid sense, really. I wouldn't dream of doing this with anyone but a good, dear friend, and when I think of good, dear friends, I think of you, just as Nathan did.''

She rolled her eyes. "Doing it a bit too brown, Parker."

"Not at all! I mean it. We are friends, aren't we?"

"Well, of course we're friends, but that's hardly a basis for marriage."

"But it is! It's a far better basis for marriage than love or passion."

"Oh, really?"

"Sure. Of course. Love's a much too volatile emotion for the kind of intimacy marriage means. Why, nobody in their right minds would try to live together if they were in love! And passion, well, that's just a fleeting, shallow, physical thing. Half the marriages in this world begin in passion and end in acrimony! No, really. I wouldn't consider marriage with anyone but a very good friend. And when you get right down to it, Kendra, you're about the only real friend I've got. Well, the only real friend of the right gender, anyway."

She folded her arms. "Right, and if I believe that, you've got a bridge you want me to consider buying."

"Scout's honor," he said, holding up two fingers.

"You were never a scout."

He hung his head as if wounded. "All right," he admitted, lifting it again, "I was never a scout, and I *do* know a lot of women. I just don't know any—except you—whom I trust enough to marry and help me raise this little girl, even for six short months. Now that's the God's honest truth."

She couldn't find it within herself to disbelieve him, foolish as that was, but still she resisted him. Her sense of self-preservation was finely honed, and she had no doubt at all that Parker Sugarman could be a serious threat if she allowed him even a small measure of influence over her heart. No doubt at all. In fact, she'd have to be certifiably insane to marry such a man, whatever the motive. He was a wanton womanizer, a sexual athlete of professional caliber, a party animal, a completely self-centered male. Well, maybe not completely self-centered. He had been very good to Nathan, both big brother and father figure, and despite his life-style, Nathan had turned out all right. Nathan had turned out fine, actually. Maybe Parker could do the same for Nathan's daughter, and maybe Darla could return the favor in a way that Nathan had not been able to.

But she'd be a fool to count on that. She'd be a fool to count on anything but trouble with Parker Sugarman. And yet she couldn't tell him to forget this crazy scheme of a sham marriage. She couldn't tell him yes, and she couldn't tell him no; so she told him nothing at all. She just sat and watched him watch the sleeping infant that he held so very carefully, as if not only her life but his depended on keeping her safe and comfortable. Oh, Lord, was she really starting to consider this insanity?

He looked up suddenly then, a strange intensity in his brown eyes. "Will you come with me tomorrow to the service? Will you ride with me? I mean, Edward will be there, but I need someone who will hold my hand, someone to help me say goodbye."

The funeral. God, she hated funerals, and this one promised to be a real torment, but she couldn't skip it. She would never do that, but she had intended to attend with her father—and Kate. Kate would be going, of course. So why did Dan need her? Might as well make herself useful to someone.

She clapped a hand over Parker's shoulder. "Sure, I'll go with you. That's what friends are for, isn't it?"

He turned his head, lifted his shoulder and pressed his lips to her fingers. "I knew you wouldn't let me down," he said.

She swallowed a sudden lump in her throat and managed a slight smile, but inside she was quaking. Something told her she ought to be running fast toward Africa, but instead she was sitting on the floor looking at the last man in the world she ought to marry—and wondering what that kiss might have been like if they weren't just friends.

Chapter Four

The long black limo swung off Walnut Hill Lane and glided past the country club. Parker took Kendra's hand in his and managed a smile, despite the weight of exhaustion on his haggard features.

"Thank you for coming by Dad's to pick me up," she said. "I turned in my apartment key this morning."

He shook his head. "I should be thanking you—for finding me a baby-sitter."

She shrugged. "We were lucky. Cheryl's aunt just happened to be free."

"Well, she was a godsend. I was at my wit's end. I never realized how difficult it would be to find a competent sitter for a single afternoon. I can't imagine what I'm in for when I start looking for full-time help."

"It can't be easy."

"I'm afraid that's an understatement. I've already called a couple of agencies. I think it would be best to have someone come to the house, don't you? I'd hate to haul an infant out every morning."

Kendra smiled benignly. "Millions of parents do it every morning," she pointed out gently. "If I'm not mistaken, Candace and Nathan did it several times a week, too."

Parker sighed. "I remember them saying that they couldn't afford in-house help. If I'd realized what that meant then, I'd have paid for it myself. Thankfully, I can afford it."

"You couldn't have known," she assured him, but he merely stared out the window, silent.

Kendra realized that they were driving past the memorial park and cemetery, where two small, dark green canopies had been erected side by side on the plots Parker had chosen and paid for with a personal check. He turned his head away casually as they drove by, but his hand tightened on Kendra's, the knuckles on both their hands turning white with the pressure. Just south of Northwest Highway, the pressure lightened. The limo made an abrupt turn to the west, then two blocks later glided to a stop.

Parker took a deep breath as the funeral director hurried forward to open the door. He looked at Kendra and smiled weakly, his hand sliding under her elbow.

"Here we go."

Kendra nodded and slid from the opulent car onto the sidewalk, straightening the drape of the simple black wrap skirt she wore with a black silk T-shirt and a yellow, white and black plaid jacket with black velvet lapels. She had pulled her dark hair into a chignon at the nape of her neck and wore a small black pillbox hat with a wisp of veil upon her forehead. Sheer black stockings and black velvet pumps with two-inch heels completed her outfit. The overall effect was neat but soft with a touch of primness. She had no idea how sexy that made her or how many male eyes slid over her compact five-foot-six-inch frame. Parker got out and stood next to her, his fingers finding and mingling with hers.

Several people surged toward them simultaneously. Walt and Dennis were in the forefront, but Edward and the Randles were right behind them. A number of arms surrounded and slid off them. Condolences were murmured. Parker's hand clutched hers tightly as he nodded acknowledgments and whispered replies. Finally, the funeral director stepped forward and stated in that silky voice peculiar to those in his profession, that all was in place and it was time to enter the church. Parker nodded and tugged at Kendra's hand. They started forward in tandem. The crowd milling about on the church lawn turned en masse and started up the steps leading to the sanctuary. Edward fell in on Kendra's other side, his large, bulky form familiar and oddly comforting considering how assiduously she had avoided him in recent months.

"You look good," he said out of the corner of his mouth, as if fearing it might be crude to compliment someone at a funeral.

She tried but failed to manage a smile. "Thanks."

They had reached the bottom step of the impressive porticoed church front. Parker slipped his hand from hers and laid it against the small of her back. Sensing his need for comfort and support, she slipped an arm about his waist. He responded by moving his arm to her shoulders, his hand clasping her upper arm possessively. Edward slid a speculative look their way, and this time she managed a slight, dismissive smile. He frowned beneath the thick curve of his mustache, then rubbed a hand over his face as if to physically erase it, and targeted his gaze on the movement of his feet.

They were perhaps halfway up the steps when the minibus tore around the corner and screeched to a stop in the center of the street directly in front of the church. Parker, Kendra, Edward and three or four others automatically glanced backward to see what the hubbub was about as Pendletons of every shape and size spewed from the vehicle into the street. The children, in Sunday clothes, scrambled noisily to the sidewalk, where the littlest one fell, scraping various parts of her skin. Sandra Pendleton was right behind her, but she neither stooped to inspect the damage nor slowed her stride.

"The lesson," she said smoothly to the bawling child, "is that haste can be dangerous."

Only at the foot of the steps did she halt to await the girl's slow, painful progress. Meanwhile, the girl's siblings clambered up the steps past the knot of gape-mouthed mourners and spilled noisily into the church. Mother and daughter began the ascent. A second later, Heath Pendleton trotted up behind them, having managed to park the van.

"What's going on?" he asked his wife, his voice containing obvious concern.

"A typical exercise in endurance," came the reply. "She's well ahead of the norm here, no doubt due partly to sibling example. Nevertheless, such perseverance is quite remarkable at her age. Obviously we ought to be encouraging her toward more physical endeavor. I'll have a devil of a time finding flash cards depicting females involved in physical occupations, but it can't be helped."

Heath Pendleton nodded his head in understanding, then glanced down at his daughter. "Want me to carry her?" he asked his wife.

Sandra shook her head. "Not yet. I don't want to rob her of achievement."

"Achievement!" Kendra gritted involuntarily, and Parker instantly tightened his hold on her arm. It was precisely then that the Pendletons drew alongside their group and, led by Sandra, halted.

"Where's Darla?" she queried of Parker.

He loosened his hold on Kendra's arm slightly, as if forcing himself to relax. "Just where she ought to be," he said. "Home."

Dr. Sandra Pendleton smiled thinly. "That's exactly what I'd expect of you, Parker. You don't even realize what benefit attending her parents' funeral could be to the child."

"I don't see any benefit in it for an eighteen-week-old infant," he confirmed.

"Of course you don't, Parker," she retorted, "but a properly trained adult could see to it that the experience is encoded in the brain for recapture later."

Parker literally smirked. "Oh, sure," he said drolly. "No doubt that theory is embraced by everyone but extraterrestrials and us troglodytes."

Dr. Pendleton was not amused. "A child whose possibilities are limited," she quoted sagely, "is a child with limited possibilities."

"And a child with scraped knees is a child in pain," Parker replied sadly.

Sandra Pendleton drew herself up tightly. "Pain is one of nature's most adept teachers," she snapped. "Self-caused pain teaches caution. Self-conquered pain teaches perseverance, stamina and self-reliance."

"And a lack of care teaches a kid that she's worthless and deserving of pain," Parker contended. "I know damned well *you* had a mother who kissed your sores and made them better."

"My mother was as well-meaning and well-informed as any other of her generation," Sandra declared angrily, "which is to say, not very well at all! Behavioral science has taught us that—"

"Behavioral science has taught some of us one thing and some of us another," Parker interrupted. "It's a matter of interpretation and perspective, and I don't mind telling you that yours are downright screwy! What's more, lady, I intend to make certain that you'll never get a chance to test them on my niece."

"My niece, as well," she reminded him coldly.

"Granted," he said with deadly calm, "but Nathan and Candace named *me* her guardian, and as far as I'm concerned, that's that."

"We'll see," Sandra told him, and with a nod of her head she signaled her husband that he was now allowed to pick up the sniffling child standing quietly between them.

Parker dropped his arm from about Kendra's shoulders and balled his hands into fists. He gritted his teeth, then by breathing deeply managed to stop. "She won't have her, Edward," he said. "Sandra Pendleton will not practice her lunacy on my Darla! Do you hear me?"

Edward bowed his head and glanced up at Kendra doubtfully from beneath furrowed brows. "I hear you, old buddy," he said softly. "I hear you." And then he looked away guiltily.

A fear of immense proportion seized Kendra in that moment. She saw suddenly just how unlikely Parker was to win custody of "his" Darla and just how distasteful Sandra Pendleton's parenting techniques were to one reared by loving, doting parents. In a flash, she remembered the pain of scraped knees and the pleasurable comfort of a mother who had folded her close and promised relief. She remembered praise for treatment endured patiently and the pride that came afterward. She remembered, too, shamelessly milking every last drop of sympathy from her parents before the scabs formed and the suffering became more liability than boon. They were memories of such sweetness that they woke in her a nostalgia so sentimental as to bring tears to the eyes—and grow apace the fear that Darla Sugarman might never know such nostalgic sweetness if robbed of her uncle's inept but loving care. Kendra could safeguard that child's future by marrying her uncle. The thought lodged in her mind like an annoying jingle that, once heard, could not be forgotten.

Parker helped quiet it for a moment when he seized her hand and squeezed it. "No point in standing out here," he said gruffly. "Let's go in."

She nodded and began climbing steps again. With each one that fell away beneath her, she heard that inner voice telling her what she already knew. She could fix everything by marrying him. Six months was all it would take, a half year out of her life. He might not be the best of fathers, but it wouldn't be for lack of trying. On the other hand, Sandra Pendleton might not be the worst of mothers. Again, not for lack of trying. But that was unfair.

Sandra sincerely thought she was correct. She sincerely believed her ideas were superior to the collective wisdom of countless generations of traditional mothers, and that conviction meant not a thing to a little girl in need of the traditional hug and a bit of commiseration.

They reached the top of the steps and walked sedately beneath the portico supported by towering columns, then through tall, elaborately carved doors and down the long vestibule. At the open door to the sanctuary, the funeral director awaited them. Organ music drifted through, the tune dignified, solemn and hauntingly beautiful.

"A moment please," the director intoned, scanning the congregation to be certain that all were settled properly.

At the end of the aisle, Sandra Pendleton was leading her noisy brood to the foremost family pew, leaving the one directly behind for Parker and his friends. Once they were all ostensibly seated, the director nodded. Parker squeezed Kendra's hand, and together they started that long walk toward the two identical coffins resting side by side in the midst of a bank of flowers before the altar rail. Kendra heard sniffling and muted sobs and whispers from either side of the aisle, and when she glanced at Parker's profile, she noted a tiny muscle trembling in the hollow of his jaw. She slid her free hand over the inside of his elbow and received a squeeze of her captured hand in return.

At last they reached the end of the second pew and halted. Parker stepped back slightly to allow her to enter before him. Then Edward followed and squeezed past her to sit at her side, while Parker settled himself on the other, next to the aisle. At some unseen signal, the organ music faded away and the throbbing sound of a harp smoothly picked up where the last organ note had left off. Suddenly the voices of a mixed choir lifted in song, the beauty of the harmony so overwhelming that the words themselves seemed of little importance. Kendra closed her eyes and let the music soothe her—until a slight bump against the pew immediately ahead brought forth a screech of pain. The littlest Pendleton had just learned an unpleasant lesson about fidgeting while bearing scrapes upon one's elbows. In an apparent attempt to quiet the crying child, Sandra Pendleton lifted her onto her lap, but the little one continued to weep. After a few moments, the oldest Pendleton child, a boy of about ten, turned a censorious expression on his injured sibling.

"She's acting like a baby!" he grumbled.

His mother turned a complacent look upon him. "Yes, she is."

"Well, she'd better cut it out or I'm going to pinch her!" he hissed.

Sandra turned her attention back to the choir. "Pinching is not acceptable," she said calmly, but she shifted her sniffling daughter to her husband.

He took the child onto his lap, and there the little girl leaned back against his chest and brought her feet up onto his knees, hugging her legs with her arms. Presently, she wiped her eyes with the backs of her hands, breathed a shuddering sigh and popped two fingers into her mouth. A few seconds later, she was asleep.

The service lasted slightly less than half an hour, and when it was done, Kendra found herself with a new appreciation for Parker's taste and sensibilities. The whole thing was carried off with decorum and dignity, from the opening chords of music to the closing words of prayer. The only really uncomfortable moments came when the caskets were opened for the final viewing. Contrary to custom, Parker elected to view the bodies first. Kendra was sure that he had crushed her fingers by the time they made the brief, obligatory pauses at the foot of each casket. The Pendletons were right behind them, the older children whispering and jostling as they approached the altar. Parker clearly did not wish to linger to witness whatever havoc they might wreak. Switching his grip from her hand to her elbow, he steered Kendra toward the side door that had been opened for them. Before they made good their escape, however, the littlest Pendleton, carried in her father's arms, was somehow awakened and set up a frightful shriek.

For several moments, Sandra and Heath Pendleton talked to their daughter in calm, level tones, explaining that there was nothing to fear, that Aunt Candace was neither cold nor in pain, but that she could not wake, sit up or speak. Finally Sandra began to grow impatient.

"You're too intelligent to carry on like this," she said sternly. "We discussed the clinical details of death at length only yesterday."

"Clinical details," Parker muttered, and before Kendra knew what he intended, he had left her there by the door and was striding purposefully back the way they had come. He walked straight to Heath Pendleton, but his softly spoken words, whatever they were, were for Sandra Pendleton alone. She stiffened as if he had struck her, but when he reached for her daughter, she made no protest, merely watched as the little girl went willingly into his arms and buried her face in the curve of his shoulder. As he carried the child to the door, he caught Kendra's hand and pulled her along with them. "There, now," he said the instant they stepped down into the hall. "You can cry all you want."

The terrified cries abruptly ceased, and the child turned a damp, tear-stained face up at him. "I don't like that!" she declared stoically.

Parker's smile was grim. "Neither do I. In fact, I understand exactly how you feel. But there really is nothing to be afraid of, I promise. If you should have a bad dream or two, remember that. Okay?"

"'Kay," she said around her fingers, laying her head against his chest.

"Good girl."

They wound their way through corridors that led to a back door. The limo waited for them, having been parked on an apron of cement adjacent to a covered walkway. They went to it and leaned against its fender. Parker sighed wearily, and the subdued child in his arms mimicked his action. He smiled at Kendra over the crown of the little one's head, and she smiled back, thinking how natural he seemed with that child in his arms. She marveled, knowing that only one day earlier she would have scoffed at such a notion, but that was before he had brought Darla to her apartment, before he had asked Kendra to marry him. She knew now with dreadful certainty what she was going to do, and the knowledge did nothing to cheer her.

Suddenly Sandra Pendleton burst out onto the covered walkway, her brood close behind her. Indignantly, she stalked over to Parker and glared up at him. Her eyes narrowed, and she was huffing and puffing through her mouth, but she mastered the obvious desire to scream invective at him and lifted her chin.

"I . . . regret the disturbance," she said stiltedly. "Now let me have my daughter."

Parker's expression remained blank as he handed over the child. Then quite deliberately he switched his gaze to the child, smiled warmly, tweaked her cheek and winked. The little girl beamed at him. Kendra rolled her eyes. Was there no female of any age whom he could not charm? Well, apparently there was one. Sandra Pendleton shifted the girl to her hip and fixed him with a belligerent stare.

"I'm well aware," she said caustically, "that you disdain both my efforts and my intentions, but I implore you to abandon this selfish stance you've taken and release Candace's child into my care. Whatever you think of me, I am far better able to care for an infant than you are, and you must know it!"

Parker shook his head. "I don't know any such thing."

"I know why you're doing this!" she exclaimed. "You're jealous! You've frittered away your life on pleasures and parties, and in your shame and grief you're striking out at the only accomplished person within your reach. But think of the child! Think of her future."

"That's exactly what I am doing!" Parker retorted. "I'd rather see her go to a rank stranger than become material for your zany psychological experiments."

"How dare you—"

"You leave me no choice!" he shouted. "Besides, I made a promise to my brother and sister-in-law! This was their idea, you know, not mine!"

Sandra sneered, curling her upper lip in a most unattractive manner. "Nathan and Candace were sweet people," she said, "but they were both as pathetically ignorant as you. I know what they said and thought about my work! But the day will come when I am vindicated, Parker. Mark my words."

"Maybe," he said evenly, and his voice took on the ring of steel, "but it won't be at Darla's expense. Mark *my* words."

Sandra turned suddenly to Kendra. "You look like an intelligent woman," she said. "Make him see reason, please, before it's too late. The child is already woefully behind. Candace just wouldn't listen, you see. She couldn't seem to grasp the concept of education beginning in the womb! But I'm sure I can bring little Darla up to speed with a relatively short period of intensive training, provided I can get to her quickly enough! Don't you see? You must help me. You must help Darla."

Intensive training for a four-month-old? Kendra was well aware that her mouth was hanging open, and she didn't bother to close it. Instead she covered it with her hand and shook her head. "Sorry," she managed to choke out, barely mastering an absurd desire to giggle, "I'm afraid I'm just one more speck in a sea of ignorance."

Sandra stepped back, eyes narrowed to slits, jaw working side to side. She cocked her head and regarded them both snidely. Finally she sniffed and put her nose in the air. "I'll see you in court, then," she said to Parker before turning on her heel and striding away.

One by one, her wide-eyed flock followed. Last of all went Heath. A quiet, burly fellow with a passion for horticulture and too much colorless hair about his ears, he had always seemed the defenseless, long-suffering type to

Kendra. The weak, apologetic shrug he gave them as he turned away did nothing to dispel the impression.

Parker waited skittishly until they were out of earshot before he vented the temper threatening to explode. "She's crazy!" he exclaimed, poking holes in the air with a rigid finger. "No! She's not crazy—she's ambitious, egotistical!" He turned on Kendra, spreading his hands beseechingly. "Don't you get it? This isn't about Darla. This is about Sandra! She's going to try her theories in court. She's going to dazzle some poor, naive judge with her psychobabble, and after he hands over the kid—against the wishes of her deceased parents—*Dr.* Pendleton will happily thumb her nose at her critics! What better way to prove the validity of her screwy ideas?" He clapped both hands to his head. "God, I feel sorry for those kids!"

Kendra sighed, utterly defeated. "I see what you mean," she admitted reluctantly.

He dropped his hands. "You do?"

She nodded. "I guess Nathan and Candace were right after all. She is rather...extreme."

"That's putting it mildly!"

Kendra cravenly changed the subject. "What did you say to her that made her let you take the little girl out of there?"

He folded his arms smugly. "I asked her if she was trying to impress everyone with her parenting skills, and because she was, she had no real option but to shut the kid up any way she could, even if it meant letting me take her out. To tell you the truth, I think she wanted Heath to do it, but because it went against her rule about being able to reason with properly trained children, he just didn't catch on. You should have seen the look she gave him when I took the kid."

Kendra remembered the way the child had gone into his arms without the least hesitation, as if she trusted him on sight. For the first time, Kendra admitted to herself that he had the makings of a wonderful father. Too bad that he just wasn't decent husband material. Nevertheless, she was going to have to marry him. She just couldn't let Sandra take the baby away from him. If only there was some other female who could do this! On the other hand, maybe there was. Well, it was worth a chance, anyway. She bit her lip, mentally seeking the best approach. They were in the car on the way to the cemetery when it came to her.

"Parker," she said carefully, "are you still interested in getting married?"

He sat up straight, the weariness and pallor momentarily banished from his face. "Absolutely."

"Well, I was wondering then," she hurried on, "if you'd considered Jeanna?"

The sudden rise of his brows told her clearly that he had not, and she pressed on, making her case.

"I couldn't help noticing that there's some tension between the two of you and I thought that perhaps you had... that *she* had... grown more fond of you than was wise, perhaps."

His smirk was blatantly arrogant. "You could say that."

Kendra swallowed down an unexpected spurt of indignation. "Then surely that would work in your favor now. I'd bet that if you asked her, she'd—"

"You'd win that bet," he told her flatly, "and that's precisely why Jeanna Crowe is the last woman I'd ask to do this for me."

Kendra looked at him in utter confusion. "You *want* a woman who *doesn't* want you?"

"I want a temporary wife," he snapped, "someone with enough compassion to help me protect Darla from Dr. Frankenstein-in-a-skirt, someone who won't cling to my neck like a wet scarf once the objective is accomplished, and trust me, that is *not* Jeanna Crowe!"

The words fell out of her mouth before she could stop them. "You had an affair with her, didn't you?"

He glowered at her. "Yes."

"And she didn't want it to end, did she?"

Something kindled in the depths of his chocolate-brown eyes, and he shifted slightly toward her. "No."

"You hurt her!" she accused.

He flexed a muscle in his jaw. "She hurt herself. 'Fun and games, Parker,' she said. 'Just fun and games.'"

"But you knew she hoped it would become more," she whispered. "You knew she was hoping for love!"

He stared at her a moment longer, and then he blinked and turned away. "Yes," he said.

She felt tears burning her eyes. It was the day, she told herself, this damned difficult day! What did she care if he'd had "fun and games" with Jeanna? She didn't. She simply felt sorry for her friend, foolish, silly Jeanna. For Parker, she felt nothing but contempt. And that was exactly why she had to do it. She was probably the only female in the whole blasted city who was immune to that fatal Sugarman charm. She could keep Darla out of Sandra Pendleton's "laboratory" and fulfill the last wishes of two of her dearest friends, and she could do it—she'd be damned if she couldn't!—without sacrificing either her heart or her dignity to Parker Sugarman's libido, which was saying a lot more than any of his "play partners" could say.

She took a deep breath, folded her arms, and crossed her legs. "Six months," she said, staring straight ahead. "Not a day more. Not one day more."

He put his head back, then raised it stiffly, swallowed and swallowed again. "Thank you," he said softly. "From the bottom of my heart, thank you."

She glanced to the side. He turned his head away, but not before she saw the tear squeezed from his tightly closed eyes. Instantly she felt her hastily erected barriers crumbling, but she wouldn't believe he was that moved. She wouldn't. It was the day, she told herself, this damned difficult day. She pressed her knuckles to a trembling lip and watched Dallas slide past the limousine window.

Chapter Five

"And so we've agreed," Parker said reasonably, his fingers plucking at the knife-edge crease of his slate-gray slacks, "only you will ever know the truth about this marriage."

Edward leaned forward, braced his elbows against his desktop, and templed his fingers beneath his chin, regarding both Parker and Kendra with the blandly thoughtful expression that had suckered so many unknowing opponents. Kendra glanced guiltily down at her lap, reading all too clearly the temper boiling beneath the calm exterior. Parker crossed his legs and lifted his chin slightly. Edward abruptly dropped his hands to the desktop and glared at Parker.

"You son of a bitch," he said. "You sorry son of a bitch."

Parker grimaced, uncrossed his legs and leaned forward. "You're the one who told me to get married."

"So you immediately go out and arrange to marry the one woman I've ever wanted. You put a mighty high price on friendship, *old buddy*."

Parker sighed in the manner of one forced to counsel a particularly dull child. "The two of you broke up ages ago. Besides, you know perfectly well this is not a romantic situation. It's merely an agreement between friends, a *temporary* arrangement. She's going to help me keep Darla, help me take care of her until I figure out what I'm doing. Then we'll each go our separate ways. It'll seem to everyone else that a friendship of long-standing was spurred into a romance by a mutual tragedy but that the marriage simply didn't work out. After six months or so we'll quietly secure a divorce."

"What's wrong with an annulment?" Edward asked sharply.

Parker shrugged. "Whatever. Makes no difference to me."

"Oh, I think it might," Edward answered, his voice dripping with sarcasm. "A divorce can be had for the flimsiest of excuses—or none at all—but an annulment is a little more difficult to attain, especially if there has been sexual congress."

Kendra felt her cheeks turn to red. "No one need worry about that," she said flatly, keeping her gaze trained on the hands that nervously smoothed the brown suede skirt she wore with matching boots and a cowl-necked sweater of deep gold. She had pinned her hair up in a loose swirl at the crown of her head and let the shorter tendrils fall where they may. One of them now tickled the back of her neck, but she felt too self-conscious in the presence of these two very familiar men to even lift a hand to dislodge it.

She was already deeply regretting her decision to go through with this scheme. Facing Edward was difficult enough. Facing her father and pretending that she had fallen desperately in love with Nathan's rapscallion brother would be next to impossible. But she understood that the marriage must look real and permanent in order to sway the court. Sandra Pendleton would attempt to discredit them as it was. For that reason and that reason only, she had just that morning called Devon Hoyt in New York and had her name removed from the roster of the U.N. medical team. He had been polite but most distressed and had pressed her for a reason.

She hadn't wanted to lie to him, but since she couldn't tell him the truth about her impending marriage, she'd decided not to mention it at all, saying instead that the sudden and tragic death of two dear friends had made it necessary for her to change her plans. She had apologized profusely and told him that she hoped to eventually be able to renew her commitment to the team. When he had blurted that he had so been looking forward to seeing her again, she had felt a sharp stab of guilt and muttered that she, too, would have liked to have renewed their acquaintance. He had begged her please to rethink, but when she had told him weakly that it wouldn't be possible, he had told her that he would need written notification of her withdrawal. Writing that letter had been one of the hardest things she had ever done. And now this. She wondered if she could possibly be more miserable and decided that she probably could. She sighed and stilled her hands.

"Let's get this clear," she said, tension making her snap when she only meant to be adamant. "I'm doing this to keep Sandra Pendleton from gaining custody of the baby. To tell you the truth, I don't know if Parker can take care of Darla or not, but I suppose I'll know soon enough, and if he can't, I'll be there to help until other arrangements can be made."

"There won't be any other arrangements," Parker interjected tersely.

She inclined her head, unwilling to argue the point. During the past night, she had determined that the helpless infant must be her first priority, and she intended to stick to that determination come what may. It had occurred to her at some point during her hours of rumination after the difficult matter of seeing two dear people laid to rest that she would have a considerable amount of power in this situation. Parker dared not let the true circumstances of this impending marriage come to the attention of the court if he intended to acquire and keep custody of little Darla. Therefore, if she saw during the marriage that Parker was not going to be a proper guardian and caretaker, she could see to it that other arrangements were made for the baby. All she had to do was admit that the marriage was a ruse and testify that Parker was unable to discharge his duty to the child. She had even prepared a defense for her own culpability in the matter of the marriage, that being that she believed Sandra Pendleton an even greater risk to the child than Parker. She just didn't see any point in telling all this to Parker. Why make an enemy of the man with whom she would be living for the next six months? Besides, the most important thing at the moment was quelling Edward's anger. It would be up to him, after all, to make their argument in court.

She lifted her gaze to meet Edward's glower. "As I was saying, I'm doing this for Darla and for no other reason. This will be a marriage in name only. We'll live together, and we'll share responsibility for the baby for six months—and only six months. Then I'll be free to get on with my life by renewing my commitment to rendering medical aid in Africa. I expect to do it with a clear conscience *and* an annulment."

Edward met her gaze levelly for several seconds then abruptly switched his attention to Parker. "And what have you got to say to that?"

Parker crossed his legs again, ankle balanced on knee, and plucked at the hem of his slacks. "Nothing, except . . . Nothing."

Edward nodded. "Good. Keep it that way. Then I may not have to take your head off your shoulders."

Parker dropped his foot to the floor and sent his friend a warning glance. "Just do your job and mind your own business and we'll all get through this with as little difficulty as possible."

"That," said Edward, leaning back to lace his fingers casually across his middle, "is exactly what I intend to do. This whole thing being my idiotic idea to begin with, I think you'll agree that it *is* my business, especially as my reputation as an attorney could be at stake."

"Now listen here, White..." Parker began angrily, but Kendra had had enough for one morning.

She shot up to her feet and scolded them both with a divided look. "That's quite enough from both of you. Let's get one thing straight, gentlemen. *I* have the final say here. Without my cooperation, this marriage does not even take place, let alone maintain itself long enough for your purposes. It will go as *I* determine it will go, and I think I've made myself plain as to that. Now I would appreciate it if we could get out of here. I have a great deal to do today. Not only do I have to prepare to get married tomorrow, I have to see about getting my job back, and I promised Cheryl's aunt that we wouldn't be gone long. We're going to have to find another baby-sitter right away, I'm afraid."

Having said her piece, she stepped past Parker, who scrambled to yank his feet back out of her way and follow. Edward, too, came to his feet and moved toward the door.

"I'm just looking after your best interests," he mumbled, catching at her sleeve.

"*I* happen to be the client," Parker reminded him.

"That could change," Edward rumbled.

"Oh, for crying out loud!" she snapped. "This is difficult enough without the two of you acting like petulant schoolboys. Knock it off!"

Edward had the grace to look sheepish. "I just don't want you hurt."

Parker was downright combative. "Nobody's going to get hurt!"

"I know you!" Edward shouted, getting in his face. "You're the one who uses women like Kleenex and tosses them away as soon as you're done!"

"I resent that!"

"I resent you hitting on the one woman who means anything to me!"

"Oh, grow up! It's over. It's been over a long time. And I'm *not* hitting on her, I'm just marrying her!"

Just marrying her. Kendra caught her breath, surprised at the pain in that callous remark. Not hitting on her. Not interested in her personally. Just marrying her. "That's it," she said softly, and walked out, ignoring the gaping stare of Ed's secretary, Brenda, Edward's rumble and Parker's shout.

"Kendra!"

She walked on, fast, hearing Parker's parting shot at Edward.

"Some best friend!"

She walked past the receptionist and across the smartly tiled foyer to the hand-carved door with the heavy, leaded glass inserts and out onto the stoop, down the steps and along the sidewalk. Traffic whizzed by on Oaklawn Avenue.

Parker caught her before she reached the corner and the parking lot set discreetly among the trees and wrought-iron lamps. "Just where do you think you're going?" he asked.

"Africa."

"Come on now, honey..."

"Call me honey again and I'll break your jaw!" She would, too, if she had to use a tire iron. She jerked free of his hold and glared down at the toes of her boots.

"I thought you were going to help me," he said plaintively.

"I thought you were going to behave like a human being."

He closed his eyes, counted silently to ten and opened them again. "What'd I do? Ed's the one who started braying like a jackass. I just..." He stopped, sighed and pinched the bridge of his nose. "I'm a little touchy, all right? For Pete's sake, these last four days have been hell!"

They had, of course. She cooled. It wasn't anything anyway, just a little feminine pique. She usually had better sense, but then it had been a difficult four days. She lifted a hand to brush along the thick, sloping ridge of his shoulder.

"We're both a little touchy." She felt him relax and took her hand away.

"Truce?"

She nodded. "Sure. Why not? We aren't supposed to fight until after the wedding anyway."

He smiled, turned and slid an arm about her waist, urging her forward. "We're not going to fight at all," he said. "We're friends, remember?"

"I remember, but I wonder if Edward will."

He frowned and kicked a pebble that had found its way up onto the sidewalk. "Why did you break it off with him?"

She thought of all the sane, sensible excuses she'd been giving everyone since the break up, but somehow she couldn't make herself repeat them. Then she told herself that she just didn't know why she'd found it increasingly impossible to think about living with Edward White throughout the rest of her life, and to a certain extent that was true. But there was something else, and she knew it, something lurking just beneath the surface of the vague doubts and dissatisfactions. It didn't make much sense, but suddenly she had words for it and she just blurted them out.

"He's too much like my father." But she loved her father, adored him. He was a solid, steady, dependable man, just like Edward.

Parker dropped a look on her, his mouth quirking up on one side. "Dan's a good man," he said. "I'll never forget what he did for Nathan, taking him into the business like that, putting his faith and trust in him, but if you don't mind my saying so, I always found him a little...well, dull."

Dull, she thought. Solid, steady, dependable. Comfortable. She lifted a brow at that. "I guess," she said testily, "given your playboy existence, that my father's wholesome life-style and long, uneventful marriage to my mother must seem pretty tame, but it's just what ninety-nine percent of the world holds its breath and hopes for."

"Including you?"

"Of course, including me."

He shook his head, grin widening. "I don't think so, Nurse Ballard. If that were the case, you'd have married good old, dependable Edward White months ago, but instead you went looking for adventure in Africa—or would have if I hadn't tossed an orphaned infant into your lap."

She didn't like the fact that he'd come so close to pegging something she'd dared not voice aloud. What was wrong with her anyway, tossing aside a perfectly wonderful man like Edward White and then marrying a libertine like Parker, never mind the reasoning? Edward had pleaded for deliverance, too. Edward wanted, needed, a wife, someone to press his shirts and order his house, someone to talk to on long, quiet nights. Edward had promised her stability and normalcy and . . . comfort. She shook her head, scattering the unwelcome thoughts back into the fuzzy netherworld of semiconsciousness. One thing had nothing to do with the other. She wasn't marrying Parker because she wanted to. She was marrying Parker because of Nathan's darling Darla. She stuck her chin out and resorted to the old excuses.

"I didn't marry Edward because I discovered that I'm just not ready to settle down. I want my life to count for something. I have valuable training that should be put to good use before I settle into domestic bliss. Once I'm tied down to a family of my own, it'll be too late."

The look in his eyes was blatantly skeptical, but he only said, "And what about Edward?"

"Edward will find someone else," she said confidently, and in her mind she added, *someone dull*. The unbidden thought sent a guilty flush to her cheeks, but she pretended a sudden exuberance to cover it. "We'd better get moving. I have a thousand things to do."

He held her at his side for a moment, his hand clamped into the curve of her waist; then he smiled and nodded. She slipped away, hurrying toward... She didn't know what she was hurrying toward anymore, or even what she was running from.

They were married late in the afternoon by a judge Edward knew. The three of them went in, Edward gnashing his teeth and glaring, and had it done in short order. Two clerks in the office signed the license as witnesses, Edward refusing to do so while muttering something about his license to practice law. Parker knew, even if Edward did not, that it had much more to do with losing. Edward was an excellent attorney, a great racquetball player, a good competitor in almost any arena, all because along with that fine mind he possessed an absolute loathing for loss. Edward played to win, which was to say that Edward actually *played* very little at all. He did not love Kendra so much as he hated to lose her, or at least it seemed so to Parker, not that it mattered a great deal, for Parker knew something else: Kendra and Edward were wrong for each other, totally wrong.

Kendra was an uptight little thing who needed someone fun and uninhibited to loosen her up. Edward was an uptight *big* thing who also needed someone fun and uninhibited to not only loosen him up but to challenge him, as well. It was all very tidy, because it allowed Parker to feel not in the least guilty about marrying his best friend's ex-fiancé. Very tidy. Especially as the ex-fiancé, now new wife, was a pediatric nurse who nurtured no illusions about him and yet possessed a strongly passionate nature of which she was just barely even aware, and Parker had decided somewhere along the way that there would be no annulment. A divorce, yes—amicable, timely, civilized—but no annulment. But there wouldn't be a wedding night, either.

Such a campaign would require a great deal of finesse and careful planning. The first time would have to be an accident, or as close to it as seduction could be, anyway. It must be an anomaly, a moment of foolishness coupled with overwhelming urges. After the initial tumble, he saw no reason why they could not continue to enjoy themselves until it came time to part. But first he had to show her that sex, in proper perspective and under the right conditions, was harmless, a thing unto itself, which could be kept carefully separate from the marriage, such as it was, and even from the friendship, which he did treasure, especially after she had very generously married him. He began with the kiss that came with the pronouncement of their binding.

Not too ardent, but not perfunctory, either. It had to be engineered precisely, with just enough clinging of the lips to demonstrate possession. He did not take her in his arms. Instead, he placed his hands upon her shoulders, and then moved one of them carefully to the side of her head, gently cupping her ear, his fingers lightly infiltrating the fine strands of rich brown hair with its shimmers of bronze and copper. He canted his own head to the precise angle and leaned forward slightly, settling his mouth against hers and closing his eyes. She tasted sweet, very, very sweet, and as clean as sun-dried linens. He felt a heady thrill of anticipation and smiled as he pulled away from her. Her gaze was solemn and troubled and closed.

After the "wedding," they returned to Edward's office where they relieved a besotted Brenda of a fussy baby. Kendra checked Darla's diaper, which was dry, and gave her a little formula, then carefully calmed her. Her every movement was efficient and knowledgeable.

Parker watched with keen satisfaction. His wife. His baby. Playing house could be fun. He grinned, well aware how out of character this was for him. But babies did things to people. Besides, she was all he had, this little scrap of humanity. He watched Kendra patting her tiny back as she rocked to and fro, and he saw himself down through the years with Darla, his darling Darla. He saw her as a jet-haired, potbellied ballerina with big doe eyes and a gamin smile. He saw a confident tomboy with a swinging ponytail. He saw a budding beauty ready for her first dance. Himself he saw as a fatherly patron of the arts, a softball coach—or maybe soccer—a wise and knowing dance master, a best friend and buddy, just a little superior, older, loving. He saw himself and her, and he imagined it would be just as it had been with him and Nathan, a little more complicated, perhaps, but essentially the same.

The baby went to sleep against Kendra's shoulder and was carefully tucked into the car seat, which was doubling as a carryall. To his amazement, Kendra's embarrassment, and Edward's chagrin, Brenda and the receptionist had taken it upon themselves to fetch in a bottle of bubbly with which to toast the bride and groom, the assumption being that the recent tragedy had rendered a proper reception in poor taste. They did their best to make it a festive single drink, but despite their efforts, Kendra's lips barely touched her wine and Edward didn't even make a pretense of sipping. Parker drank and smiled and tried to be happy enough for all of them.

"We should go," Kendra said after a few minutes. "Dad is expecting us."

The dreaded meeting with Dan Ballard. Parker refused to let it trouble him. He had enough troubles just now. The deaths of his brother and sister-in-law were a constant ache that grew at times to a great, tearing, throbbing pain that momentarily robbed him of sanity and strength. And then there was Sandra Pendleton. He could not rest while any threat remained to his guardianship of Darla, and yet somehow he had to live under that threat until it was settled once and for all. Months, Edward had said. The court would appoint an attorney to represent the child's interests. Studies would have to be done, opinions solicited, recommendations made. It scared the hell out of him. But he had Kendra, his secret weapon in the fight against Dr. Pendleton and her crazy notions. His wife. How remarkable that he should have a wife.

He picked up the car seat and carried Darla to the door. Kendra followed with the diaper bag and a warm blanket to tuck around the baby. He paused, and she tucked, flipping the end of the blanket up over the baby's face as protection from the cool air of early evening. They walked to the car, a sporty silver two-door with all the extras. He wondered if it was sensible enough for a man with a family. Would the court care what sort of car he drove? He made a mental note to ask Edward. Surely a station wagon wouldn't be necessary.

They buckled in the baby and took their places. Kendra looked pale and nervous. Before he started the engine, he reached over and squeezed her hand. "You're a good woman. Nathan always said what a good woman you are. And you're a good friend, too. I promise you won't regret this."

Her expression did not change, and yet sadness seemed to come over her, a deep, welling grief that filled her eyes and shadowed her face.

He was startled. "Kendra?"

"Oh, it's nothing," she said, and the tears started to fall.

"Kendra!" He put his arms around her and pulled her as close as the bucket seats would allow. "I'll make it all right, I swear."

She laughed huskily. "It's so silly! I guess I had more girlish dreams than I realized. Oh, and Parker, my father wasn't even there. I got married and my own father wasn't even there!"

He didn't know what to say to that, how to restore her "girlish dreams." He just held her close, his nose buried in her fragrant hair, and wanted to kiss her. Oh, how he wanted to kiss her! After a few seconds, she wiped her fingers across her cheeks and drew away.

"All right now?" he asked.

She nodded and gave him a stilted smile that quickly faded. "It would be so much easier if we didn't have to pretend."

"Yes," he said.

"But Edward says it's necessary. The court wouldn't take kindly to being duped."

"No," he said.

She patted his thigh, which made him instantly uncomfortable in the most lascivious way. "We'd better go."

He started the engine and drove her to her father's house.

It was an older home off Walnut Hill Lane, a rather stately place despite its size and mixed style. Less than two thousand square feet, he could only call it a Tudor ranch, a mixture of brick, wood and rock with high, overhanging windows and narrow eaves. The lot was good, covered in trees and gently sloping for excellent drainage. The house itself sat rather far back from the street, which made room for a wide, curving drive without sacrificing a showplace lawn. Dan Ballard had done a lot of gardening, landscaping and general maintenance since his retirement, and it showed. The place was picture perfect. Parker noticed a sleek, expensive "status" car parked in the garage beside Dan's sensible, late-model sedan.

Kendra noticed it, too, and grimaced. "Kate's here. I think she's living here, and he just doesn't want to admit it."

Her vehemence surprised him. "Kate?" he said questioningly.

"Oh, they started up four or five months ago, and it's... I don't know. Something's strange about it. She's nothing like my mother, and he's... It's like she has this *hold* on him."

"And you don't like her," he said.

"It isn't that."

"Isn't it?"

"No. It's... it's creepy, is what it is."

"Do you want to go and come back later?"

She shook her head. "No, I told you. He's expecting us."

He parked the car close to the house, then got out to open Kendra's door and unbuckle the baby. They were standing at the door side by side, car seat and baby in his arms, diaper bag in hers, when Dan opened it. He smiled, and they both smiled back.

"Parker, how are you?"

"As well as can be expected, thank you."

"Come in, come in. Don't stand out there in the cold night air." Dan fussed around them as they got inside with all their paraphernalia. "How is she, the little one?"

"Fine, I think."

"Sad thing, terrible thing. I can't bear even to think of it still. Such wonderful young people."

"Yes, sir," Parker said. "The very best."

Dan herded them toward the living room. Kate was standing before the fireplace in a slim silk pantsuit she had definitely not worn to work unless her work was very unusual and highly titillating. Parker swept an appreciative eye over her. She was tall and elegant, blond by design and several years older than him, which still put her at least a decade under Dan Ballard. She exuded a fierce, unmistakable sexuality. A very interesting woman, he would have to say. Kendra hated her. He could sense it in the air, and he knew that Kate could, too.

Parker set the baby in her car seat on the coffee table. Introductions were made. They all sat down, he and Kendra on the couch, Dan in the big chair opposite them, with Kate perched on its arm. Parker laid his hand deliberately on Kendra's knee and sent her a secret look from the corners of his eyes. She settled more comfortably next to him and pretended to relax. He traced the indentation just below her kneecap with the tip of his finger and felt the tremor that he had started beneath his palm. Satisfied, he looked at Dan and began.

"We have a rather startling piece of news."

"Not so startling really, when you think about it," Kendra said quickly.

He smiled at her and lifted his hand from her knee to drape his arm about her shoulders. "It's all right, darling," he said. "We're adults, after all, and we've known each other a long time."

"All of our lives practically!" she interjected a bit too brightly.

Dan and Kate looked at one another.

Parker tightened his arm about Kendra and took the plunge. "Kendra and I were married this afternoon."

He could not have stunned them more effectively if he'd fallen to the floor in a fit. For a long moment, neither of them moved or spoke or so much as breathed, and then he smiled, that charming, full-of-the-love-of-life smile of his, and Dan Ballard bought it hook, line and sinker.

"Married, for the love of God! Parker, my boy, my...son-in-law!" Suddenly Dan and Kate were on their feet again.

Parker nudged Kendra up, smiling, his eyes holding hers as Dan Ballard wrapped him in a bear hug and Kate folded her in. Parker couldn't tell what Kendra was thinking or feeling, but he was pleased, immensely pleased. He was even relishing his role, which was easy enough to do, considering that it wasn't permanent. When everybody had hugged everybody and exclaimed enough to wake the baby, they all took their seats again. Kendra held Darla and comforted her absently, her eyes flitting from one face to another while Parker fielded a barrage of questions.

"It's been coming on for some time actually," he lied as easily as buttering bread. "I think we both knew it but neither of us wanted to admit it, and then the accident... I guess we just suddenly realized how much we meant to each other." He gave Kendra a long, full look. "I certainly realized how much I need her." He took a breath and switched his gaze back to Dan. "We're going to raise Darla ourselves." He thought it best not to say anything about Sandra Pendleton's intentions just yet. Let them get used to the idea of the marriage first. "Maybe have one or two of our own eventually." That was laying it on a bit thick and he knew it, but what the heck.

Dan Ballard was positively jubilant by this point. "I can't believe it," he said to no one in particular. "Thank God she's not going to Africa! Holy cow, I guess I'm the next thing to a grandfather now, aren't I?"

"She's a beautiful baby," Kate said, leaning forward with her elbows on her knees and her hands twined together.

"Yes, she is," Kendra said softly, "very beautiful."

Something about the way she said it, the wistfulness of it, or maybe just the sincerity in it, went through Parker like a bolt of shimmering light. He looked down just as she looked up, and something behind her eyes leapt out at him. A yearning, a need. He leaned over and kissed her, his hand at the back of her head. She opened her mouth beneath his and, briefly, kissed him back. It was over in an instant, a heartbeat, two, no more, but it was enough to send a hot, wild lust through him, a raging, desperate need to feel and taste and invade her naked flesh. No annulment. No annulment, no way.

Parker looked at Kendra's father and smiled and knew he was everything people had ever called him, and he smiled some more.

Chapter Six

"Leave the crib here," Kendra said. "I'll move into the other room."

Parker shook his head. "Let's think this out, shall we? There will be home studies, Edward said. People coming in to look us over. Will they think this is a real marriage if they see you living in one room and the baby and I in another?"

She fixed him with a flat stare. "You're not suggesting that you and I sleep in the same room, are you?"

He pursed his lips. "No, not exactly. But you will have to put your things in here. It has to *look* like we're sleeping together. Of course, one of us will be sleeping here in the master suite, and one of us will be sleeping on the extra bed in the baby's room."

"And which one of us gets to get up with the baby every night?" she asked cryptically.

He smiled. "We'll take turns. I have to work tomorrow, but I'll be glad to go first if you like."

"How magnanimous," she retorted coolly. "But I have to wonder what you're going to do if I don't get a permanent shift at the hospital. Get up with the baby every night?"

He made a doubtful face. "Surely you're higher up on the totem pole than that."

She mimicked him, pulling a doubtful face of her own. "I wouldn't count on it. Chances are I'll be in at the bottom again."

He sighed. "Well, we'll cross that bridge when we get to it. Meanwhile, will you do the honors tonight, or shall I?"

"You have to work tomorrow," she reminded him sweetly. "I'll get up with the baby tonight."

He smiled, and she knew without a doubt that she'd played right into his hands. But what the heck? He *did* have to work tomorrow.

Kendra helped Parker partially dismantle the crib and maneuver it out of his bedroom and along the gallery, which was separated from the living area, as was the kitchen and dining area, by tall plaster columns. They wrestled the awkwardly rolling bed past the powder room to what had been until this moment the guest room. It didn't fit. Parker had sacrificed space in the less used portions of the house for the large, elegant, open living area where he liked to entertain crowds of people. The guest room, now the baby's room, was the smallest in the house. Kendra looked at Parker and shrugged. Wordlessly, they moved to the bedside table, lifted it and hauled it out of the room.

Next went the darling antique curio cabinet in the corner, followed by the small, satin-covered armchair. The four-drawer dresser had to be moved to another wall, with the mirror to follow later. Finally, they shoved the full-size bed up against the wall and positioned the crib next to it.

The baby was sleeping in her car seat, safely tucked into the corner of one of a pair of long, white couches in the center of the living room. Parker transferred her to the newly made-up crib, removed her tiny soft-soled shoes and tucked her in without waking her, while Kendra began to unpack her necessary personal belongings and put them away in the master bedroom, making room as she had to. Parker was almost depressingly neat and organized, his slacks on one side of the closet, shirts on another, coats and vest in their own areas, shoes lined up neatly on the floor around the perimeter. Kendra shoved them all together and hung her own jumbled belongings haphazardly upon the rods.

In the bathroom, his razor was laid neatly next to his toothbrush in one drawer, his hairbrush and comb in another. The bottles in his medicine cabinet were all positioned carefully with their labels turned out for easy reading. His hair dryer hung on a hook behind a door on the underside of the sink. Kendra dumped all of his things into one drawer and her own in another. She stuffed her medicine bottles into the cabinet and shimmied the door until it closed. She slung her hair dryer, curling rod and hot rollers into the cabinet beneath the sink, tossed a can of hairspray in on top of them and hung a plastic bag of extra cosmetics on the hook with Parker's dryer. Her shampoo and conditioner were stashed into corners of the shower. That left only the dresser drawers to shuffle around and stuff with panties, bras, slips, gowns, scarves, stockings and the comfy old clothes in which she lounged around the house.

Parker came into the room and glanced around him. He smiled with pleasure at a room that looked exactly as he'd left it. "All done?" he asked.

"All done," she said.

He rubbed his hands together. "Good. Let's have dinner."

She smiled as she walked past him. "Fine. What are you making?" She pretended not to notice as his eyebrows shot up.

They had warmed-over pizza out of the refrigerator and a salad cobbled up from canned peas, lettuce, radishes and shredded carrot. He seemed determined to make it a festive affair, putting out fringed cotton napkins, white stoneware and candles, along with marble-handled flatware and stemmed glasses filled with fragrant red wine. He lit the candles, and they sat down to enjoy an adequate but pleasant meal. The handle on the front door rattled faintly, then the doorbell rang three times in quick succession. Finally a fist pounded on the closed door. A thin, shrill cry came from the bedroom and quickly built in volume. Parker hung his head. Kendra pushed her chair back and said, "I'll get the baby."

"I'll kill whoever's at the door."

She had to laugh as she hurried in one direction and he in another. She returned to the kitchen with the baby hiccupping against her shoulder to find Edward sitting in her place, sullenly sipping her wine and munching her pizza. Parker set another place for her and shared the pizza off his plate, placing his own wine close to her hand. She smiled her thanks and sat down.

"What's up?" she asked offhandedly, lowering the baby to her lap.

Parker slanted a look at Edward. "He was just wondering how your father took the news."

She bounced the baby gently on her knee and reached for the wine glass. "He was thrilled," she said drolly, "absolutely thrilled. He considers Darla the next thing to a granddaughter and waits breathlessly for us to produce the real thing."

Edward choked on his wine, coughing a spray of it into his napkin. Kendra sipped hers, grinning wickedly over the rim of the glass at Parker, who cleared his throat to derail a laugh. She put her wine down and picked up a piece of pizza, nipping off the end with her front teeth and transferring it to the back of her mouth for chewing. Parker picked up her glass and sipped from it, his eyes on hers. For some reason she felt warm all over when his lips touched the rim, but she denied the feeling and switched her gaze. Edward put his elbows up on the table and looked from Parker to her mournfully.

"I'll never forgive myself for this," he said. "It's all my fault for suggesting he find a wife. I should have known he'd go to you. I should have known."

She smiled sympathetically. "I'm a big girl, Ed. I make my own decisions and I live with the consequences."

He didn't seem in the least cheered. "*We* could have thrilled him," he said. "*We* could have given him grand-children."

She didn't pretend not to understand. "No, Ed, we couldn't."

He looked at her a long moment, then slowly nodded and stood, thumb and small finger massaging his temples as if he had a headache. "You just call if you need me. You know all the numbers."

"Thanks. I'll remember that, but it's going to be fine. The hard part's over now, and it's going to be fine."

He looked at her as if memorizing her as she was at that moment, as if he expected some remarkable change to alter her before he saw her again. She smiled, and he turned away, dragging his feet toward the door. The baby bur-bled, calling Kendra's attention down to her lap. She made sheep's eyes at the little thing and tickled her under the chin while Edward made his exit. She looked up to find Parker smiling at them, his forearms folded against the edge of the table.

"You look good with her," he said softly, "like you be-long."

She felt a drop of icy fear slide down her spine and in-stantly raised her barriers. "I should," she said. "I've handled children of all ages and sizes throughout my ca-reer. That's one of the reasons I'm here, isn't it?"

He just looked at her and reached for the wineglass, leaning back from the edge of his chair. "One of the rea-sons."

She kept her expression carefully neutral, weighing that answer with the memory of his arm draped possessively about her shoulders while they sat on her father's sofa, the feel of his mouth on hers and the weight of his hand on the back of her head. She thought how happy her father had been to hear that she had married this man, how completely accepting of it he was. She thought how right it had felt to sit in her father's living room as a married woman with this man at her side and his infant in her lap, and she wondered if she was sane, if Edward saw much more clearly than she realized, after all. She had given up Africa for this.

No, not given up, she promised herself, merely postponed. She would go to Africa in six months, the marriage annulled, the baby safely placed and cared for, her obligations to three good friends met in full. Her conscience would be clear, her heart light. She would even find a way to make it all right with her father and Edward. Everything would be fine if she just kept these things in mind.

She looked at Parker, lounging on the edge of his chair, his dark eyes holding her image in their black centers. He was devastatingly attractive, his hair waving away from his handsome face, long arms and legs bunched with muscles even in relaxation, soft shirt molding to the sleek, hard planes of his chest. She looked at him and congratulated herself for recognizing the danger there in that lean, hard body and sculpted face. She looked at him and knew this wasn't going to be as easy as she wanted to believe.

"It's time this little one and I put it to bed," she said, lifting the baby in her arms as she stood. "Thanks for the dinner. Good night."

He said nothing as she walked away, just smiled down into his wine as if he knew a secret he wasn't about to tell.

She carried the baby back to the bedroom, changed her, zipped her into a sleeper and laid her on her side, patting her tiny back until the lids lowered over her eyes and her breathing deepened and evened. She was a good baby and so very beautiful with her black hair and eyes and ivory skin. Kendra smiled down at her, then tiptoed away to gather her things for the night. She shed the jeans and T-shirt she'd traded earlier for the pearl-white suit with the gold braid that she'd worn to be married in and slipped into a long nylon shirt with a simple V neck and short sleeves. She brushed out her hair, twisted it up and fastened it atop her head with a butterfly clip, then went into the bathroom to brush her teeth, wash her face and moisturize her skin. She padded back into the bedroom on bare feet, folded back the covers on the bed, and turned out the light. With a sigh, she slid between the sheets, piled both pillows together and settled down to sleep.

Ten minutes later, the door onto the gallery opened softly, casting a distorted rectangle of light onto the carpet and foot of her bed. Parker walked into the room and over to the crib, where he leaned his forearms on the rail and gazed down at the baby. He stood that way for a long time, smiling to himself and moving his gaze over the tiny form. Finally he leaned forward and placed a feather-light kiss on that dainty brow, then he straightened and turned away. A single step carried him to the bed. He turned and sank down onto the edge of it, the mattress pitching slightly beneath his weight. He stretched his arm across her and planted a hand upon the mattress near her hip, leaning slowly forward to kiss her cheek and nuzzle her with his nose.

"You smell wonderful," he whispered, before drawing back a short space. "Sleep in tomorrow if you can, and I'll see you about five in the afternoon. I'll leave the office number next to the phone in the kitchen. It's a private line. You can call if you want. Oh, and I'll leave some money on the counter, too. Do whatever you want about dinner, okay?"

She nodded, and he reached up to release the butterfly clip holding her hair. It tumbled down, and he smoothed it away from her face, rubbing the silky strands between his fingers. He smiled and leaned forward again, kissing her gently on the mouth. Then he stood and looked down at her.

"Sleep well, and take care of my little girl for me—wife." He turned and moved quietly from the room, taking the light with him.

As the door closed, Kendra let out her breath and lifted a hand to her chest. Her heart was racing so hard and fast that the whole room seemed to vibrate with it. She closed her eyes and tried not to feel his hands smoothing her hair away from her face, his lips on hers, the heat of his breath. "You smell wonderful," he had said. She bit her knuckle and forbade herself the luxury of fantasy.

The baby woke Kendra twice in the night. The first time she slung on her bathrobe and stumbled into the kitchen to warm a bottle. The second time, she stumbled in her nightshirt, the bathrobe fallen in a forgotten heap beside the bed. She was dismayed the second time to find that the last diaper had leaked, soaking the infant from chubby knees to nonexistent waist and the bed sheet in a large circle beneath her. She propped the bottle long enough to get a dry pad beneath the baby and her clothing changed, then cuddled her close while Darla sucked down three ounces of milky formula, burped and dropped into a sound sleep. Kendra laid her in the center of her own bed while she stripped away the crib sheet and mattress pad, only to find that she had nothing with which to replace them.

She searched the bathroom, the dresser and the laundry room off the kitchen. She looked through the closet that opened onto the gallery and made a cursory check of the coat closet in the entry foyer before turning reluctantly toward the master suite. She tapped lightly at the door, waited and turned the knob, pushing the door open with infinite care. Six feet into the large chamber, she found herself standing in thick darkness, wondering where to look first. Mentally, she went over all the furnishings in the room: the entertainment center, the dresser, the wardrobe, the nightstands, the chairs, the chaise, the massive king-size water bed with its unique sleigh-style frame hinting obliquely at Egyptian influence. The contents of the dresser she knew well. The wardrobe then. The doors squeaked softly as she pulled them open.

"Ken'ra?"

She whirled, staring into the dark shape of the bed. She waited, but no other word came. She canted her head, taking stock. His voice had sounded heavy and thick, the syllables slurred and indistinct. Could he possibly have spoken in his sleep? She tiptoed closer to the bed, bending forward at the waist in an attempt to discern whether or not he slept or merely waited. He sighed and shifted slightly. *Sleeping,* she thought, and bit her lip, wondering if she should wake him or continue searching in the black shadows. He mumbled something unintelligible, and she decided to wake him. Moving about the room while he muttered in his sleep smacked too much of voyeurism for comfort.

She whispered his name, but he made no response. She spoke a bit louder, wanting to penetrate his slumber but not startle him out of it. He rolled onto his side, facing her. "Hmmmm?"

"I need sheets for the crib. The baby wet—"

He rubbed a hand drunkenly over his nose. "Hmmmmm?"

"Sheets for the crib."

Nothing.

She sighed in exasperation and reached far forward to nudge his shoulder. He rolled over onto his back, his hands coming up to fasten onto her arms. Effortlessly, he pulled her to him. Her thighs hit the high, heavy frame of the bed, and she toppled over on top of him, knocking the breath from her lungs in a near silent whoosh as the bed dipped and rocked upward again. He slid his arms around her, one across her shoulders, the other against the small of her back.

"Come here, honey," he muttered, shifting his hips beneath her. His breath was hot against her temple, his chest hard beneath her breasts, the long lump of his sex pressed intimately into the softness of her belly. The bed undu-

lated beneath them, and she gasped. He sleepily followed
the sound to her mouth, sliding his tongue inside and
sucking lazily at her parted lips. Of its own accord, her
body relaxed, warming to the erotic pulse of his as they
rode the gentle swell of the water bed. His hand slid down
to cup her buttocks, pulling her higher as he thrust against
her. She felt the hard length of him like a jolt of white-hot
electricity through the cotton sheet and her nightshirt. Instinctively, she recoiled, recognizing the danger and her
own vulnerability in a crystalline burst of clarity. She
pushed up onto her knees, one hand planted in his midsection just above his navel. The bed roiled, nearly throwing her down atop him again. He doubled up sharply,
impelled by the weight behind that hand in his midsection
and effectively threw her off.

"What—" He levered his upper body weight onto one
arm and spread his legs in an effort to stabilize the bed, his
other hand pushing into his hair. "Kendra?"

She scrambled off the bed, knocking her knee painfully
on the frame in the process. "Sheets!" she gasped. "Crib
sheets!"

"Sheets?" he repeated dumbly.

"For the crib, dammit! I need sheets for the crib!"

She could see him thinking as he lay there on the gently
undulating bed, his arm bent beneath him. She knew the
moment he realized the condition of his body and the reason for it, the moment he found an answer for her.

He pushed his arm from beneath him and lay back on
the bed. "Bottom drawer." He pointed toward the opened
doors of the wardrobe. "Front left corner."

He would know *exactly* where they were. She whirled
and stalked to the cabinet, fell down on her throbbing
knee, yanked the drawer out and grabbed the neatly folded
square from the front left corner. She shoved the drawer
closed and leapt up to her feet, heading for the doorway.

He went up on his elbow again. "Kendra?"

She paused, not daring to turn back. "Hmm?"

"What happened?"

She deliberately misunderstood him. "The baby wet the bed."

Silence, and then he said, "Oh."

She nearly collapsed with relief. "Sorry-I-woke-you-good-night."

Safe in the baby's room, she put her back to the door and pumped calming oxygen into her lungs.

What happened?

What *had* happened? She shook her head. Nothing—except she'd felt him hard and ready beneath her, and her treacherous mind had whispered, *"Husband,"* and her body had almost believed it. God help her if her heart hadn't believed, too, for an instant. And for an instant, she had been his, wanting so badly to have him buried inside her, wanting so badly to make pretense *real*. When had she started wanting him? When had she *not* wanted him? Wild, sexy, provocative, arrogant Parker, who had had so many women wake him from a sound sleep that he automatically started to make love by rote when the opportunity presented itself. Had she always wanted him in some dark, secret part of her, always been drawn by the lure of forbidden fruit, the excitement of that dangerous eroticism? She knew she had, but she knew, too, how utterly foolish it would be to fall victim to that allure. She lay awake well into the morning, trying to ignore the heat that smoldered deep inside her body and kept turning her mind to fantasies of what it might have been like.

Kendra was sleeping the sleep of the exhausted when Parker crept into the room the next morning to take a look before he left for work. Darla, too, was slumbering contentedly—on her back, he noticed, though he clearly remembered Candace saying that infants should be put on their sides or stomachs to sleep. He shrugged, quite sure that Kendra knew what she was doing, and put it out of his mind. Though he wanted to, he didn't kiss the baby, for fear that he'd wake her and put an end to Kendra's rest. Kendra herself looked as if she could sleep through a small invasion on her person. He bent, smoothed the hair from her face, and kissed the slight indentation of her temple. It was not enough. He wanted so much more. He wanted to touch her in all the intimate places of intense pleasure. He wanted to make her smile, make her sigh, make her pant and scream and scratch his back with her nails.

He had thought for a dreamy, confused moment last night that she wanted the same thing. He had awakened to the wonderful idea that she had come to him, that he was to have his wedding night after all. When the truth had penetrated the fog of sleep around his sex-drugged brain, he'd felt the kind of deep, distressing disappointment that he'd thought he'd left behind him in adolescence. He'd lain awake quite a while pondering that. He'd had almost as many failures with women as successes—any honest man did—but he'd never before felt the kind of depressing disappointment that had swamped him last night. It didn't quite make sense unless... Being married, having a wife and all the attendant rights was a strangely erotic phenomenon, except that Kendra wasn't *completely* his wife. Yet. But she would be. He'd felt it when he'd put his tongue in her mouth and her body had melted against his like hot wax to flame.

He closed his eyes, remembering again the shocking weight of her breasts, much heavier than he'd realized, and the inviting suppleness of her belly. He'd been surprised by the narrowness of her waist, the lushness of the curves above and below, the long slender limbs. She did not dress to accentuate her assets, his little wife, and he found himself strangely pleased with that. He'd felt as if he'd held a secret in his arms last night, a very sexy, very female secret, the depths of which he had not even begun to plumb. He brushed his lips against the corner of her mouth and made himself leave.

He was eager to get into the office, eager to bring some normalcy back to his life. He wanted to settle into the new office, see his name chiseled into granite alongside those of the other partners. He needed to work, to design again, building the vision in his mind and transferring it to paper, watching it take shape stage by stage until it stood before him, a *livable* work of art. He'd been giving thought lately to redesigning his own home yet again. He just hadn't planned on a baby when he'd come up with this latest rendition. Besides, he loved playing with the basic plans, seeing what he could come up with, given the parameters of a fifty-year-old original structure. He studied different ideas on the drive downtown to work.

Over its many transformations, he'd given the elevation of the house a decidedly French flavor via a hip roof, stucco, cornice detailing and paned glass windows, while producing a sleek modern look inside with the aid of recessed lighting, raised ceilings, multilevel floors and a score of thirty-inch columns. He was thinking now that he might add a room or two. After all, he really ought to maintain space for guests, and Darla would soon require a place to play where the clutter of children's things would not disrupt the general orderliness of his—their—home.

Orderliness. He shook his head over the discoveries made behind the neat facade of his bedroom this morning. Who'd have thought his delicious little wife was such a slob? He'd already made some adjustments in the bathroom, but that closet was going to take some time. How on earth did she ever turn herself out so attractively from such a muddle? Well, he was sure she'd take the hint from the improvements he'd made in their bathroom arrangement and do something about that closet. Perhaps she would even fold some of those things she'd crammed into his dresser drawers. He wasn't bothered by the obvious incompatibility of their organizational styles. His was by far the superior, and she was bound to see that. Kendra was nobody's fool, after all.

He parked in his new reserved space in the tiny parking lot next to the ultramodern granite-and-glass high rise designed, built, owned and operated by his firm. He strode along the sidewalk, briefcase and plan tube in tow, aware that he was not quite as ebullient as he ought to be on his first day as a partner in one of the area's most distinguished and successful architectural firms. But then, that was understandable, all things considered. No matter what he did, he could not rid himself of the black knowledge of his brother's death. And yet, his dissatisfaction felt oddly foreign to the tragedy. Ah, well, one could but endure until the clouds lifted.

He pushed through the heavy glass door into the building, crossed the empty lobby to the elevators and slid his bright copper executive key into the executive's elevator lock. The door opened immediately. He stepped inside and pushed the top floor button. The elevator whisked upward silently and floated to a stop. The door opened, and he stepped out into the plush, quiet luxury of the executive floor. The receptionist leaned forward and smiled welcomingly, pushing a button on the underside of her desk. Doors opened on every side and people stepped out to greet him.

"Mr. Sugarman, welcome back."

"Good to see you again, Parker."

"So sorry about your brother and his wife."

"Is there anything we can do?"

"Welcome to the executive suite, my boy. We've set you up in a nice quiet office right around the corner." The last came from the senior partner, who ushered him away from the others. They turned the corner and came to a sterile cubicle containing only a desk and a telephone. "Your secretary's space," he was informed. "You'll also need a drafting assistant, of course." He was shown another space, somewhat larger and with a door, then was escorted on to his own office.

It was a large, airy room, the outside wall of which was composed entirely of glass. The view was not particularly spectacular, but that would come as he moved on up the corporate ladder. He looked around him, quite pleased. He'd picked out the decor and furnishings himself, of course, but he'd been unable to supervise the actual outfitting. He saw that his eye and sense of style had not betrayed him. His drawing board was set up near the window wall, everything laid out and waiting for him. A desk, chairs, file cabinet, planning table and bookcases were artfully arranged to make the most of the remaining space. He laid his briefcase on the desk, left the plan tube on the drawing table and hung his coat on the rack he'd ordered for that purpose.

"You'll want to begin interviewing for that secretary and assistant," the senior partner said. "Just call down to personnel, and they'll send up the qualified applicants."

"Thanks," Parker said, moving around behind his desk to sit down, "but I'd really rather get right to work. I've got a few ideas for the Bronson project."

The senior partner pursed his lips thoughtfully, then slipped his hands into his pockets and made a little shrug. "Suit yourself. Some of the fellows and I would like to take you to lunch to celebrate your first day as a partner. Would eleven-thirty work for you?"

"Anything will work for me," Parker said, flicking open his briefcase and removing papers.

"Eleven-thirty, then. Oh, and Parker, my condolences."

He spread his hands on the top of the desk and nodded. "Thanks."

The other man went out and closed the door. A sudden silence descended and with it a sudden loneliness. Parker sat back in his chair and stared out the window wall of his office. *Oh, Nathan,* he thought, *what have you done to me?* He got up and wandered over to the drawing board, but the urge to work had vanished with his enjoyment of the day. He slid his hands into his pockets and stood staring down at the parking lot.

Were they still sleeping? he wondered. Would Kendra wake and remember with the same flood of feeling as he what it had felt like last night? Would the baby fret and make a picture of him in her mind? Could she possibly miss him? It occurred to him that he hadn't told anyone that he had married and taken his brother's child to raise. He would tell them at lunch.

Lunch. It seemed an awfully long time away. The hours looked as long as aeons from this rarefied perspective. He closed his eyes, feeling a little ill, his stomach churning. He ought to get a danish or something and a cup of coffee, but he didn't really want anything to eat.

He only wanted to go home and gather them both safely into his arms.

Chapter Seven

He was surprisingly tired, not that he'd accomplished a great deal. For some reason, he couldn't stop thinking about Nathan and Candace and Darla and Kendra. He had lost the first pair, and he wanted to be with the second. He wanted to know they were all right. He wanted to know they were safe. He wanted to know he wasn't going to lose them, too. But he was going to lose Kendra eventually, of course, in a way. He was going to lose her excellent services in caring for his niece, and he stood to lose her friendship as well, unless he could control his sex drive. He'd given it lots of thought during the day, and he'd come to the conclusion that seducing her would be a huge mistake. Sleeping with her would make the marriage all too real. Emotions that should be absent could well become engaged. The divorce would be just that, a real divorce with all the attendant baggage. The friendship would cease to exist, and after the losses he had recently suffered, he was just not ready to contemplate that. And yet the very idea of denying himself the pleasure he knew he could find in her bed was as hurtful as the thought of being alone, truly alone.

He told himself he was blowing the sex thing way out of proportion. He had been crazy for certain women before but never like this. It was just the circumstances, the grief, the loss, suddenly finding himself alone in the world except for a dark-eyed cherub who couldn't even understand that a battle was about to be waged for the privilege of caring for her. It was just that Darla and securing their future together had had to come first, that Kendra's friendship and generosity had filled those needs when none other's could. It was gratitude and desperation and proximity and the novelty of actually being legally bound to her. It was the idea that she was his in ways no other woman ever had been. It was sharing his home and Darla with her. It was the way she looked at him sometimes and the way she looked, period. It was a peculiar kind of insanity that he simply had to wait out, rise above and put behind him. He could do that. He had to.

The emotional turmoil was taxing, far more so than he had imagined. It was only natural, therefore, that he should long for home and those awaiting him there. He drove a little too fast on the way back to the house, and he realized that it made him nervous. He couldn't forget that it was a traffic accident that had taken the lives of the two people closest to him. Yet he kept feeling his foot depress the accelerator. And he kept hoping that they would be as happy to see him as he would be to see them.

He came in the back way, turning the car down the alley to access the garage behind the house. He pulled in, killed the engine, dropped the remote garage door controller into his breast pocket, grabbed the handle of his briefcase and the plan tube that contained the drawings he meant to go over that evening and got out. He slapped the garage door controller against his chest as he headed for the house and heard the screech of the door as it lowered behind him. He stepped up into the back hall and walked around the corner, thrilled with the soft glow of light and the wonderful aroma that greeted him. She was cooking. The pleasure of that washed through him and opened a hole in his stomach.

A very pleasant sense of anticipation gripped him, and he stood for a moment wondering if it would be terribly corny of him to call out that he was home. He decided against it in case Darla was asleep. They hadn't had much chance yet to establish a routine, and he didn't want to derail any attempts on Kendra's part to start them along that path. He stepped down into the living area, crossed it, and stepped up again into the dining area. He could see enough between the columns separating dining area and kitchen to see that Kendra was seated at the breakfast table. A slimly jeaned calf, a bare ankle and a small foot encased in a leather flat were swinging rhythmically side to side between the table's legs. Parker smiled to himself, taking a perverse pleasure in the delicate turn of that ankle, and stepped up into the kitchen.

Edward White was sitting next to her, a sappy grin on his face, and his hand was covering hers where it lay against the tabletop. Kendra was speaking softly to the baby, who rested atop the table in a yellow plastic seat Parker had never seen before. A sharp, hot anger shot through him in the instant before Kendra looked up, smiled and said, "Guess what?"

The words just tumbled out of his mouth. "Company for dinner?" he asked acidly.

She looked slightly amused. "I rather doubt it, but since you've brought it up... Ed, would you like to stay for dinner?"

Edward leaned back in his chair. "Sounds good. What's on the menu?"

"Scampi."

Parker could have whooped.

Edward made a face. "You know I hate seafood."

Kendra had the grace to look embarrassed. "Yes, well, I wasn't really thinking about that when I planned tonight's menu, and to tell you the truth, I didn't really make enough for three.''

Parker instantly buoyed. "Oh, sorry about that, babe,'' he said, not sounding the least contrite. "Guess I'll have to start checking out these impulses with you beforehand, hmm?''

"Yes, and I'll try to do the same on *your* nights to cook,'' she replied pointedly.

He laughed. "Deal." He set down his briefcase and plan tube in the corner and rubbed his hands together. "Boy, am I famished.''

"Don't mind me,'' Edward said amicably.

"I won't,'' Parker assured him, crossing the floor to lean against the table and smile down at the baby.

Her face instantly broke into a smile, one little eyebrow crooking up as if to ask where he'd been keeping himself all day.

He kissed the top of her head. "Hello, sweetheart. Miss me?''

That eyebrow fluctuated expressively.

He smiled. "Yeah. Me, too." His eye caught an heretofore missed detail just then, and he looked questioningly at Kendra. "What's this?''

She rolled her eyes. "That, my dear man, is called a bib.''

"I know *that*. I meant that gunk all over it.''

"Ah. Well, now, that is the remnants of our very first solid meal, er, her very first solid meal. Actually, semisolid is a better description. It's sort of a rice mush. The directions are on the box. And if all goes well, next week we can start her on a little applesauce.''

"Oh, yeah? Real food, huh?'' He looked at the baby again. She seemed awfully small for that stuff to him. She didn't have a tooth in her head, for Pete's sake. "You sure she's ready for this?'' he asked warily.

Kendra smiled. "That's what I was going to tell you. I called her pediatrician today and explained things to him.

I knew who she was seeing because I recommended him to Candace, and anyway, he had me bring her in."

"She's okay, isn't she?"

"She's fine, but since she's not on breast milk anymore, he thought it might be best to go ahead and start her on solids. She's about the age they start them anyway, and it might help her sleep better through the night. I asked him to recommend a formula, too, since we've been sort of playing Russian roulette in that respect. He did, by the way, so I bought some of that. Oh, and I bought this little seat, too. It's a lot easier to move around than that car seat, and I wanted to keep her with me while I was making dinner, you know."

"Great," he said, straightening and smiling down at her. "You've been a busy girl today. How'd you manage, though, without a car?"

Edward raised his hand just as Kendra slid him a glance. "Well, I called Ed, of course, and he brought me his car."

Of course. Parker's gaze went to his buddy at the end of the table. "Helpful fellow, aren't you?" he muttered, then regretted it.

Edward smiled. "I told her I'd be here for her."

"Us," Kendra said quickly. "I mean, we're all friends here, aren't we?"

Parker glared at Edward and kept a clamp on his tongue. Edward glared back, then relaxed a bit and shrugged. "Sure. We're all friends. Just good friends, all three of us."

Kendra seemed to breathe easier. "Right. Of course. Anyway, Brenda dropped him off on her way home so he could pick up his car, and that's the whole story. Simple. See?"

Parker nodded, his gaze on Edward. "I see. I see just fine."

Kendra took a deep breath. "Well, I'd better get this little sweetie cleaned up and put dinner on the table."

"I'll clean her," Parker volunteered, once more tamping down his temper. "She just needs a face wash."

"Better check that diaper, too," Kendra said, getting up.

"I can do that," he commented, engaging Darla's attention just to see her smile.

Edward took the hint and excused himself. Kendra thanked him for the use of his car and walked him to the door, which set Parker's teeth on edge. But at least she was quick about it. He had just worked his hands under the baby and was lifting her to his shoulder when Kendra returned. She smiled at him and went about her business. That rankled for some reason, not that he was expecting her to throw her arms about his neck or gush a private welcome or anything.

He carried the baby into the bedroom and laid her in her crib, then removed the soiled bib, cleaned it and left it to dry on the edge of the bathroom sink before gently cleaning her face with a warm, damp washcloth and checking her diaper. She was wet. No surprise there. She always seemed to be wet. He changed her and carried her back to the kitchen. Kendra had the table set and dinner dished up when he got back.

"Smells great," he said. "You've gone to a lot of trouble here, and I was expecting you to order in. This is a nice surprise."

She shrugged, looking pleased. "Scampi isn't so much trouble, really. I bought the shrimp already shelled and deveined. I just hope they haven't been warming too long. I *hate* rubbery shrimp."

He chuckled. "I didn't know you had it in you to hate anything."

She cocked her head. "Do I hear a compliment there?"

"Absolutely."

"Well, thank you very much."

"Thank *you*," he said smoothly. "If you weren't such a loving, caring person, we'd be in a pretty pickle right now. Wouldn't we, princess?" This last he addressed to the baby, who had taken a grip on the end of his nose. He grinned and kissed the underside of her chubby little wrist, breaking her grip, then turned her to face Kendra. "What shall we do with this while we eat?"

Kendra picked the seat up off the floor and placed it on the table between their plates. "How's that for ringside seating?"

"That's great as long as she doesn't try to steal my shrimp," he quipped, carrying her over and placing her in the plastic seat.

"I don't think she's fully grasped the concept of eating anything that doesn't come through a nipple."

"It was a bit difficult, was it?" he asked walking around to pull out her chair for her.

"Let's just say that she was probably wearing more on the outside than I managed to get inside." She sat down and allowed him to help her move the chair forward. "Thank you."

"My pleasure." He took his own chair, spread his napkin and picked up his fork.

"I hope you like it," she said, watching him scoop up rice and spear the first shrimp.

He took the first bite, chewed and closed his eyes, letting the combined flavors of butter, garlic, parsley and lemon fill him. After a long moment, he swallowed. "I *love* scampi," he said, digging in again, "and this is some of the best I've ever had."

She beamed at him. "Thanks. I love it, too. That's why I decided on it. This is sort of a celebration, actually."

He lifted his brows. "Oh? What are we celebrating?"

She put her fork down and leaned forward eagerly. "I got my job back! Well, not the same job. They'd already filled my old spot, but they were eager to hire me on again."

Her job. Suddenly all sorts of problems popped into his head. He put his elbows on the table and let his fork dangle over his plate. "Ah, it's kind of soon, isn't it?"

"What do you mean?"

"Well, for starters, what are we going to do with the baby?"

"What do you think? We'll have to get a sitter. We've discussed this."

"I know. I mean, we sort of discussed it. I know you said you were going to try to go back to the hospital, but I thought... well, I thought..." He realized suddenly that he'd thought she'd change her mind, that Darla would charm Kendra just as she'd charmed him and she would just put off going back to work until... He put his fork down, unwilling to think about the future beyond the next few weeks. "Listen, you don't have to work if you don't want to."

"But I do."

"No, I mean, I can certainly support all of us. Heck, I'm a partner now, you know. It just isn't necessary for you to work."

She took a deep breath, obviously getting a hold on her temper. "Parker," she said slowly, evenly, "you don't seem to understand how important my work is to me. What I do is important, and I love it. I went to school to be a nurse, and I'm a good one, a darned good one, if I do say so myself, and I just have no intention whatsoever of giving that up. I hope I've made myself clear."

"Very," he said tightly, sensing that this subject could get hot quick if he didn't watch it. He concentrated on his food, but the taste seemed less refined and less smooth than before. Nevertheless, he managed a few bites before he felt compelled to broach the subject again. "I guess we'd better start looking for someone suitable to watch the baby. I'll call the agency again tomorrow."

"Good," Kendra said, working on her own plate. "Maybe they can send some applicants over tomorrow for you to interview."

"Tomorrow!" he exclaimed. "I can't interview baby-sitters tomorrow. I have to find a secretary and an assistant."

"Well, I can't do it," she said. "I have to go in tomorrow."

He was aghast. "You can't go in tomorrow! You have to watch the baby!"

"I watched the baby today!"

"What's that supposed to mean?"

"It means that tomorrow it's your turn!"

His mouth fell open. "Who said anything about taking turns?"

"You did!"

"But I didn't mean in the daytime, too!"

She sat back abruptly and folded her arms. "Oh? I guess you thought you'd *married* a baby-sitter then."

He sensed a trap. "N-not exactly."

"Then you don't expect me to put my whole life on hold for the next six months?"

"N-no, I only... That is..." He stopped and licked his lips. "Holy cow, Kendra, they just made me a partner! I can't go laying out of work now."

"But they know what's happened," she argued. "Didn't you tell them about the baby?"

"Of course. I told them about the baby today. The other partners took me to lunch, and I told them about the baby—and you."

"And?"

He targeted his gaze on his plate. This was not going to play as well as it had the first time. He pulled a deep breath. "And the senior partner said that it was sure a good thing I had you to step in and help out since new partners just naturally work the longest hours and get the most difficult accounts."

She looked utterly exasperated. "And it never occurred to any of you that I just might not be right here at your beck and call, did it? Of all the sexist, chauvinistic..."

"They think this is a real marriage!" he snapped. "What was I supposed to do, tell them the unvarnished truth? You know the courts are going to be checking me out! They're bound to ask a few questions around the office."

"Even *real* wives work, Parker," she pointed out smartly, "and even the reigning playboy king of the Western world ought to know that!"

That stung. He slapped his napkin down on the table and shoved his chair back. "Dammit, that's not fair!" he shouted defensively.

The baby jerked and started to wail, her reedy little voice sounding startled and frightened.

Kendra jumped up and glared at him. "Fair," she retorted. "You don't know the meaning of the word. And now look what you've done! Well, fix it yourself, Parker Sugarman. I'm *not* primary caregiver here, and you might as well face it!" With that she swung around and marched out of the room.

He grimaced, the fight already gone out of him. "Hell," he said, reaching across the table and picking up the baby. He put her against his shoulder and jostled her uncertainly. "Don't cry, honey. It's all right. It's okay. Come on now. That's enough. I feel bad enough already." He patted her back and kissed the top of her head and held her close, wondering what had happened to that happy feeling that had filled him when he'd first walked in the door. Obviously he had a lot to learn about this marriage business, not to mention babies and women. That part surprised him. But then, he hadn't really thought about women beyond the pleasures they afforded and how to avail himself of those pleasures when the mood struck him without getting tangled up in ways that had seemed unnecessary at the time. Suddenly he realized that time was past.

He was married. And even if he wasn't, he'd still have Darla to think about. The old days of freedom and indulgence were over. He now had responsibilities to someone other than himself. More surprising still was the realization that even if he could change it, he wouldn't—short of bringing her parents back, of course. This little one was his, and he'd fight God Himself for her if he had to. No one and nothing was ever again going to take someone he loved from him if he could help it, no matter what he had to do.

"Okay, princess," he said to the little one snuffling against his chest, "if that's the way it has to be, that's the way it has to be. The partnership be damned. You're what counts now."

He held her to him and rocked her gently side to side, marveling as the love flowed through him. It was unlike anything he'd ever felt, and it made all the hassle worthwhile, *all* the hassle. He sighed, preparing himself to make an apology he'd never thought to make. The playboy king of the Western world was about to abdicate his throne.

Kendra threw herself on the bed, clenched her hands in the covers and tried not to sob. It was useless to try to stem the tears. They had taken her by surprise in the kitchen, so much so that all she had been able to do was run away to hide them. She was so mad, and she was so *hurt*. What a fool she was to let him hurt her, to believe, to hope, even for a moment that he might value her for herself, for who and what she was, that he might see her as something more than a baby sitter, a nanny with job security—for six months, anyway.

Six months. She moaned, inaudibly castigating herself. It was all her fault, all her own stupidity, and she hadn't even realized it until just now. Of course he couldn't stay home with the baby tomorrow. Any idiot would know it, and yet she had gaily told the nursing supervisor over the phone that she wanted to get back to work as soon as possible. She had said it while holding the baby on her lap, while stroking that dark, silky hair and listening to the gurgling babble as little Darla played in fascination with her own fingers. She had said it while her heart contracted with pure affection. She had said it while a vision of Parker pulling her to him in his bed shimmered before her mind's eye.

Only now did she realize that she had been setting up a test. She had wanted him to say, "Yes, darling, whatever you want, need, expect.'' But he had said, essentially, ''Oh, are you a nurse? Well, you can't be, because I need a convenient baby sitter.'' Of course, that was exactly what she was. She had agreed to be that and had no right to expect more now. He had made it perfectly plain from the beginning, and it was foolish in the extreme to hope it might have changed just because he'd awakened from a sound sleep, found a half-dressed woman bending over his bed and been moved by sheer rote to take advantage of that fact. And he *had* just been made a partner. It was pure selfishness for her to ask him to risk that.

But that didn't make her hurt less, proving once again how very foolish she was. Still, she had no one to blame but herself. After all this time, as well as she knew Parker Sugarman, to think that he might have changed so drastically overnight was nothing short of lunacy. She suddenly wished quite desperately that she could just pick up the phone and call on Nathan. No one could ever talk sense to her quite like Nathan. She could almost hear him now, saying, ''Ken, you make omelets with eggs, not lemons. Parker's a lemon for a woman like you. You can peel him, squeeze him, grind him to a pulp, but you'll never be able to make an omelet with him. Now if lemonade was your thing, you could make a sweet, sweet lemonade with him, but you're an omelet girl, and that's a fact.'' She could laugh and say, ''How true!'' and believe it, and everything would be all right again. But Nathan was gone. Nathan and Candace were both gone far beyond the reach of a telephone. Suddenly she was sobbing, missing them both, wanting them both. She didn't even hear Parker enter the room, didn't know he was around until he called her name.

''Kendra. Aw, honey, don't.''

She sat up abruptly, forcing a halt to her tears and rubbing them from her face. He was standing at the foot of the bed, the baby held against his chest with one arm. She thought, ludicrously, how well he did that now. ''Never mind," she said. "It's all right. I was a dope, but it's all right now."

He walked over to the crib and gently laid Darla on her back. He gave her a soft, squeaky, terry-cloth teddy bear to play with, cooed reassurance, kissed her on the forehead and turned away to sit on the edge of the bed by Kendra. "It is all right," he said, laying a hand upon her shoulder. "I apologize. I've thought of no one but myself for so long that it's sort of difficult to remember that I now have...a family. And family should come first, I *know* that, but I'm still discovering how to make it happen. Just bear with me for a while, please. I'll do better, I promise."

She couldn't believe her ears. Parker Sugarman apologizing for being Parker Sugarman? She shook her head, truly bemused. "I don't understand. I mean, I was the one who didn't think. You have all these new responsibilities, and you've just been taken on as a partner. Of course you have to go to work."

"No. No, I'll stay home tomorrow. It's only fair, just as you said."

"But the partnership—"

"Isn't what matters most," he said gently. "If I've learned anything from what happened to Nathan and Candace, it's that people matter most. Darla is what matters most now. Darla and *you.*"

"M-me?"

"Of course, you. Who else but you? After all you've done for us, everything you've given up, put on hold..." He moved his free hand to her lap and folded hers inside it. The other crept up to lay against her neck, his knuckles skimming her earlobe.

Her heart fluttered, the stirrings of hope she didn't dare give wing. Inexplicably, that thought brought fresh tears to her eyes. "You're the one who's changing your whole life to take on a baby."

"Not just *a* baby," he said with silky earnestness, "my brother's baby, Nathan's baby."

The mention of Nathan's name, so recently mourned, set her bottom lip to trembling. "I miss him. I miss them both so much."

"I know," he said, sliding his arms around her. "Me, too." He kissed the top of her head. "Oh, God, I want to wake up and find it all a bad dream. I couldn't bear it without you and Darla."

"Yes, I know," she said thoughtlessly into the hollow of his shoulder. "That's why I had to help you keep her."

"Is it?" he said, suddenly gripping the hair at her nape to tug her head back.

She looked up into soft brown eyes that swept her face before locking into her own blurry gaze. She knew it was her turn to speak, knew there was something she ought to say, but she could not seem to think what it was. She could not seem to think at all. She could only feel, his arm about her, his chest against her breasts, his thigh alongside hers, his hand spreading to cradle the back of her head. She could feel his heart pounding, or was it hers? His eyes tugged free, shifting downward, and she shuttered hers, feeling his gaze upon her mouth until his own was there, soft at first, and sweet, so sweetly gentle that she ached beneath it. And then it changed. A subtle increase in pressure, a simple slanting, a parting of lips, and it was if he breathed fire into her, as if he sent flames licking down into the core of her being, into the very woman's center of her body.

She felt her nipples peak and harden, her hands clench in the fine fabric of his shirt. Her thigh began to tingle. The skin on her back rose up into gooseflesh, and her heart slammed against the wall of her chest and went into convulsions. She felt herself sinking back onto the bed, felt his hands begin to explore. That was when the trembling began, and when his hand closed over her breast and he drove his tongue into her mouth, she jerked against him, electrified. She pushed her hands up into his hair, pulling his head down and opening her mouth wider for his tongue. He slid a knee between her legs, shifting his weight to press his groin to hers. She moaned, feeling his heat hard against her, wanting so much more of it and pushing upward to gain it.

He ground his mouth against hers, his body following suit. Then he was lifting the hem of her T-shirt and tearing at his own clothing, while balancing his weight on his elbows and plying her mouth with such desperation that in some part of her mind she began to pull back from him, to fear slightly what they were doing, so that when he wrenched away to yank his shirt off over his head, she was able to put her hands against his chest and push him away. He hit the floor with one foot and stumbled backward, his shirt in his hand, confusion on his face. She realized simultaneously what they'd almost done here and that her shirt was pushed up under her armpits, exposing her breasts clad only in the thin silky covering of her bra. Face burning, she scrambled up onto her knees and tugged her shirt down. When next she glanced up, it was to see that self-same realization dawning on him.

"Oh, God," he said, closing his eyes, "Oh God, oh God, oh God. Kendra, I didn't mean to... It wasn't my intention to..." He pushed a shaking hand through dark, waving hair, and swallowed audibly. "We're both in a highly e-emotional state right now. W-we... I... It's the situation! Married, not married...caring so much..." He pushed out a breath harshly and looked up at her. "Lady," he confessed, "you're a hell of a temptation!" He grinned crookedly. "And we both know I'm not very good at resisting temptation."

One corner of her mouth quirked up into a smile. "Well, you're right about the state of our emotions just now, and no doubt the situation lends itself to..." She gulped. "As for temptation, I don't really think you've had much practice at resisting, but...you weren't exactly alone in that this time."

"I hope I wasn't alone in it any other time, either," he quipped.

"Probably not," she muttered, wondering how many others he had found tempting enough to lead into temptation.

"Look," he said, leaning forward to plant his hands on the bed, "I came in here to say I was sorry. You were crying. I wanted to hold you. Then I wanted to kiss you. Then I wanted to make love to you." His voice softened. "I still do, but I know it's not the best thing for us. I don't want to hurt you, and I don't want to lose what we already have. You're my best friend now. I need that. I need you." He straightened, turned his shirt right side out and began unbuttoning it. "So," he said, "I'm going to stay home tomorrow and interview baby-sitters, and you're going to do what you do best—besides looking gorgeous, I mean, and taking care of Darla and cooking great scampi and rescuing my butt." He slung his shirt on and held out his hand. "Come on," he said, "dinner's getting cold."

She smiled to hide the conflict taking place inside of her. He had given her exactly what she'd wanted, and yet having it just seemed to create greater needs in her. She almost wished they'd finished what they'd started, almost wished they weren't just friends. But no, that was nuts. She'd have to be crazy to let herself feel more for him. She'd have to be certifiable to fall in love with Parker Sugarman. Well, she just wouldn't do it. This was one time he would have to succumb to temptation all on his own, if it came to that. She lifted her chin and put her hand in his. He pulled her off the bed and onto her feet.

"I'll get the baby," he said, releasing her a bit too quickly.

She swayed, then righted, holding her determination around her like a protective cloak. She put on a smile. "I'll rubberize our shrimp in the microwave."

He gathered up the little one, glancing at Kendra with twinkling eyes. "Ah," he said, "an exemplary wife indeed!"

"But a better best friend," she reminded him gently.

He looked away, then nodded, and came back with a smile that didn't quite cover the desire in his eyes. Kendra turned and hurried from the room, uncertain which of them was the worse liar.

Chapter Eight

"None of them would do?" Kendra asked, slipping off her shoes so her tired feet could breathe.

Parker shook his head and dropped down on the sofa next to her. "You wouldn't believe who the agency sent over here. The first one came at 10:00 a.m.—with liquor on her breath. She likes a 'nip of the Irish' in her coffee. It went downhill from there."

"That was the best? That couldn't have been the best of them."

He lifted a hand, palm out. "As God is my witness. I tell you, it was a nightmare, One of them had, and I quote, 'extensive experience.' She had four kids of her own. Of course, they're all living in foster homes now. The state said she neglected them, but, hey, a woman's got to work, doesn't she?" He shook his head woefully. "I swear to you, Kendra, I couldn't have left Darla with one of today's candidates if my life had depended on it. I called the agency and told them not to bother sending over anyone else. We'll try another one, or we'll just put an ad in the paper...something. I don't know." He sighed and leaned his head back against the couch. "So how was your first day back at work?"

She grimaced. "Tough. It's been a while since I was involved in primary care, you know, real nitty-gritty stuff. There's this one little girl, made me think of Darla, you know? Black hair, a face that's all eyes. She's in a cast from the waist down. Well, I noticed she was all alone. Most of the kids have parents, adults of some kind with them, during the day, anyway. So I took a few extra minutes, tried to talk to her. She just looked at me with those big, black eyes. Finally she muttered something. It was Spanish, Portuguese, I guess. Turns out she was visiting here with her parents from Brazil. There was an accident—just like Nathan and Candace—and now her parents are dead, and she's all alone in a strange country, while the authorities try to contact relatives on another continent. Oh, Parker, I wanted to bundle her up and bring her home with me. What if she doesn't have someone like you who'll take her in and love her?"

He just looked at her; then he sat up and wrapped his arm around her, pulling her close to his side. "I bet you rescue stray puppies, too, don't you?"

She smiled. "I've been known to."

"You want me to have Ed check into this little girl's situation?"

"Oh, could you? He'd do it, wouldn't he?"

Parker nodded and kissed the top of her head, before leaning his cheek against it. "Thank God tomorrow is Saturday. I couldn't face going into the office after today."

Kendra rolled her eyes up at him apologetically. "I have to work tomorrow, Parker," she told him softly.

He groaned. "Blast!"

"Nursing's not a nine-to-five, weekday job."

"I know, I know. It's okay. I just thought we could do some shopping for the baby, get her settled in a little better. I'd like her room to look a little more like a nursery and less like a guest room before the court starts snooping around.''

"Well, I don't have to go in until one. We'll get up and start early."

"The stores don't open until ten," he pointed out.

"So we've got two hours, anyway."

"All right." He nodded and patted the top of her arm. "Then maybe we can all go out for dinner after you get home."

"Parker, I won't be home before ten at night—more like half past, actually."

He shook his head. "Damn! Aren't we ever going to see you anymore?"

She hoped he couldn't see how good that made her feel. "I have Sunday off," she told him lightly, and was rewarded with a pleased smile.

"Great! We're taking Darla to church."

"Church?"

"That's right, church. I'm turning over a new leaf here, remember. Besides, Ed told me I had to."

"And you do everything Ed tells you to," she said doubtfully.

He kissed the tip of her nose. "I'm married, aren't I?"

"For the time being," she answered, regretting it immediately.

His brown eyes clouded, but then he smiled. "I made dinner. Lasagna. I hope you don't mind frozen."

"Not when I'm this hungry," she said, getting laboriously to her feet. "I'll set the table."

"Done."

"Well, I'll look in on the baby, then."

"She's had her cereal and she's napping. I think I tired her out today. We played a lot between prospective kidnappers."

"Okay," Kendra said, "then I guess I'll just change and eat."

"It'll be on the table when you get there."

* * *

It was on the table when she got there, along with a bottle of Texas Red, a tossed salad and garlic toast. She hadn't enjoyed a meal so much in a very long time. It was heaven to eat something she didn't have to cook herself or that wasn't carried in.

They took their time with the meal and cleaned up together afterward, blowing handfuls of soap suds and popping dish towels at one another. When the baby cried to let them know she was awake, Kendra went in to get her, while Parker warmed a bottle. Kendra had her changed and was kissing her tummy when Parker carried the bottle into the room. Darla's face lit up and her mouth went to work before the nipple even got there. They laughed at her and were shocked to hear her laugh back, a real belly laugh. "Just like a real kid," Parker said wonderingly, and then they laughed again while Darla got down to serious eating. Fifteen minutes later, they were both lying on the bed with her between them playing peek-a-boo and kissy-feet, when they looked up and found Edward standing in the bedroom doorway.

"Doesn't anyone around here answer the doorbell?" he asked grumpily.

Kendra scrambled off the bed, tugging at the bottom of the sweatshirt she wore with her jeans. "Edward! You frightened me."

Parker folded his hands behind his head and crossed his ankles. "The only time you use the doorbell is when the door is locked," he said pointedly.

Edward shrugged. "All right, so maybe I knocked."

"And maybe you just walked in, expecting to catch us at what you're expecting to catch us at."

"Parker," Edward said, "you have to realize that I've got a stake in this, too."

Parker bounded up into a sitting position. "Like hell. This is my house, my kid, my *wife*."

"And I'm your lawyer, your friend and *her* ex-fiancé."

"Emphasis on the 'ex,'" Parker retorted.

"Get out, both of you," Kendra said sharply. "I've had a long day, and I want to go to bed. What I *don't* want is to listen to the two of you argue. Now go."

Parker glared at Ed, and Ed glared at Parker, neither willing to make the first move. Kendra rolled her eyes. Finally Parker spoke up. "You don't have to sleep in here tonight. I will."

She shook her head. "Uh-uh, no way. The deal is we take turns, and tonight's my night with the baby."

"The baby's not ready to turn in."

"Fine. You take Darla with you. When she's ready, you bring her in. Meanwhile, I'm going to soak my weary bones in a tub of hot water, and if I hear any shouting in there, I'm calling the cops."

Parker switched his gaze from Edward to her, sighed and got up, scooping the baby up as he went. He strolled around the end of the bed toward the door, pausing as he passed Kendra to kiss her hard on the mouth. "Get some rest," he said.

She gave him a look meant to draw blood and said through her teeth, "I will. Good night."

Not to be outdone, Ed waited for Parker to pass him, then leaned forward and kissed her lingeringly on the corner of her mouth. "Sleep well," he told her softly.

She said nothing to that, just watched mutely as he went out and closed the door. Why did it have to be like this? They were both so stubborn, so proud, so *competitive,* and she'd be damned if she'd let them fight over her like two dogs fighting over a bone, especially when neither of them really wanted her. They just didn't want the other one to have her! Suddenly she thought of the little girl in the hospital.

Yanking open the door, she stepped out onto the gallery. They were in the kitchen, glaring at one another as they popped the tops on a pair of beers. She stepped up into the room.

"Parker, remember the little girl from Brazil?"

He snapped his fingers. "Right. I meant to ask you if you knew her name."

She nodded and gave it to them.

"Better write it down, hon."

While she found a piece of paper and a pen, he explained the circumstances to Edward, who shook his head morosely.

"What're you two doing, opening an orphanage?"

"We just want to be sure she's got someone," Parker said. "If she needs a place to stay after she gets out of the hospital, it's not out of the question."

Kendra wanted to throw her arms around his neck at that moment, wanted to laugh and kiss him and tell him he was wonderful. Instead, she slid a glance toward Edward, stepped up close to Parker's side and settled for a covert squeeze of his arm. He smiled at her as he brought the rim of the can to his mouth. She smiled back and mouthed the word, "Thanks." He gave her a barely perceptible nod and a wink. Her smile broadened as she stepped back and turned away. She bade them good-night once again and slipped off to her bath, happier than she had been in a long while.

It couldn't last, of course. By Monday, they still had not found a baby-sitter, though a woman in the church nursery had given them several names and phone numbers to try. Kendra got another nurse to take her shift for her and spent the morning on the telephone. She managed to locate a woman whom she felt might be acceptable, but she could only watch the baby for the remainder of the week and only in her own home. It was better than nothing, so Kendra made an appointment with her for that evening. She and Parker took the baby and drove over to the woman's house near Love Field airport. The place was small but neat and clean, the woman's references exemplary. A middle-aged widow, she cared for her feeble and ailing father. At week's end, she was scheduled to drive him out of state for an extended visit with her brother and his family. They engaged her for the remainder of the week.

It was a nightmare in logistics. With only one car between them, Kendra's unusual hours and hauling the baby back and forth to the sitter's, they were all exhausted and harried. Parker found himself leaving work at odd times to play taxi driver but absolutely refused to allow Kendra to ride the bus, contending that the only people who rode the bus in their neighborhood were day maids and teenagers with revoked driver's licenses. Kendra was not so proud, but Parker wouldn't stand for it, saying he'd disrupted her life enough as it was without putting her through the agony that was public transportation in Dallas. She tried engaging a cab, but that proved unreliable as her hours kept changing and cabs were invariably late.

Parker determined to buy her a car, and she agreed that would be a workable option; they could simply resell it after six months. But then they got into an enormous hassle over what type and age the second car should be. He insisted that they look at only new or late-model cars with good safety standards and all the amenities. She wanted to go for an old clunker that would require a minimum outlay of cash. He would not have "his" kid riding in some old bomb. She would not have him spending a ridiculous sum of money on some luxury auto when all she required was basic transportation. They wound up shouting at each other until the baby erupted into anxious screams, then made up while calming her. Something had to give, and they both knew it.

Kendra made the decision to quit her job again. Going back had been ill considered to begin with, and she was likely going on to Africa in a few months anyway. It was true that she had counted on being able to come back to her job after Africa, and quitting a second time in such short order would be a black mark on her record, but she considered that just recompense for the way she'd handled things anyway. Besides, Darla had to come first, and after being dragged out several times a day during cool, damp fall weather, she had developed a troubling case of sniffles. Kendra determined to tell Parker of her decision on Friday evening but wouldn't inform her supervisor until Monday, by which time she hoped to have lined up a substitute for the coming week, allowing the supervisor a little time to find a permanent replacement.

Parker was there to pick her up about ten on Friday evening, a sleeping Darla snugly belted into her car seat. The car was waiting outside the west entrance of the hospital when Kendra and her co-workers exited. Parker got out and came around the front end to open the passenger door for Kendra. He had been doing that for the whole work week, and the other nurses had taken to kidding her about it, saying that she should enjoy such thoughtfulness while it lasted because their own husbands had forgotten such things existed by, according to general consensus, the end of the first month of marriage. Kendra had had to wonder if Parker would be one of those "forgetful" husbands and had concluded that he wouldn't. Such thoughtfulness was part of Parker's persona and accounted for much of his appeal to the opposite sex—and old habits died hard, as the saying went. She had to admit that charm had benefits she hadn't considered before.

This particular evening, however, Parker did not content himself with the simple gallantry of opening a door. He stepped forward, took her hand and pulled her into his arms for a quick kiss. They were treated to giggles and hoots for that little demonstration. Embarrassed, Kendra gave him a reproving look.

"What's got into you?" she demanded softly.

He flashed her a grin, eyes twinkling. "Tell you later. Meanwhile, let's give 'em something to really think about, hmm?" So saying, he urged her arms up about his neck, wrapped her in a tight embrace and kissed her long and passionately, until her knees threatened to buckle and leave her lying in a puddle about his feet.

She barely heard the cheers, applause and shouted advice. Even after he was finished with her, she had trouble catching her breath and focusing her attention. In fact, he had her in the car and was driving away before she came to herself enough to even be annoyed.

"What the heck was *that* about?" she finally snapped.

He put his head back and laughed. "Aw, come on. They enjoyed it. You enjoyed it. I sure as hell enjoyed it. And it reinforces the image of the happily married couple. No harm done."

"I don't enjoy being made a public spectacle," she said firmly. "And you haven't answered my question."

He rolled his eyes grinning. "Can't put anything over on you, can I? Okay, okay. I'm feeling great because I've done something that's going to solve all our problems."

That was unexpectedly welcome news. She shifted in her seat. "Really? What did you do? Did you hire a permanent sitter?"

He shook his head.

"You bought a car!" she accused, and he laughed out loud.

"Nope. It's better than both of those ideas combined."

She furrowed her brow. "What does that mean? For Pete's sake, Parker, spit it out, will you?"

He brought the car to a stop at a red light, then reached over and squeezed her hand before answering. "It's the perfect solution," he said sincerely. "I've just taken an extended leave of absence from my job."

Her jaw descended as the significance of his announcement dawned. "No! Parker, you didn't!"

His smile grew softer, his grasp upon her hand warmer. "I knew you'd take exception. That's why I didn't tell you I was considering it. But, honey, this *is* the best thing. Believe me, I've thought it all through, and I *want* to be at home with the baby."

"But, Parker, the partnership!"

He shrugged. "So it's on hold for a while, and maybe I won't be able to keep it after all. It doesn't matter. I'll still have my job, and in the meantime, I won't go without work. Heck, I've already lined up a couple of private clients, jobs I can work on at home. It'll be a little cramped for a while. I thought I'd just set up shop in the dining room. We can store the furniture for now. Anyway, the place needs remodeling. It's just not set up for a kid, and we need at least two more rooms, a playroom and an office for sure, and we could really use another bedroom, too."

The car behind them honked, the light having turned green already. Parker turned his attention back to the street and got them moving again with an apologetic wave of his hand to the other driver, while Kendra tried to digest what he'd said. It just seemed so radical to her, and she had to tell him so.

"I have a better solution," she told him. "I had already made up my mind to it, in fact. I'll quit my job."

He shook his head. "Oh, no. I knew that was coming up, and I won't have it."

"But, Parker—"

"No. I'm dead set on this. You've already quit your job and then gone back to it once because of me. I won't have it a second time. What you do *later* is your own business, but as long as I have any say about it, you'll do what you love to do—and that's pediatric nursing. Besides, Kendra, I meant it when I said I *want* to be at home with Darla. Nothing in the world is more important to me. She's all I have . . . except for you," he finished huskily.

Kendra caught her breath, remembering that passionate kiss in the hospital parking lot. Was it possible? No, and she was foolish to even think that way. Parker was changing, true, but he was still Parker with Parker's basic instincts and Parker's basic personality. Seduction was second nature to Parker Sugarman. She wasn't even sure he realized he was doing it at times. And God knew this situation was rife with the possibility of that very thing. She steeled herself to say what she had to.

"You do have me . . . for now," she pointed out evenly. "But it's a temporary arrangement, Parker, and you shouldn't forget that."

A muscle flexed in the hollow of his jaw, and she thought for an instant that she had angered him, but he spoke then, his voice calm, reasonable. "I haven't forgotten. How could I when we don't even sleep together? Not that I haven't been tempted, of course." He flashed her a smile. "But that's just me, you know, and anyway it's best like this. I know that, and I'm terribly grateful for this time you're giving us."

Just him. It wasn't her at all. It was just the way Parker was, panting after everything in a skirt. She tried not to be disappointed. She tried very hard. She didn't quite manage it. "Just so long as you remember the ground rules," she told him cuttingly.

That muscle flexed again, but he didn't say anything, just kept driving. They drove into the garage from the alley. They usually did and would continue to with winter coming on, but it kept them from noticing any cars parked in the front drive. So they were both surprised when Edward met them at the back door, his hands jammed down into the pockets of his overcoat.

"What are you doing out here so late, Ed?" Parker asked a little testily.

The big man shrugged. "I need to speak with the two of you about the custody case, and I knew Kendra wouldn't be home before now."

Kendra shot Parker a troubled glance and took the baby from him. They were leaving the car seat in place these days. It saved time. Parker unlocked the door and motioned her to go ahead of them. She stepped up into the hall and quickly carried the baby into her room, where she unwrapped her, checked her diaper, which was thankfully dry, and tucked her into bed on her side. By the time she rejoined the men, they were sitting on opposite sofas, their elbows on their knees, hands folded in concern.

"What's happened?" she asked, seating herself next to Parker.

He leaned back and draped his arm lightly about her shoulders. "It's nothing we didn't expect," he said, but worry had put an edge to his voice. "The Pendletons have formally filed for custody of Darla."

She bit her lip and automatically placed a comforting hand on Parker's leg. "It'll be okay," she assured him.

He nodded, but Edward said, "That's not all." With their attention fixed on him, he went on. "They're asking for court-ordered visitation."

"Visitation!" Parker erupted. "They didn't have to do that. They can see Darla anytime they want as long as they don't try to leave with her."

"I know that," Edward said, "and that's exactly what we're going to tell the judge."

Parker leaned forward again. "Are you telling me the judge might say I have to hand her over to them, let them leave with her? That's insanity! We might never get her back!"

"Not necessarily," Ed said in that calm, sure voice of his. "First of all, the Pendletons aren't going anywhere. They have a home and business here. They're not going to take off with her in the dead of night. Moreover, this whole thing just might work in our favor. Darla is an infant. It's not unusual for visitation of infants to be restricted to the infant's home. This is Darla's home, and it can't hurt anything to have that established by visitation decree of any other court document. But I might as well tell you that the Pendletons are bound to know this. Their lawyer is one of the best. I know him well, and he's not the type to let the details escape him, so they know they'll likely get an in-home order, which tells me that they want it that way."

"Meaning?" Kendra asked.

Ed gave her a direct look. "Meaning they suspect this marriage is a sham and are hoping to find proof of it during their 'unlimited' visitations. That's what they're asking for—unlimited, unrestricted visitation. They aren't going to get it. We're asking for prior notification, custodian's convenience, all the usual stipulations, but we are *not* going to fight the order itself. That would be implying that we have something to hide, which we do, of course, but we can't let them know that. You following me?"

Parker nodded, taking Kendra's hand in his. "Just tell us what to do."

Ed glowered and ran his hands through his short, spiky hair. "You're already doing it. You're acting like a pair of love-sotted newlyweds."

Shocked, Kendra pulled her hand from Parker's, who slid her an oddly sad look before targeting his gaze on the floor.

"Is there anything else?" she asked in a voice husky with discomfort.

Ed made a face. "How's the hunt for a competent sitter going? It's really important, guys, that we find someone who'll come down squarely in our corner."

"Don't worry about that," Parker said flatly, and he went on to bring Ed up-to-date on the decisions he'd made.

To Kendra's surprise, Edward was very supportive. "Good move," he said. "Excellent move. Just be sure you know what you're doing. We don't want the Pendletons to be able to document shoddy care or neglect on your part."

"No fear on that score," Kendra assured him. "Parker's good with her, and he's learned a lot these last couple of weeks. He's read a couple of baby-care books I've brought him, too."

"Besides," Parker said, "she's just a phone call away if I need advice, and that ought to count for something."

Edward nodded. "Sounds like we've got all the bases covered, then. Parker, I'd get right on remodeling the house, if I were you. You might want to consider moving into Nathan's place while the work's being done, though."

Parker shook his head. "I'd rather not—too many memories for my peace of mine. Besides, that cracker box offends my aesthetic sensibilities." He chuckled, adding, "Hey, I have a professional reputation to maintain, especially if I'm going to support myself in the life-style to which I've become accustomed, financially speaking, of course.''

"Of course," Ed agreed dryly, getting to his feet. "You might as well face it, old buddy, the good times are over for you.''

Parker shook his head. "There's more than one kind of good time, Ed, and I like my life just fine right now.''

Ed looked mournful. "I was afraid you'd say that.''

Kendra rolled her eyes. "He's talking about the baby, sap.''

"Is he?" Edward asked, gazing down at her. "If that's so, just be sure you don't admit it to anyone else.''

"If she did," Parker said, "I would very convincingly make a liar of her.''

They both looked at him, neither doubting him but for very different reasons. Kendra knew to what lengths he would go to keep Darla now. He had for all intents and purposes scuttled his partnership in one of the finest, most renowned architectural firms in the southwestern United States so that he could be home with her. He was attending church, remaking his life, about to remodel his house. Kendra did not doubt that he'd make her appear a liar if it suited his purposes and protected his niece. She did not seriously consider that he might be regretting the temporary nature of their marriage. She would not dream that he was coming to view her as a very large, very pleasant part of his life. She could not fathom that he might be coming to love her. Edward could not believe anything else.

When Edward was gone, Parker got up and went to the bedroom to check on the baby. He came back shaking his head.

"I've been meaning to ask you something," he said. "I've been reading about this SIDS stuff and about whether or not the baby's sleeping position has anything to do with it. The British, they're saying to sleep a baby on its back, but for years now, American doctors have been saying to sleep them on their stomachs, so lately—and

Candace mentioned this to me—the prevalent recommendation is a compromise, sleeping the baby on its side.''

Kendra nodded, pulling the pins from her hair and combing her fingers through it. "You're absolutely right," she told him. "So what did you want to ask me?"

He leaned forward over the back of the couch and ran his fingers lightly through the hair at her temple. "Well, whether or not you've been putting her down on her side or some other way."

She cocked her head. "I always put her down on her side. Why?"

"You do it that way this time?"

"Yes."

"Well, she's lying on her back in there."

Kendra smiled and pulled her feet up beneath her. "Really?"

He nodded. "And this morning when I got her up to go to the sitter's, she was sleeping on her stomach."

"Is that right?"

"Uh-huh. Do you suppose that means something?"

She grinned at him. "It means that she's learned how to turn over, Parker."

He looked purely surprised. "Oh, I hadn't thought of that."

"I can see that you hadn't," she told him, trying not to be too amused.

He straightened and hooked his thumbs in the rear pockets of his jeans. "She's kind of young for it, isn't she?"

"A little, maybe."

He nodded. "Yeah, that's what I thought. She's a fast learner. You can tell, the way she mimics your facial expressions and everything, the sparkle in those big eyes."

Kendra couldn't help it; she had to laugh. He glowered at her.

"What's so funny?"

"You are," she told him. "Who would ever have thought it? Parker Sugarman as proud papa."

He colored slightly, two spots of ruddy pink high on his cheekbones. "It's not that," he said. "It's just that she's special, you know."

Kendra nodded. "I know. She's very special."

He smiled, and the conversation just seemed to die a natural death. Kendra took a deep breath and pulled herself up off the couch.

"Well, I'm going to bed," she said. "Tomorrow's another day."

"You wouldn't be off tomorrow, would you?" he asked suddenly.

"Ha. I wish."

"You're working, then?"

"Afraid so, and I've got to go in early, too."

"Well, that's not so bad," he said, sounding unusually eager. "I mean, if you're going to be off in time, maybe you'd like to take in a movie or something."

"A movie?" Now that was a thought. She couldn't remember the last time she'd actually gone to a movie. Then reality set in. "But what about the baby?"

He scratched an ear. "I think I know where we can find a sitter. Your dad called this evening to complain that he hadn't yet gotten to see much of his almost-granddaughter. I suggested tomorrow evening might be a good time, and he said it sounded good to him. Kate will be there, so he wouldn't have to handle it all on his own."

Kate. Kendra felt an automatic surge of resentment. "I don't know if that's such a good idea," she grumbled. "Kate isn't exactly the motherly type."

Parker brought his hands to his waist and just stared at her. That look was so knowing, it made her uncomfortable.

"What?" she snapped, and he shook his head.

"Dan said you'd make some kind of protest."

She grimaced and pushed a hand through her haair. "He knows I don't like her."

"Anybody who's ever seen the two of you in the same room together knows that. What I don't understand is why. She's a nice woman, attractive, intelligent and it's obvious that your father is crazy about her."

"*Crazy* is the operative word there," she declared.

"I still don't get it. It looks pretty mutual to me. Heck, they can hardly keep their hands off one another, from what I saw."

"That's just it," Kendra said testily. "He was never like that with my mother."

Parker ran his eyes over her face. "Was your mother like that with him?"

Miserably, Kendra shook her head. "No."

"Well, then, maybe that's the way she wanted it."

Kendra wrapped her hair into a knot at the base of her neck and let it fall free again. "It doesn't really matter, and I don't want to talk about it anymore. I'm tired." She turned and started toward the bedroom, but he caught her by the wrist and pulled her around to face him.

"I think you need a night out on the town," he said. "Let's go out tomorrow night. Your dad can watch the baby. If you don't want to see a movie, we'll do something else. We'll go dancing. Want to go dancing?"

Dancing. She smiled at the thought of it, slow dancing in a dimly lit room filled with music. Dangerous. She shook her head. "We really ought to make it an early night. We have to get up for church on Sunday morning."

He shrugged. "Okay, a movie, then. Maybe we can work the dancing in later."

"Later," she said, and he smiled.

"Then it's a date."

A date. Ludicrous thought. They were married—sort of. So what could it hurt. "It's a date," she said, pulling away. "Good night."

He just stood there smiling and watched her walk out of the room.

Chapter Nine

She wore a simple sweater dress of jade green with a wide collar that clung to her shoulders and showed off the pretty bones that came together in a small V at the base of her throat. She left her hair down, pulling it back on one side with a heavy, tortoiseshell comb, and wore long, dangling earrings made of multicolored beads. She fitted a pair of suede, sling-back heels to her feet, and clipped a heavy gold bracelet on her wrist. Parker whistled when she stepped out onto the gallery. She blushed, more pleased than she wanted him to know, and tossed him her black wool coat. He caught it and held it open for her to slip into. She did so, ignoring the way his hands seemed to linger at her shoulders. They went in together to get the baby and attendant paraphernalia.

Kendra was amused to see that Parker had dressed Darla in her frilliest pajamas, a strawberry pink jumper with rows of soft white lace sewn around an appliqué of a teddy-bear ballerina. He had combed her hair forward, framing her cherubic face with delicate wisps of hair that was gradually turning from inky black to dark, dark chocolate. He had slipped a softly gathered satin band around her head, leaving the flowered pink bow resting at a saucy angle above her left eye. She was the cutest thing breathing, and with that indefinable sense all females seemed to possess, she knew it. Her big black eyes sparkled with the knowledge. The wisps of her eyebrows rode up and down on it, inviting every observer to agree with her personal assessment. Kendra certainly couldn't resist. She picked her up and dandled her in the air, telling her how wonderful and pretty she was. Darla preened and smiled, her chubby little fists pushed up her chin in the classic pose of innocence. Kendra's heart contracted and abruptly expanded with love.

She was shocked, momentarily overwhelmed by feelings she had never before known. A lump rose in her throat. Tears misted her eyes. A sense of rightness and homecoming seized her simultaneously with one of fear. This was not her child. This would never be her child, unless by some miracle... But she dared not think of that. She dared not let gratitude and lust mislead her into believing in love, not with Parker Sugarman.

She handed the baby to Parker and busied herself gathering up the diaper bag, blankets, toys, the baby seat and various other items for baby care. While she was doing that, Parker zipped Darla into a heavy blanket sleeper that would keep her warm on the trip, then they all trooped out to the car, settled in and were off.

Dan opened the door of his house even before the car came to a complete stop before it. He was obviously so eager to see them that Kendra felt a pang of guilt. She looked at Parker with apology in her eyes.

"Maybe we should skip the movie and stay here."

He reached across the car to tap the end of her nose with a forefinger. "No way. You need this night out. *I* need this night out. We playboy kings don't reform without a few lapses, you know."

She tried to smile, to share his humor, but she was feeling shaky in a way she couldn't quite describe even to herself. Her smile was tremulous at best, and it did not help when he cupped her face with his palm and looked questioningly into her eyes. "I—I guess I'm just tired," she offered halfheartedly.

"You'll feel better after you relax a couple hours. Come on. Let's not keep him waiting, hmm?"

They got out of the car, gathered up the equipment and the baby and hurried into the house. Dan greeted them with bear hugs and hearty words of welcome. Kate hovered in the background, an intrusive, unwelcome shadow. After a perfunctory greeting, Kendra simply tried to ignore her as she explained the intricacies of infant care to her father, who laughingly reminded her that he'd had a bit of experience in that area, albeit nearly three decades past. To her surprise, he didn't even give them a chance to sit down and chat but hurried them on their way, saying they didn't want to be late for the movie. Kendra noticed that as he closed the door behind them, he winked at Parker, who merely chuckled when she sent a suspicious look his way.

"Subtlety is not your father's long suit," he said. "All right, I confess. I called him and asked if they'd like to baby-sit so I could have you to myself for a while."

"Why?" she demanded, and he looked utterly dumfounded.

"Why? Because you're my wife, my best friend, my closest adult companion. You speak in real words, think in complete thoughts and you attempt to laugh at my jokes. Much as I love my darling niece, she's not my idea of good company—yet."

Kendra found that answer appropriately soothing. She relaxed a bit. "Okay, so what movie are we going to see?"

He smiled. "You like foreign films, don't you? There are a couple playing at that great old theater over on Inwood. I thought we'd go there. They've got a cozy little bar next door where we can wait until the movie starts, if you want.''

She shrugged. "Sounds fine."

Something about his smile sent little shivers of alarm through her, but she pushed them away. She was overreacting again. What could happen? He draped his arm about her shoulders and turned her toward the car. Her footsteps dragged only slightly as they approached.

A half hour later, their movie tickets in his pocket, they sat side by side at a table the size of a dinner plate. They were sipping bourbon and cola when Dennis Scherer and his date walked in. Any hope that they might escape his notice was instantly banished. Indeed, his gaze seemed literally drawn to their particular corner, and to make matters worse, Parker raised a hand high in the air and waved. Dennis and his date made a beeline for their table, pausing only to steal chairs for themselves.

"Well, well, if it isn't the newlyweds!" Dennis exclaimed, placing his chair across from Kendra. "Ah, allow me to introduce my date. Mandy, meet Mrs. and Mrs. Parker Sugarman."

Parker had gotten to his feet as soon as they'd drawn near, and he now stepped around the table to hold Mandy's chair. "Nice to meet you, Mandy. This is my wife, Kendra." Just before he seated himself once more at Kendra's side, Parker shook hands with Dennis. "Good to see you again, Dennis. How's it going?"

Dennis sat down and dropped his elbows onto the table, eyeing them both pointedly. "It's okay," he said. "We've all been missing Nathan and Candace, of course. Man, I can't tell you how bad I feel about that."

Parker inclined his head and wrapped his arm around Kendra's shoulders. "Thanks. I still can't quite believe it, you know. If it wasn't for Kendra, I'm not sure what I'd do."

Dennis nodded pensively. "Yeah, I can see that, but talk about a shock, man. You two really kept the lid on this thing. You could've knocked me over with a feather when I first heard you'd tied the knot."

Kendra cringed inwardly. Now that the moment to lie had again arrived, she wasn't sure if she could go through with it, but Parker evidently had no such scruples. He tightened his embrace and turned a look on her that all but virtually shouted love. His mouth curved upward in a gentle smile.

"I don't think we knew it ourselves," he said to Dennis. "It just sort of blindsided us. At least it did me." He leaned close and pressed a kiss into the hollow of her temple.

Kendra dropped her gaze, unable to look either Dennis or Mandy in the eye. Her hands were clasped tightly together beneath the table. Parker's free hand covered them, then gently pried them apart. With his thumb, he began to stroke her palm and the inside of her wrist. The soft, languid movements quickly became the focus of her attention. Her heartbeat began to slow and a sensuous warmth spread through her. Soon she felt utterly relaxed and yet was pleasantly tingling in various places. He neither slowed nor sped the rhythm of his stroke but kept it a gentle, constant physical caress, all the while speaking with Dennis and his date in a calm, measured tone of voice. Kendra didn't even bother to try to follow the conversation, just sat within the clasp of his arm and allowed him to stroke away her worries and embarrassment and doubts.

When Dennis and Mandy rose to leave, Kendra realized she'd laid her head upon Parker's shoulder. It felt heavy as lead when she lifted it and smiled a farewell. Dennis leaned across the table and kissed her in the middle of her forehead.

"I'm so happy for you," he said. "Try not to overdo it. Kiss the baby for me. I'll see you soon."

She nodded, wondering what she'd missed, and pulled a deep, cleansing breath of air. Parker's hand was clasped firmly over her wrist. She felt limp as a dishcloth. She turned to him with a bemused expression. "I guess I'm more tired than I realized."

He smiled and nuzzled the hair over her ear with his nose, saying softly, "We can skip the movie if you want, just go home and put our feet up, put on some music."

The heat of his breath was causing her skin to tighten and tingle. She thought of sitting next to him on the sofa in the living room, the lights turned down low, music playing softly in the background, him touching her this way. Her breasts began to ache, her legs to tremble. She gulped.

"We've already b-bought our movie tickets."

He didn't argue, just smiled and rose from his chair, pulling her up with him. He draped her coat over her shoulders, wrapped his arm around her and steered her toward the exit.

The theater was packed, but they found two seats near the back and slipped into them. If Dennis and his date were attending the same movie, Kendra saw no sign of them before the lights went down and the previews for coming movies began. As before, Parker draped his arm about her and took her hand in his.

Soon she was caught up in the action and subtitles, the scenery and the interesting camera angles of a superb French drama set in a former century. When the hero and the vulnerable, unsuspecting heroine finally came together in a rare moment of privacy fraught with sexual tension, Parker began to stroke her palm and wrist again, but this time his touch journeyed far up the inside of her arm, invading the hem of her sleeve to stroke almost as high as her elbow, while his other hand gripped the top of her shoulder, his fingertips sliding beneath the collar of her dress to rest provocatively against the delicate bones there. When the big-screen hero finally worked himself into a position to kiss the reluctant object of his desires, Kendra closed her eyes, feeling that kiss all the way down to her toes, but it was not the actor whose face she saw on the other end of that kiss. It was Parker. It was her husband, and that realization did nothing for her peace of mind.

She crossed her legs and shifted slightly away from him. He crossed his own legs and leaned with her. She took a deep breath, shrugging lightly in an attempt to dislodge his hand. He slid his fingertips along her collarbone and up her neck to rest, comfortably splayed, against the curve of her jaw and the sensitive skin below and behind her ear. She imagined he could feel the beat of her pulse, the swift, erratic rush of blood through her veins, that he knew how deeply she was affected by his seemingly casual touch. She wondered if he was taunting her or simply bent on seduction. She knew he had been celibate since they'd been married, probably since Nathan had died, and Parker Sugarman was not a man resigned to celibacy. Nathan had told her once, only half kiddingly, that Parker slept with a different woman every night of the week, and she didn't doubt it. She didn't, at that moment, doubt it a bit.

When the movie was over, she was relieved beyond words, wanting only to get out of there and put some distance between them. Unfortunately, the whole darned audience seemed of the same mind, and whoever was at the end of their row didn't seem inclined to push out into the stream of those rushing for the exits. They were forced to stand between the rows of seats, shuffling their feet in place, waiting for a chance to move. While they did so, Parker rested one hand in the curve of Kendra's waist and the other on her shoulder, his fingers again resting inside the edge of her wide, ribbed collar. He stepped up close, his chest to her back, and held her against him. His touch was light, caressing and amazingly possessive. It was all she could do not to lay her head back on his shoulder and turn her mouth to his. Finally they began inching forward, and a few seconds later stepped out into the aisle and turned toward the exits. The traffic was lighter now, people strolling rather than pushing and rushing, but Parker took her hand and pulled ahead of her, tugging her behind him as he wove his way through the remaining crowd with unseemly haste.

They reached the corridor, but instead of slowing his pace, Parker picked it up. By the time they made the lobby, they were practically running. He paused and threw her coat over her shoulders, then grabbed her hand and yanked her out onto the sidewalk. Trotting now, he headed down the block toward the car. Within moments, Kendra was winded, the lusty pull on her senses and the pell-mell flight combining to rob her of breath. She called a halt, feeling her toes slide forward in her shoes as she dug her feet in.

"Parker—" she gasped.

He swung back, the expression on his face intense, almost pained. With a muttered curse, he clamped a hand on her arm just above the elbow and pulled her forward. An instant later, he shoved her sideways. She turned slightly, stunned, and he pushed her backward into the dark shadows of a recessed door. She felt the cold, smooth, hardness of polished granite at her back, and then he engulfed her, his hands in her hair, tilting her face, his mouth possessing hers, his body pressing her against the stone. He held her head tightly to his as if fearing she would pull away, and plunged his tongue into her mouth. Her hands were on his shoulders. She could feel him trembling. She could feel the desperate need driving him to plunder. She pushed her hands up and slid them about his neck.

He groaned and relaxed, loosening his hold. His mouth slid from hers and fixed itself just below the curve of her jaw, where his fingertips had rested earlier. "Kendra, you're making me crazy." He breathed the hot words against the sensitive skin of her throat, his nose nuzzling her. "I'm losing my mind, wanting you, needing you. It wasn't supposed to be this way! Damn you, it wasn't supposed to be this—"

His mouth covered hers again, wet and seeking. He pressed against her, thrusting his hips forward, grinding against her. His hands dropped to her sides, and she felt him gathering great handfuls of her dress, tugging the skirt higher and higher until he could push himself between her legs. One hand slipped under her thigh. Stocking slick, it seemed to shape itself to his hand, then raised effortlessly at his prodding. He slid his hand down her leg, guiding it around him, tucking her foot between his thighs just above the backs of his knees. He thrust against her hot core. Mindlessly, she wound her arms around his neck and hung on for dear life, great waves of desire racking her. His tongue imitated his action, stroking in and out of her mouth, delving deeper and deeper, opening her for his exploration. Automatically, she shaped her mouth to fit his, undulating her own tongue beneath it. His hand slid up her leg and to the inside of her thigh.

When his fingers first touched her there, a jolt of electricity shot through her, followed by moist, white-hot heat. He stroked her, much as he'd stroked her wrist, through her panties and hose. Her head fell back, and she cried out mindlessly, lights flashing behind her closed eyes. He kissed her cheek, her ear, the curve of her shoulder.

"Go wild for me," he said, trapping his hand between them as he thrust against her. "Go wild for me, baby, please." His voice was husky, shaking. His hand closed over her breast, squeezing rhythmically as his other hand stroked, and he thrust against her.

She kneaded his back and shoulders, head thrashing side to side, a pressure building in her. "Parker!"

"Yes, love."

"Parker! Oh . . . !"

He seized her mouth with his, inhaled her breath, gave her his own, grinding his palm and hips against her. She closed her hands in his jacket, twisting the fabric as the lights flashed and the pressure within her exploded and radiated. The waves swept through her, each smaller than the last, until she was utterly drained, emptied of all but a lazy warmth. He pressed against her, pulling at her mouth, supporting her with his body. Gradually, little by little, he pulled away from her, his hands traveling up her body to her face. He cupped it gently, his fingers splayed against the sides of her head. She covered them with her own as he sweetly plied her mouth, tongue sweeping its moist cavern and slowly retreating. At last he broke the contact completely, rocking back on his heels. She leaned into him, her head bowed, cheeks flooding with heated color. His arms came around her. He rubbed his chin against the top of her head. She could feel him shuddering still and wrapped her arms around his waist.

"If I survive this," he told her, chuckling, "it will be a damned miracle."

She turned her cheek against his chest. "I'm sorry."

He took a deep breath and pushed it out again. "I'm not." He dropped a kiss into her hair. "Let's get our kid and go home."

She nodded, not wanting to move, not wanting to face what waited for them. He stepped back and turned her within the clasp of his arm, his motions a little awkward, a little stiff. She knew he was far from sated, struggling for control. He seemed to steel himself then stepped out of the shadows and turned down the sidewalk. There were only a few cars left in the parking lot. The silver coupe sat alone beneath a street lamp. He unlocked the door and held her arm as she bent and stepped inside. He didn't look at her when he got into the car, didn't speak, just started up and pulled away, tires squealing against the cold pavement. They seemed to fly, catching all the green lights, silent in the night. She closed her eyes, too exhausted to think or even feel. When they pulled up in front of her father's house, Parker put the transmission into Park but left the engine running.

"Wait here," he said, and got out of the car.

Long minutes passed, during which Kendra did not lift her head or open her eyes. She began to remember, to relive what had happened in that darkened doorway. Had people walked past them on the sidewalk? Had they snickered behind their hands or moved on into the night, oblivious? Had they heard her cries of ecstasy, peered startled into the black shadows? Shame washed through her. Her face and neck and even her breasts burned with embarrassment. By the time Parker came with the baby and as much of her gear as he could carry, Kendra had entered into the lowest depth of self-loathing and blame. How could she have let him do that? How could she have come to climax there in the shadows, clinging to him, mindlessly allowing her body a response she had not even dreamed was possible? She felt ill, physically nauseated.

When he got back into the car, the baby safely belted into her seat, Kendra turned her face away. She felt him staring at her, felt him silently pleading for a look, a sign of acceptance, anything. She couldn't give it to him.

They drove home in silence, more slowly than before, almost ponderously, it seemed to her. Parker turned the car into the alley, the lights bouncing off poles and fences, trash cans and pavement. He shut off the lights as the car rolled into the garage and came to a halt. Kendra pulled her coat closed with one hand and groped for the door handle with the other. Suddenly Parker's shot out and clasped the back of her neck. He pulled her toward him, leaning close.

"Don't let's sleep alone tonight," he said huskily. "Please, not tonight."

She fixed her gaze on the steering wheel, eyes and throat burning, and shook her head. "I can't!"

His hand tightened on the steering wheel. "Can't? We're married, and you can't? You want it just as badly as I do, and you can't? What are you afraid of, Kendra? That it'll feel so good you'll want it more and more, again and again?"

She closed her eyes. "Don't...oh, don't!"

"Don't?" he echoed roughly. "You didn't say don't back there in the shadows, Ken. You didn't say don't then!"

"Stop it!"

"Just let me love you. Just let me inside you and—"

"Stop it!" She spoke more sharply, more loudly, than she'd intended. The baby made a tiny sound of surprise and gathered breath for a wavering cry.

Parker dropped his hand from the back of her head and slammed it against the steering wheel. "Damn!"

Kendra recoiled, shrinking away from him. The baby wailed and sobbed brokenly. Parker yanked his keys from the ignition and tossed them into her lap.

"Take the baby into the house," he groaned out. "I said take the baby into the house!"

She grabbed the keys and yanked the door open. She leapt out and slammed it shut, took one step and yanked the back door open. She gathered up the baby as quickly as she could with shaking hands and limbs, left the bag and backed away from the car.

"Lock your damned door!" he told her harshly. "I mean it, Kendra. Lock it!"

She turned and ran for the house, the baby's cries muffled against her shoulder. She could hear him cursing, hear the blunt sounds of his fists as they hit the steering wheel. She fumbled the key into the lock, somehow got the door opened and got herself and the baby up and through it. Cradling the baby against her, she stumbled down the hall and turned onto the gallery. She blundered into the darkened bedroom and collapsed on the end of the bed, rocking the baby, jabbering senselessly. The baby thrust her fingers into her mouth, turned her wet face into Kendra's chest, snuffled and quieted. Kendra held her and rocked her until she was sure that she slept, then lifted her tiredly into the crib.

With trembling fingers, she unzipped the blanket sleeper to check her diaper, found it dry and sagged with relief. After a moment, she zipped the sleeper up again, then pulled the blankets from the crib and dropped them on the floor. Only then did she stumble to the door, close it and lean against it. Her hand pressed to her mouth as the tears fell and the sobs began. She put her head down and tried to stifle the sounds. After a long while, she moved to the bed and fell against it, but she did not lock that door. She would not lock that door. If he came to her, she would throw her arms around him in welcome. She would love him with every fiber of her being, every cell of her body.

It was what she longed to do, what she needed to do, despite the danger. He would break her heart. She knew that as she knew her own anguish. He would make love to her with his knowing touch and his expert ways. He would take her to paradise, fill her with passion, drain her with pleasure. He would make love to her, but he would not love her, and she would die. She would simply die. But she couldn't lock him out. No matter how hard she tried, she couldn't lock him out. He got in with a smile, a soft word, a stroke of his fingertips. He undid all her careful defenses with a look, an insinuation, a kindness.

She sobbed into the pillow, hoping he would come, praying he would come, terrified he would come. After a very long time, the tears stopped. She heard the baby sigh in her sleep, heard the tick of a clock somewhere, heard the central heating unit cycle on and then off again. She heard the rustle of the bushes beneath the window, the faint whistle of wind as it rounded the corner of the house. She heard traffic far away on Central Expressway or maybe Preston Road. She heard a thousand sounds, and none of them were those of Parker entering the house. She listened until sleep stole sound away.

Then, somewhere in the night, dimly, a baby cried. *Darla.* She struggled toward consciousness, her body drifting upward ahead of her mind. She tried to say that she was coming. Her arms and legs felt like lead weights, but she made them move, dreamlike, the distances and effort required to gain them distorted by the deep-water aura of exhaustion. Her eyes wouldn't open, and when she tried to make them, tears leaked out. Then there were other hands pushing her down, another voice telling her to stop, to wait. She sighed, and her mind seemed to jump ahead. The baby needed her. It was her turn, her night. Darla would be frightened, wondering why someone didn't come. Did babies wonder, or were their fears nameless, thoughtless voids of sheer panic? As if in answer, someone said that it was all right, and it was because, miraculously, the baby had stopped crying. A dream, Kendra thought, a bad, bad dream. No, that wasn't right. It must have been Parker, dear, dear Parker, whom she loved, whom she couldn't love. She was sure of it a moment later when she felt his arms about her, lifting her.

"Parker," she said.

He told her to shut up. She was going to the other bedroom. He would take care of the baby.

"Sleeping," she mumbled. If he replied, she didn't hear it, but somehow she thought the baby must be sleeping. That wasn't the important thing, though. He had come, and somehow she had to make him understand. Nothing was more important than that he understand. She tried to lift her head, but only her eyelids would move. Her gaze drifted painfully over floating walls and columns and lights until it found his face. He needed a shave. His jaw looked hard as steel beneath the shadow of his beard.

"Parker," she said. He seemed not to hear, but she couldn't stop the words, even though they were slurred and garbled. "It's because I have to leave. Six months, and I have to go. I couldn't bear it. I couldn't bear it if it was good."

His nostrils flared. A muscle worked in the hollow of his jaw. "I know," he said. It came again on a sigh. "I know."

She closed her eyes and felt the bed undulate gently beneath her, felt cool, cool sheets. It was heaven, and it was agony. She wanted to tell him that she would bear it anyway, that not having him was too hard, too painful. She wanted to tell him that he was her husband, that in her heart he would always be her husband. But the deep, warm waters were closing over her, and she couldn't find him. She was adrift, alone. Lost. All lost.

Chapter Ten

She hadn't locked the door.

Parker put down his mechanical pencil, hooked his elbows on the rim of the tilted board and bowed his head. She hadn't locked the door, but she was still going.

Six months, and not a day longer.

It had seemed like such a long time, all the time in the world. It *had* seemed that way, and now... He straightened and looked down at the little mischief-maker in her playpen. Somehow he couldn't seem to get any work done unless she was sleeping or right here with him, and even then it was a pretty iffy situation. She was up on all fours, *urrr*ing like a motorcar, swaying back and forth as if building momentum for that first real gain of ground. She'd get it figured out pretty soon, and then he wouldn't dare put her down without first throwing up barricades and stashing away everything she could possibly lift, reach or knock over. As it was he spent all his time wiping her chin and taking things out of her mouth or putting them in, that or changing her diaper, and from the smell of things, it was time to repeat that one now.

He got down off the tall chair, bent and lifted her, his hands under her arms. She threw her head back and squealed, her fist going straight to her mouth to be slurped and smeared. She had seemed so sick that night after the movie that he'd called the doctor. Gas, he'd said, a hot water bottle for her tummy, liquid analgesic, and call him on Monday. When Kendra had awakened that Sunday morning to find them on the couch, Darla asleep on his chest, she'd been angry beyond any reason. It had been her night, she'd insisted, but he'd listened to Darla scream for long seconds before he'd gone in to find Kendra trying to get up, eyes swollen, tears still in her eyes.

He'd quieted the baby momentarily and carried Kendra to his bed so she could get some real rest, but she must have thought he'd still had other things in mind because she'd roused enough to tell him again that she couldn't make love with him. She was going to leave him when the six months were up, and apparently nothing he could say or do would change that, certainly nothing he'd come up with in the two weeks since. He had to laugh when he remembered that he'd married her because she wasn't in love with him. He had to laugh, but he wanted to cry, only he had no right to the tears.

He popped Darla into her crib. He'd had to lower the mattress a few days ago when she'd started trying to pull up on things, so he had to put the side down now in order to change the diaper. She flopped over on her belly the instant she hit the sheet and reared up on all fours.

"Lay down, scamp," he told her, gathering the things he'd need from the bedside table.

She ignored him as usual and reached for the teddy, overextending and toppling forward onto her face. She grunted and tried to get up again. He held her down and flipped her over. She screwed up her face and prepared to scream. He grabbed the toy and thrust it into her hands.

"There! Now cool it. You smell like an outhouse." She gnawed on the bear's ear and pretended not to understand, but he knew better. She was sharp as razors, this girl. No doubt one day she'd discover the substance that would render plutonium obsolete or walk on Mars and speak the languages of peoples heretofore unknown. No doubt one day she'd stick her chin out, glare at him and say, "No!" Then he'd have to find some way to make her do whatever he meant her to without breaking either of their hearts. He'd be on his own when that day came. He wouldn't think about it. One day at a time, one moment, one crisis, one joy, one pain, for Darla's sake, because he loved her beyond all reason and she was his, all that was his.

She stopped struggling when he got the tapes on the diaper loose and locked her chubby ankles in his hand, lifting her out of the mess so he could clean her with the towelettes he'd laid to one side. She held the bear up and spit at it, in an effort to say its name or just in sheer orneriness.

"Poor bear," he said, emphasizing the *b* and at the same time hoping to convey the idea to Darla that it was ill-mannered and hurtful to spit. She dropped the toy on her face and started gnawing its nose. Well, they could work on biting later when her teeth were in and she could do real damage. He folded up the soiled diaper and set it aside for cleaning. She didn't just soil them anymore, she filled them, and he'd quickly learned they couldn't go into the trash like that. He shook out the clean diaper and hiked her rear again. Someone knocked on the door.

"Yeah?"

A construction worker stuck his head inside. "You got a lady here, Mr. Sugarman."

Parker slid the diaper under Darla and dropped her feet. She instantly flopped over. He made a grab for her and started over. "Not Mrs. Sugarman, obviously."

"No, sir."

"Mrs. Pendleton, then? *Dr.* Pendleton?"

"Can't say."

"It's probably her. Send her in." He concentrated on folding the diaper up between Darla's legs and holding her down with a splayed hand while he fixed the tapes with the other. He looked up as a short, dumpy, frazzled-looking woman came in. A stranger. He held Darla down with one hand and regarded the newcomer. "You're not who I was expecting. Sorry about that. I'm Parker Sugarman. What can I do for you?"

She stepped forward and extended a hand, the other clutching a yellow legal pad and a pocketbook. He reached for it, aborted the movement and smiled apologetically.

"Better let me wash up first."

"Oh, of course."

He secured the final tape on Darla's clean undies, lifted the side rail on the crib, picked up the dirty diaper and carried it into the bathroom, where he swished it in the toilet, peeled away the uppermost layer and flushed it, then dumped the remainder in a trash can with a flip-top lid, purchased expressly for such refuse. He soaped and washed his hands, dried them on a towel and returned to the other room.

Darla was sitting up and rattling the side rail on the bed like a convict in a bad, forty-year-old movie. She had evidently thrown the bear over the side, a favorite trick of hers, and the woman had retrieved it and was offering it to her. Darla ignored her like she didn't exist. Parker walked over to the bed and held out his hands. Darla latched onto his fingers and tried to pull herself up. He slid his hands under her arms and lifted her high over his head, delighted she hadn't ignored him. She giggled and splattered him with drool.

"Monster!" He wiped his face with his shirtsleeve, kissed her on the cheek, and settled her on his hip. "Actually she's a sweetheart," he told the woman proudly, and stuck his hand out. "What'd you say your name was again?"

She put her hand in his, disciplining a smile. "I didn't. I'm Wanda Hatcher, Department of Human Resources."

Ye gods. It'd been so long, he'd almost forgotten about the home study, and the house was torn all to hell. Great. He swallowed and put on his best behavior. "Uh, let's go back into the living room and get comfortable. I don't usually receive visitors in the bedroom, you know, but dirty diapers don't wait, and the carpenter... I was expecting my sister-in-law, well, my sister-in-law's sister, my *late* sister-in-law, that is."

Wanda Hatcher nodded. "Yes, I'm well acquainted with Dr. Pendleton."

His heart sank like a stone. He pulled out his only ace. "Uh, my wife will be here shortly. She had an early shift today, ah, at the children's hospital. She's a pediatric nurse, very good, very dedicated."

"Yes," Mrs. Hatcher said, "I understand she was accepted on a U.N. medical relief team earlier in the year."

They entered the living room and he indicated that she should sit down, thankful that the protective plastic had been removed from the sofas that morning. She sat and smiled, her legal pad on her knee. He sat down opposite her, shifting Darla to his lap. Darla leaned over and bit his thumb. He removed it from her mouth and wiped it on his shirt.

"Uh, the U.N. thing, yeah, she was all set to go to Africa and rescue starving babies. She hated to give it up."

"Why did she?"

He licked his lips, tried to relax, assuming an air with which he was becoming more and more uncomfortable. The old charming Parker had disappeared, and he hadn't the least idea where he'd gone. He'd just ceased to exist, apparently. The new Parker could only make the best of it. He draped an arm along the back of the couch. "When my brother died," he said carefully, "all our lives were turned upside down. We, Kendra and I, decided we couldn't wait that year meant for Africa. She knew him, see. In fact, they were very close. Nathan and Candace were two of her dearest friends. We were all friends, had been, well, practically all our lives. And then they were suddenly gone, and we knew, we both knew, that they expected me, us, to take care of Darla if anything happened to them, which it had. It was selfish of me, I know, but all I could think to do was to marry her right away. We kind of held each other together there in the beginning, but it's better now, thankfully. I don't know what I'd have done without her." Darla was squirming like a worm. He kissed the top of her head and momentarily stilled her. "Or this one," he added, smiling.

Ms. Hatcher nodded, took a pen from her purse and wrote something on the legal pad. Suddenly Parker's heart was in his throat. Wanda Hatcher looked up.

"I expect you'll be having one of your own," she said, looking directly at the baby.

He gulped, misery washing over him. "Uh, not, not right away. That is, I don't . . . We haven't—" He felt his face coloring. It was the most horrific experience of his life. He had stilled the words, but he was absolutely certain that the truth had been exposed, that it was written all over his face for anyone to read. An imbecile could see it. A maiden aunt could see it. The most inexperienced schoolboy, innocent of his first wet dream, would know at a glance that he had not managed an act of *sexual congress* with his own wife. The ladies' man. The playboy king of the Western world. What a joke! He could seduce dozens of desperate women, but he couldn't make one good, sensitive, caring woman love him, and that woman being his own wife! He looked down in his lap, beyond the dark little head, to the tiny hands playing a clumsy patty-cake with his own much larger one, and for the first time he wondered if he was doing the right thing, keeping Darla with him, trying to be the parent his brother could have been. Maybe he just didn't have what it took. Maybe he was lacking in something basic, some fundamental element of his personality. Maybe he just wasn't worthy of the kind of goodness his brother had been. Maybe—

A sound from the back of the house interrupted his train of thought. He pushed a hand over his face, willing the color to recede, and turned his head just as Kendra stepped out onto the gallery from the back hall. She was smiling brightly, her rich brown hair woven into a French braid from the crown to the nape. She was wearing a white uniform dress, white stockings and a white cardigan sweater, a sexy angel of mercy in rubber-soled shoes. Just seeing her there calmed him somehow. He felt the longing swell within him and reach out for her. As if in response, she lifted her hand in greeting and stepped down to cross the room.

"Hi, honey!"

Honey? Oh, of course. He glanced down at the baby, quite certain that greeting had been for her. To his surprise, however, Kendra walked around behind the couch where he sat, bent and slid her arms around his neck. She gave him a quick hug, then placed her hands beneath his chin and tilted his head back for a hard, upside-down kiss on the mouth. He was speechless.

"Uh, ah. H-hi."

She smiled at him, then switched her gaze to the baby. Laughing, she clapped her hands together lightly and spread them. "Come here, darling." Darla swiveled and bucked, reaching out for her. Kendra snatched her from his lap and dandled her briefly in the air. "Ooh, I missed you today. Give me sugars." She kissed the baby noisily under the chin. Darla giggled and drooled. Kendra pulled a terry washcloth from her pocket, saying, "Look what I found in my pocket today. Look what I found." She wiped the baby's chin with it and put it back in her pocket. Carrying Darla, she walked around the couch and sat down next to Parker, *right* next to Parker, practically in his lap, in fact. She looked at the other woman, smiling. "Sometimes things get caught in pockets while in the laundry. Does that ever happen to you?"

The woman chuckled and smiled, thoroughly disarmed. "Yes, yes, I'm afraid it does."

Kendra laid her head on Parker's shoulder, then lifted it again. "Well, I'm not complaining. Parker usually does the laundry, you know. He's the one at home, and I'm working these crazy shifts at the hospital. I don't know what I'd do without him, actually. I'm just thankful it wasn't a pair of men's shorts I pulled out of my pocket today at work." She laughed, and the other woman joined her.

Parker was suddenly aware that his mouth was hanging open. He quickly snapped it shut, hoping it hadn't been noticed. The thought occurred that he hadn't made any introductions, and he hastened to correct that lapse in manners. "Oh, uh, Kendra, this is Martha, no, *Wanda* Hatcher—sorry—"

"No problem."

"Ms. Hatcher is with the, ah, Department of Human Resources. Ms. Hatcher, my wife."

Kendra beamed at the other woman. "So nice to meet you, Ms. Hatcher. I take it this is in the nature of a home study. We were told someone would be by."

Ms. Hatcher smiled reassuringly. "I was just having a conversation with your charming husband. He tells me that the two of you probably won't have any children of your own."

Kendra looked mildly shocked. "Oh, no, I'm sure that's not what he meant." She sent him a smile and slipped her hand into his. "We're just not in a hurry. We want to give Darla our complete attention for a while. We'd feel the same way if she were our natural child, wouldn't we, sweetheart?"

She squeezed his hand, and he stumbled into following her lead. "Ah, yes, a-absolutely. That's what I was saying when... She's absolutely right. I know that the majority of the experts would say that Darla was too small to suffer any real trauma over her parents' deaths, but we just want to be absolutely certain that she's secure in her own little heart that she's loved and treasured here. She's all the more precious to us because of who her natural parents were, you see, and we don't want her ever to feel as if she's 'an extra' or the odd one in the family, if you take my meaning.''

Wanda Hatcher nodded, scribbling furiously. "I understand, and I couldn't agree more," she said, "but I want to be certain about this. You *don't* intend to raise her as an only child?''

Parker opened his mouth, but the lie just didn't come out. He took a deep breath, searching for some satisfactory yet honest answer. He hadn't found one when Kendra jumped in to save them both.

"Our intention," she said smoothly, "is *not* to raise her as an only child, but of course, one never knows for sure what lies in store. However, I, for one, think it would be a crying shame if Parker were not allowed another child. He has such a gift for children. He is just wonderful with her.''

Wanda Hatcher lifted an eyebrow. "I must say that I was pleasantly surprised to see the ease with which he deals with her.''

Kendra laughed. "Oh, you haven't seen anything," she declared. "He's better with her than I am. He's never too tired to get up with her. He's never upset with her, never thrown for a loss. You'd think he had been doing this his entire adult life. He's a wizard.''

Laying it on a bit too thick, he thought, and slipping his hand from hers, he lifted his arm around her shoulders, squeezing gently. She smiled up at him.

"By the way, darling, what's for dinner?''

The switch stymied him for a moment. "Ah, dinner...dinner is lasagna.''

"Ooh, goody!" She looked at Wanda Hatcher. "I *love* his lasagna.''

He felt a little desperate. She was gushing, *bragging,* painting this perfect househusband picture, when in truth he was just barely getting it done, and businesswise, he wasn't even doing that much. A good look around ought to tell Hatcher or anyone else with a modicum of training or experience what the true tale was. Glancing at Wanda Hatcher, he cleared his throat and addressed his wife. "Um, it's just that frozen stuff that comes in a foil pan."

"Oh, I know," she replied smoothly, "but you add extra cheese and sauce and stuff, and you always make a lovely green salad and garlic toast."

"It's plain white bread with butter and a sprinkle of garlic salt," he said stiffly.

"Yes, babe, but that's more than any other husband I know of does." She looked at Ms. Hatcher. "Every woman I work with goes home at the end of the day and makes dinner. They don't believe me when I tell them that Parker cooks. I mean, they can't get their husbands to suggest an entrée, let alone cook it up and set it on the table. He just doesn't know how good he is."

Parker lifted a hand to his forehead and smiled wanly at Wanda Hatcher. "Obviously she's prejudiced," he offered weakly.

"Darned right I am," Kendra said, straining upward to kiss the curve of his jaw. "With very good reason." She smiled at Ms. Hatcher. "He's incredible, just incredible."

Parker barely restrained himself from rolling his eyes. Instead, he shifted his position slightly and latched on to the first topic that occurred in order to change the subject. "Oh, Kendra, I didn't tell you. Edward stopped by today. He...he, uh, found out something about that little girl from South America."

"Céfira."

"Right. They found a half sister, an older girl from a previous marriage of the father's. Apparently he was quite a bit older than the little girl's—"

"Céfira."

"Céfira's mother. Turns out this older half sister is able to care for the little—Céfira, and she's coming after her as soon as possible. Edward's had himself named as advocate for the child and has made a formal request for visa clearance and so forth, and, um, funds have been provided for meeting immediate needs—airline fare, housing, that sort of thing. Céfira should have someone with her by the end of the week.''

Kendra clapped her hands together. ''That's so wonderful! I'm so happy for her!'' She turned shining eyes on Wanda Hatcher. ''It's a little girl at the hospital. Her parents were killed in an auto accident while they were all here on a visit of some sort. She was badly injured, alone here in a foreign country, unable to speak the language. I felt so sorry for her, and when I told Parker, he had Edward look into it. That's our attorney, Edward White. Anyway, they've finally found someone for her, a family member, and now she won't be alone anymore.'' She turned back to Parker, her smile so bright it dazzled him. ''How much did you give him?'' she asked.

He blinked at her. ''What?''

Her smile turned knowing. ''How much did you give him to bring Céfira's sister here?''

He grimaced. What was she, psychic? ''I don't know what you're talking about.''

''Don't give me that.''

''We'll discuss this later. Right now I . . .''

He had another inspiration. ''I think we ought to show Ms. Hatcher the house.''

''All right,'' Kendra said agreeably. ''I'll just ask Edward how much money you gave him.''

Parker ground his teeth together. ''You're making a mountain out of a molehill, Kendra.'' At her skeptical look, he burst out, ''We split it, okay? He paid half, I paid half. Satisfied?''

She wound an arm around his neck and kissed his cheek. ''Thank you,'' she whispered. ''Thank you so much.'' That done, she looked at Ms. Hatcher. ''I told you, he's incredible.''

Parker dropped his brow against the crown of her head and inwardly groaned.

''Now then,'' Kendra said brightly, ''About the house. Let me explain what we're doing here . . .'' She popped up off the couch, one arm looped around Darla's middle, the other snugged beneath her little bottom. "It's going to be so great!" she enthused. "It's Parker's design, of course."

Parker got up hastily. "Uh, why not let me explain, *dear?* It is my design, after all."

"Right," Kendra agreed pleasantly. "This way, please." She didn't even pause, but began a monologue right away. "First we have the original house. The great room, which is where we're standing, is surrounded by the gallery, this raised area on three sides. Then over on this side is the dining room, except Parker's using it for an office right now. You can see the baby's playpen in there by the drawing board. And where the two steps go up, that's the kitchen, and the laundry room's off that. Don't you just love the pillars, the columns, I mean? They give it such an elegant, open feel. Now on this other side is the master bedroom. It's heavenly, a fireplace, nice big closets, a complete bath, hot tub, the works." She led the way, throwing open doors and pointing out amenities. "He's so neat," she went on. "I've never met a man so neat!"

"And you," he said resignedly, leaning in the door, "are an unrepentant slob."

She laughed. "Too true. But does he complain? No, ma'am. He just picks up after me and quietly reorganizes my messes. I tell you, he's every working wife's dream. And people wonder why women find him so attractive!"

He groaned aloud, no longer even trying to derail her.

She ignored him and breezed out the door, saying, "Now this is the powder room, and this is the baby's room. She has her own bath, not that it matters at this point, but back here..." She closed the door and went on, "Now this is where it gets really interesting. Darling, I think you were going to explain this part." She beamed at him, knowing full well that he wanted to strangle her.

He narrowed his eyes at her and smoothly picked up the narrative, pushing aside the heavy plastic sheet that covered the opening to the new addition. "This, of course, was the back hall, but we've added a small suite and a pair of rooms. Through here we have a multipurpose room, den, playroom, library. The columns help break it up in usage areas but maintain the scale and openness of the great room. And off this end, closest to the playroom is where my new office will be. That, of course, will allow us to return the dining room to its original use and still keep me close to the baby when she's playing. Then, on the other end, that's a third bedroom with a small sitting area and another bath. This extension of the original building has another benefit, too. A short enclosed walkway with extra storage space will soon connect the house and the garage. That will make getting the baby in and out of the car a lot safer during difficult weather or late at night."

Wanda Hatcher was appropriately impressed. She asked lots of little questions of no consequence, which Parker answered with his usual expertise. After that, Parker showed her a work in progress on his drawing board, getting much more technical and enthusiastic than he intended. While he was doing so, Kendra wandered into the kitchen and back. In a lull in the conversation, she interjected lightly, "Hon, have you fixed the hem on my striped skirt?"

Wanda Hatcher's mouth dropped open. Parker gulped down a spurt of laughter and turned a scolding gaze on Kendra. "No," he said laconically. "You know I'm no good at that sort of thing. I sent your skirt with the rest of the mending to the tailor."

Kendra shrugged unconcernedly. "Just thought I'd ask."

Parker turned to Ms. Hatcher apologetically. "I don't sew at all—not even buttons."

To his absolute consternation, the woman patted his arm and offered a sympathetic smile. "No matter," she said. "No one's perfect, my dear, and don't worry. I won't even bother to mention it in my report."

He was in, just like that, officially approved as a parent by the state. He was astonished. She'd bought it, lock, stock and barrel. He stared at Kendra over the other woman's head, was served up a saucy smile and a wink and promised her with his eyes both reward and retribution.

Thirty minutes and as many perfunctory questions later, Wanda Hatcher took her leave of them. Parker saw her to the door, closed it behind her and put his back to it. Kendra was standing in the middle of the room with Darla on her hip, grinning at him. He pointed a finger at her, but before he could get a word out, she pointed back at him and beat him to it.

"Now we're even, Mr. Sugarman!"

"Even? How do you figure that? Ski slopes in Colorado don't get such snow jobs!"

"And I suppose that was snow you were shoveling at my father's on the day of our wedding, hmm?"

He stared at her, then clapped his hands together in laughter. "Okay, okay," he said, strolling toward her, "so I was spreading a little fertilizer there."

"And I was snowing today," she admitted blithely. "But only a little."

He sobered and smiled at her, his hands on his hips. "It wasn't all lies, then or now."

She nodded. "I know."

"What happened changed both our lives."

"Yes, and Darla's, too."

"Darla's most of all," he agreed, "but hopefully not for the worse."

"I don't think so," Kendra said. "I think she's lucky that she has you to love her."

"I do love her," he said, taking the baby into his arms. He smoothed down her hair, which had developed a tendency to stand on end of late, and hugged her. "I love this kid like I've never loved another human being in my life."

"I know you do."

"It's funny," he said. "I loved my brother. I mean, I *always* loved him, even when he was a pesky little brat and I was a worldly wise teenager. We didn't fight like other siblings did. I honestly don't remember that we had a single argument, and I never questioned that he loved me, too. It was just a given in my life, you know, and then it was gone. I guess I thought all the love in my life died when he and Candace did. I mean, I knew Darla was precious to me. I just didn't know how much more she could mean. She was such a tiny thing then. She didn't even seem like a whole person to me, and now... Now she's one of the most important parts of my life."

"I understand," she said gently, her eyes sparkling gold and green. "I didn't expect to get quite so attached to her myself. I've been taking care of other people's sick kids for years now, and I thought this would be just like that, but it isn't. It's more, so much more."

He hadn't thought of that. He honestly hadn't thought of the feelings Kendra might be developing for Darla. She had been loving with her from the very beginning, but then that was just Kendra. Kendra was a caring person, gentle and thoughtful with everyone; well, everyone but Kate Ridley, and he still hadn't quite figured that out. More to the point, he hadn't thought how difficult it might be for Kendra to leave Darla when it came time for them to part. Might that keep her with them? He knew without a doubt that he couldn't leave Darla as his own father had left him and Nathan, no matter how much he might love another. Shamelessly, he used it.

"You'll always be as much a part of Darla's life as you want to be," he said matter-of-factly. "Of course, once you leave, it'll never be the same again. She won't remember that we were all three together like this. We can tell her, but it won't be the same, will it?"

He watched her swallow and shake her head. "No."

"Still," he went on, "you'll always be special to her. No one else will ever replace you in her life, I'll see to that—no matter what."

The eyes she turned up at him were large with tears, and he could read her thoughts in them. What if he remarried one day? What then? Could he keep her place for her in Darla's life then? For the first time since that night when he'd told her to lock her door, he willingly put an arm around her in a gesture not solely for public consumption and hugged her close, kissing her temple.

"It's all right," he said softly. "We'll work it out. We'll think of something. I promise."

She nodded into the curve of his shoulder. "Sure we will," she said, her voice bleak.

He closed his eyes, feeling the ache of desire never fulfilled, the swell of love he didn't dare reveal, the fear of losing again one of the most important persons in his life. Desperately he searched for some way to lift the cloud. Finally it came to him.

"Hey, how'd you know Ms. Hatcher was in here? I mean, you walked in loaded for bear."

She reared back her head and grinned up at him. "Derek told me."

"Derek?"

"The carpenter's assistant. He heard her say she was from the Department of Human Resources."

Parker frowned. "And he met you at the car with that news?"

She lifted her brows. "He didn't *meet me at the car.* We bumped into each other out in the yard."

"And do you often bump into each other?"

She studied him for a moment, and he didn't like it because he couldn't tell what she was thinking. "No," she finally said. "Not often."

Not often, meaning they did occasionally meet and, presumably, talk. It seemed he would just have to have a private word with Derek, the carpenter's assistant. By God, she was his wife, and until she wasn't, no construction worker or any other man was going to be arranging meetings of any kind with her. Period. It was bad enough that he had to put up with Lawyer White hanging around like a lovesick puppy all the time. He'd be damned if he'd put up with anyone else. He disengaged himself and pushed the baby into her arms.

"I have to get dinner on," he said glumly.

He didn't see the smile that followed him from the room or the hopeful gleam that suddenly shone in green-gold eyes.

Chapter Eleven

"It's your move," Kendra said.

Parker started and scowled. "I know it's my move!" he snapped. "You don't have to tell me every time that it's my move."

"Pay attention to the game, and I won't," Kendra retorted.

"This game is boring as hell," Parker said. "I can't pay attention to something that puts me to sleep."

"You wouldn't say that if you were winning," Kendra pointed out icily.

"If I wasn't bored to death, I *would* be winning," he shot back.

Edward sighed and tilted the game board so that all the playing pieces slid off onto the table. "What is it with you two?" he asked over their exclamations. "Every time I see you you're going at it like cats and dogs. It's getting old."

"You're telling me it's getting old!" Parker said, thumping his chest. "You should try living with her. On second thought, the two of you would get along just fine, you're both slobs.''

''I may be a little disorganized, *Mr.* Sugarman,'' Kendra said coldly, ''but at least that's normal, which I cannot say for your obsession with neatness! Edward, how many people do you know who dust construction sites?''

''This construction site just happens to be my house!'' Parker exclaimed, not allowing Edward time for response. ''And if you call me *Mr.* Sugarman in that tone again, *Mrs.* Sugarman, you can damned well start fixing your own dinner.''

''At least I wouldn't be eating lasagna three times a week!'' she snapped.

''You love my lasagna!'' he bellowed.

Kendra leapt up from her chair and slammed it against the table. ''That's right, Parker, wake up the baby again! It's not *your* night to get up with her!''

''Oh, for God's sake,'' he shouted back, ''if you want me to sleep with the baby tonight, why don't you just say so and stop trying to make me feel guilty for something I haven't even done!''

''Ooh!'' Kendra shook a fist at him, then turned away from him to Edward. ''Try to talk some sense into him, will you? Heaven knows I can't!''

''Sense!'' Edward said to her retreating back. ''Sense?'' He clamped both hands to his head and fell forward onto his elbows against the tabletop. ''Trying to talk sense to either one of you is like trying to negotiate with the Mafia and the FBI. And to think I was afraid you were going to fall for one another! Sheesh!'' He got up and stomped away, leaving the house without so much as a farewell.

Parker sat at the table and moved the game pieces about desultorily with a fingertip, then he swept the lot of them onto the floor and put his head into his hands. In the suddenly quiet house, he heard the faint click of a lock being set in place. That was the second time she'd locked him out in the past week, not that he'd tried to go to her. For a moment he considered kicking in the damned door, but he thought of Darla and stayed put. He always thought of Darla and stayed put, but he knew she was just the excuse that kept him from risking it all, just the excuse for taking the coward's way out, and he hated himself a little more every time he used her that way, hated himself—and loved Kendra.

Parker sat up straight, linked his hands behind his head and pressed his elbows back, stretching the pectoral muscles. Kendra swallowed and looked away, trying not to notice the firm delineations of muscle on his bare chest. Why didn't he put his shirt back on? Did he think she got some kind of charge from watching him work out with those free weights while dressed only in a pair of gym shorts, shoes and socks? She supposed that she could watch television in the bedroom, but since they'd furnished the multipurpose room and Parker had moved his drawing table and other gear in here, they'd practically been living in this one room. Besides, she was never quite comfortable in the master bedroom. That was *his* room, and she couldn't quite seem to forget it even when she had it all to herself.

Darla moved in her lap, turning her little head side to side against Kendra's breastbone. Kendra smiled and dropped a kiss on her crown. Darla abruptly threw herself sideways, forcing Kendra to catch her, and twisted onto her back, grinning. Her pink, toothless smile revealed bumps on the lower gum that were about to be teeth. Kendra laughed and lifted her for a hug. "So big!" she said, nuzzling a damp chin. "You're getting so big!"

Darla grabbed handfuls of Kendra's hair and gave her a wet, open-mouthed kiss on the forehead before twisting sideways again. Parker was doing sit-ups on the rug in front of the television and counting aloud. "One, two, three, four..." Darla took one look and decided it was great fun. She launched herself toward him, nearly propelling herself out of Kendra's lap. She seemed to have no fear wahtsoever, certainly none of landing on her head on a hardwood floor.

"Whoa! You're not just getting big, you're getting hard to handle, too. Hold on here a minute. How about a game of patty-cake, hmm?"

Parker stopped counting and reached for her. "Let me have her," he said. "We've done this together before."

Kendra handed her over and watched as he sat Darla on his stomach, facing him, against his drawn-up knees. Linking his hands behind his head again, he lowered himself to the floor, then rose again, bringing his forehead to Darla's. "One!" he said, and the baby laughed and clapped her hands together.

He did it again. "Two"

"Eeee!" Darla said, arching her back.

"Three!"

"Eeee!"

"Four!"

Darla just stared at him, eyebrows dancing, lips clamped together.

Parker laughed. "Four, scamp. Four!"

Apparently not feeling up to the challenge, Darla threw herself forward onto his chest, flopped over and rolled. He caught her and rolled with her onto his side, easing her onto her back on the floor.

"Your turn!" he declared and started counting. "One, two, three . . ."

She lifted her head slightly and kicked her feet, reaching for him with her pudgy hands. Parker laughed and grasped her two tiny hands in one of his.

"Okay, here we go." He tugged her up. "One." He let her down again and repeated the process. "Two." She pivoted on her bottom and kicked out with both legs, babbling sounds. Laughing, he did it again. "Three." He let her down and tugged her up once more and put his nose to hers. "Four."

Darla shifted her head and "kissed" him on the nose. He laughed and collapsed onto his back, Darla at his side.

She flopped over onto her tummy, pushed up onto her knees and began rocking back and forth, butting her head against his side. He lifted her so that she leaned against his chest. She turned her head and laid her cheek over his heart.

"She loves you so much," Kendra said from the couch.

He smiled and stroked her head. "It's very mutual," he said, then he suddenly snatched the baby up to dangle her above him, making outrageous eyes at her. She wiggled her brows at him, and he lowered her to blow on her tummy. She giggled and wiggled her eyebrows to get him to do it again. He complied until she was gasping between belly laughs. Finally he got up and carried her to the couch.

"Playtime's up, sunshine. Stay with Kendra so I can take a shower." He plopped her down into Kendra's lap, kissed her and automatically lifted his face to Kendra's. Suddenly his mouth was an inch from hers, frozen on its way to kiss her, too.

Her breath caught. Her heart stopped. She wanted to tilt her chin up and bring her mouth to his, but she couldn't move, couldn't speak, and then he was pulling away, straightening to run a hand down the back of his head and neck, looking embarrassed.

"I, uh, won't be long."

"Take your time," she mumbled, turning her gaze down onto Darla in disappointment.

He slipped away. She closed her eyes, holding Darla against her, while her heart thumped almost painfully inside her chest. She felt like crying, a terrible sense of loss enveloping her. She wondered if he even wanted her anymore. Perhaps the novelty of living with someone with whom he couldn't sleep had worn off. Or maybe he had just changed so much that he didn't think about it anymore. More often than not they were snapping at one another, rubbing each other raw with senselessly irritating minutiae. She had thought him jealous at points and subtly tried to play on that without visible results. At other times he had seemed possessive and was occasionally even affectionate. For a while they had even seemed like a real family, and now they were disconnected strangers pretending to be more. It hurt like hell, but she didn't know what she could do about it. This was a temporary arrangement, a sham marriage, and it was almost Christmas. Nearly half their time was gone.

Darla looked at her, her head thrown back, and pulled at her hair. "Such a pretty girl," Kendra said, hugging her. "Want your hair brushed again? Let's brush your pretty hair again." She picked up the soft-bristled brush she had placed on the end table earlier and lightly stroked Darla's glossy dark hair. It was almost exactly the same shade as Parker's now, like dark chocolate. Kendra bit her lip to stop the trembling.

Kendra had worked on Thanksgiving, treating it as if it were any other day, the result being that she was not allowed to work Christmas. The holiday, it seemed, could not be ignored. After some rather heated conversation, she and Parker decided to accept an invitation to spend Christmas with her father and Kate, though it galled Kendra deeply to think of Kate cooking a Christmas dinner in her mother's kitchen. Parker told her that she had a "real problem" that she was going to have to face sooner or later. She retorted, rather sharply, that the only problem she had was him and that would fix itself in another three months time. He had looked so wounded that she had immediately regretted her words, but somehow she couldn't say so. She dared not reveal her own vulnerability.

She got a letter from Devon Hoyt, forwarded to her by her father, whose address she had cravenly written on the outside of the envelope when she'd written to beg off as a member of his health team. The work was hard, he said, but very rewarding. It had made him think, though, seeing all these diseased, starving children, and he had concluded that bringing additional persons into this world was a very irresponsible thing to do.

Kendra looked at Darla and thought how hard Parker was fighting to keep her and how hard it would be to give her up, and she tried to picture herself with another child, a baby of her own, at some future date, and a void opened inside her. No other child could ever take Darla's place in her heart. Had Darla's parents been irresponsible to bring her into this world? She hardly thought so. Darla had enriched her life and Parker's, not to mention those of her parents, beyond measure. Any other child that followed her in Kendra's life would do the same. The problem was that she couldn't quite picture a child that she would not share with Parker Sugarman. Somehow she felt sorry for Devon Hoyt. For all his compassion, caring and work, he had missed something basic and unique and beautiful in the human experience.

Devon said other things in his letter. He wrote that he regretted not having her with him, that he'd wanted to see her again ever since she'd been a student of his, that he had put in a special request to have her join his team with the work in progress when she was able to do so. He was looking forward very much to getting to know her in a more personal way than the classroom allowed. That, he revealed, was one reason he had sought her out and offered her this opportunity. She could not even find it in herself to be flattered. Africa seemed ridiculously idealistic now. Real life was here—with Parker and Darla—and it was halfway spent. She vowed to watch her tongue and stop sniping at Parker.

When she came home late one afternoon and found the house perfumed with the aroma of pine and Parker carefully and critically decorating a small tree for the new family room, she felt the first stirrings of genuine Christmas spirit. Apparently, the tree had put him in a good mood, too, for he had prepared a special dinner. Steaks were ready to go under the broiler. Potatoes had been baked to fluffy doneness, their skins brown and crisp. Yeast rolls had been thawed and were rising on the counter, while an oblong dish of precooked asparagus was chilling in the refrigerator and a bottle of red table wine had been decanted and left to breathe on the table.

After broiling the steaks and baking the bread, they ate in the family room before a gentle fire, sitting cross-legged on the floor at the big, round, oak coffee table Parker had chosen to go with the heavy sofa and chairs upholstered in bold red, blue and green plaid. For Darla, he rigged up a feeding chair by attaching a wood lap tray to her plastic seat with an old leather belt. They stripped her down to her diaper, fixed a sectioned plate with a suction cup on the bottom to the tray and let her feed herself cooled potato without the skin, strained carrots and creamed beef. She delighted in squishing the beef between her fingers and, aided by a penchant to put everything her hand touched into her mouth, actually managed to consume a fraction of what she smeared on her face and chest. Parker seemed to literally delight in the spectacle she made, and Kendra felt happier than she had in a long time.

After dinner, they gingerly freed Darla from her chair and carried her at arm's length to a warm bath. By the time they had cleaned her up, dressed her in footed pajamas, and brushed her glossy hair dry, the child's eyelids were drooping. They tucked her into her bed, wound up a softly tinkling music box and watched in awe as her thumb found its way to her mouth. They turned out the overhead light and stood in the soft shadows until her eyes closed fully and her breathing evened, creeping from the room as the music tinkled to an end.

Parker put his arm around her shoulders as they walked across the living room to the kitchen. He didn't say anything, but he didn't have to. She knew exactly what he was feeling. It was the commonplace wonder of watching Darla grow and change before their very eyes, the small daily miracles, the delightful nuisances, the astounding depth of emotion attached to one tiny person whose communication was limited to expression and the tone of her wail. It was an overwhelming sense of responsibility and a protectiveness so fierce, it was frightening. It was love, deep, blind, selfless love for which no words had been invented.

The dishwasher was running and the broiler drying on the counter when he poured the last of the wine into their glasses, leaned his hip against the edge of the breakfast table and turned a thoughtful look on her. "You think it's okay for her to suck her thumb?" he asked, his voice betraying his anxiety.

She smiled at him, ran a finger around the rim of her glass and nodded. "The conventional wisdom is that it really doesn't hurt anything. Most babies stop when they develop other ways to comfort themselves. If she's still doing it four or five years from now, we'll start looking for ways to distract her."

"Will *we*?" he asked softly, a slight accent on the last word.

Kendra cocked her head, wondering just what exactly he was asking. She whirled the ruby liquid in her glass and picked her words. "Do you think I'll somehow stop caring about her?" *And you?* she added with her eyes.

He stared at her a moment, his eyes slowly traveling over her face; then he smiled gently and shook his head. "No more than we'll stop caring about you," he said.

She ached to reach out for him, to have his arms open and pull her against his chest, but neither of them seemed quite prepared for such a dangerous display of affection. Instead, she leaned against the table next to him, and they sipped their wine in companionable silence. Parker checked his wrist watch and drained his glass.

"Want to catch the news?"

"Sure."

They left their glasses on the table and went to the family room, where they watched the television, sitting side by side on the couch without touching, while the fire died away to embers and the Christmas lights winked at them from the boughs of the small, cheery tree.

She went into work the next day to find that two nurses in her section had come down with a nasty virus, and a third had sprained an ankle ice skating at one of the area malls. The week that followed was one of double shifts, snatched meals and exhaustion. She stumbled home in the wee hours of the morning and collapsed into bed, sometimes without even undressing. Parker stayed out of her way as much as possible, and she barely saw Darla as the little one was sleeping entirely through most nights, a mixed blessing since Kendra insisted on continuing to trade nights in her room and would have welcomed a few minutes to hold and talk to her, despite a desperate need for sleep.

On the last night of what had been a grueling experience, Kendra drove herself home, dragged her aching body into the house and slipped into the bedroom. She did not even think about whose night it was to sleep with Darla. Indeed, her mind seemed to have suspended cognitive thought. Numbly she stripped down to panties and bra and slid into bed without even bothering to take down her hair. Rolling onto her side, she curled into a loose ball, vaguely aware of a floating sensation and a line of comfortable heat at her back, but the healing sleep of exhaustion was stealing over her body, robbing her nerve endings of feeling and her mind of awareness. She sighed and gave herself up to it, confident that she was safe and just where she ought to be,

She was hovering somewhere between the deepest level of sleep and the shallowest of consciousness when the first sensation penetrated. It was nothing more than a brush, a whisper of skin on skin, that grew into a soft warmth and finally a gentle weight on her belly. She shifted slightly and felt it move up past her navel to her midsection. Even as she struggled toward consciousness, her mind was sifting through similar sensations, trying to identify the object lying against her. When it found the explanation, it blared it to every cell in her body, and the message read, "Hand." Not hers.

She opened her eyes to the softness of predawn light and rolled onto her back. Parker's arm followed the path laid by his hand as he snuggled against her, his sighing breath hot on the bare skin of her shoulder. Suddenly a multitude of sharp, intense sensations flooded her. She stiffened and gasped, levering herself up onto her elbows as his eyelids lifted and recognition flooded his expression with acute understanding. She froze, trapped by the flare of desire in eyes not hers and a body that clearly was.

For a long, timeless moment, they stared at one another, then he blinked, freeing her. Yet his arm tightened around her as she attempted to shift away. Instinctively she stilled, breathing roughly, waiting, wondering. He folded his free arm beneath his head, his gaze moving over her shoulders, bare except for the narrow straps of her bra, and up the column of her throat to her face. He smiled at the strands of hair tumbled from the once-neat bun at the crown of her head, his eyes picking out each one as if it were something to be treasured and remembered in times to come. He lifted his hand and plucked the few remaining pins, laying them side by side upon her pillow, then combed his fingers through her heavy tresses, the slow, careful movements and the gradual deepening of his breath holding her in thrall. Finally he buried his hand in the hair at her nape and splayed his fingers against the back of her head. His gaze fixed on her mouth, and he pulled her down to him, his arms sliding beneath her as he settled onto his back.

He cradled her mouth with softening lips that parted to allow his tongue to flick out and gently stroke hers. She pressed her hand against his chest and felt herself folded close, his warmth seeping into her, welling, spreading like sunshine. Then he tilted his head, widened his mouth and deepened the thrust of his tongue, and sunshine erupted into hungry flame. Suddenly, sensation seemed to leap ahead of commission. The skin of her back prickled; his hand slid down from her nape to her waist and back up again. Her breath fled through tingling lips, and his mouth moved against hers, increasing both pressure and suction.

Thought and doubt spun away upon whirlwinds of feeling and rising need.

When his hands came together in the center of her back and gently, smoothly, released the catch of her bra then separated to slide the straps off her shoulders and down her arms, she made no protest, didn't even think of it. When next his hands slid in tandem down her body, first cooling then heating sensitized skin, she reveled in his touch, so much that she barely noticed when his thumbs hooked in the elastic band of her panties and slowly peeled them down. She slid her arms about his neck and broke the kiss to bury her face in the curve of his neck as he rolled her carefully to her side, lifted her knees and eased the panties down her legs and off over her feet. Her toes curled and her teeth nipped at the curve of his shoulder as his palms cupped and lightly massaged her soles, then moved to her ankles and worked their way up her calves to her knees. She felt warm and vibrant everywhere his hands kneaded, so when he pressed her onto her back and slipped a hand between her thighs, she parted them for him.

He closed his other hand in the hair at her nape and tugged her head back to plunder her mouth, and this time she gave as good as she got, the internal flame growing hotter and hotter until it seemed to melt her from the inside out. Yet, when he sank two fingers into the molten flesh at the apex of her thighs, an explosion of heat roared through her unlike anything she had ever known before. It burned away the coverings of her nerve endings, leaving them supersensitized and aching with need. She arched her spine, head flung back, breasts thrusting upward. His mouth traveled a feverish path down her throat and across her chest to claim the rigid peak of first one turgid breast and then the other. She felt the pull of his mouth all the way to the pit of her belly, and her muscles constricted about his fingers accordingly. He groaned and pushed them deeper, flexing upward. She cried out and nearly came up off the bed, the sensation almost too sharp to be pleasurable and far, far too sweet to be pain. He did it

again, and again it swept through her, sharp and sweet.
The third time—or was it the fourth?—she radiated with
the shattering, mindless euphoria of climax. The waves
were still racking her when he slid atop her, pushed her
thighs wide and thrust himself home.

She felt at first that he would split her apart, and then
as he held himself inside her and the waves began to recede, she began to feel that the fit was perfect, their bodies made for each other. When gradually he began to
move, and she felt the pressure building surely and steadily inside her, she knew that nothing and no one else could
make her feel like this. She wrapped her arms around him
and held him tight, mating her mouth to his while he
rocked them closer and closer to completion. When the
rhythm increased and she felt the tension rippling through
his muscles, she wrapped her legs about him, as well.

"Oh, sweetheart!" he exclaimed, tearing his mouth
from hers and driving cleanly, deeply, to her core. "Kendra!"

She felt the hot, fluid pulsation within her and the
tremors that shook him, but he paused only momentarily,
resuming his strokes, his body never breaking contact at
that one essential point until, unbelievably, fulfillment
swept though her again, less intense but somehow more
encompassing than before, and sweet, so very sweet. When
at last he collapsed against her, his mouth plying hers ten-
derly, they were both flushed and breathless and sated.

After a moment, he rolled his weight from her and
gathered her against his chest, his hands lightly stroking
her skin as he whispered words of comfort and praise. He
told her how glad she had made him, how wonderful he
felt, how sleek and beautiful her body was, and how precious and unforgettable their joining remained. He loved
her hair, he said, filling his hands with it, and her face, and
the curve of her waist and the flatness of her belly, and that
sweet, wet, female place that gave him access to her body
as none other could. He had wanted this so long, he said,
had wanted to wake at her side and be free to pleasure her

as she was meant to be pleasured, to spill himself inside her, to feel the fit of her body to his.

"I need you," he said. "Oh, how I need you, more than ever, more than I knew I could."

And if he didn't say that he loved her, she didn't care, not while he held her, not while her body thrummed with the after-effects of his lovemaking. She tangled her legs with his and laid her cheek against his heart, and was content. Almost at once she began to slide into the blankness of sleep. She was tired still, achingly tired, and yet she felt wonderful, too. The thought occurred just before the blankness that if she had managed to climb into the right bed last night, she would not be feeling so wonderful now.

He kissed her awake to bright, cold light sometime later. She stretched, feeling the lazy undulation of the water bed beneath her, and let the remembered sensations of his lovemaking wash over her again. She smiled up at him, surprised to see that he was dressed, cleanly shaven and standing beside the bed.

"Good morning, beautiful."

"Good morning."

"Want some breakfast? Or should I say lunch?"

"Lunch?" She pushed up onto her elbows. "What time is it?"

"Oh, about one o'clock in the afternoon."

"One o'clock!" She started to throw back the covers to get out of the bed, remembered that she was nude and subsided warily.

Parker grinned. "Feeling a little shy this morning, are we?"

She bit her lip, trying to will the color out of her cheeks.

He sat down on the edge of the bed, crossed his legs and leaned over her, one hand planted on the mattress, the other fingering a strand of her hair. "I certainly can't see that you have anything to be embarrassed about," he said gently. "God knows you've nothing to be ashamed of where your body is concerned. You're simply beautiful, head to toe."

"Thank you."

He kissed her temple, his lips butterfly soft, and got up again. Reaching inside the closet, he brought out his own bathrobe, heavy white terry cloth with his initals monogrammed on the breast in gold. He walked to the bedside and held up the robe for her. "Up and at 'em, sweetheart. I left an omelet warming up for you in the oven."

She reached for the bathrobe. He moved it away, then back again when she lowered her arm.

"If you don't get out of that bed," he said, eyes twinkling, "I'm getting back in there with you, but as that's what I'd rather do, anyway, I won't complain."

She would prefer the latter herself, but a squeal from the other room reminded her that they were not the only ones to be considered—and she was not so sure, in the bright light of day, that it would be wise. "I think we're being paged," she said, tucking the sheet beneath her arms.

He lifted both brows. "So it seems. I guess that means you'll be getting up, then."

"I guess it does," she agreed, sitting up and swinging her bare legs over the side of the bed. With a yank, she pulled the sheet free of the foot of the bed, stood and turned, winding the sheet around her. She backed up and slid first one arm and then the other into the sleeves of the bathrobe.

Parker conceded gracefully, delivering the robe onto her shoulders. He leaned close and nuzzled her ear, whispering, "Cheater."

Uncertain how to respond, she flashed him a shy grin and lifted her hair free of the robe. He gathered it in his hand and kissed her on the back of the neck. A pleasant warmth rippled through her, and she knew that if she turned, he would take her in his arms and kiss her thoroughly. She was about to do just that when an insistent scream reminded them they were expected in the other room. They both laughed, aware that her communication skills were improving. Only a few short weeks ago, she would have resorted to wobbly, heartrending wails and genuine tears to summon them.

"Her Majesty is a bit impatient today," Parker said, smoothing her hair with his fingertips, "and I have a perfectly good omelet drying out in the oven." He stepped up next to her and offered her his arm. "Shall we?"

She belted the robe, slipped her arm through his and squeezed, then released him. "You go on. I'll be right there. I just want to wash my face."

He looked at her searchingly for a moment, then nodded. "Okay, but don't be long."

She smiled. "Promise."

He left her, and she padded into the bathroom, performing an abbreviated morning ritual while pondering what she'd done, letting him make love to her. She couldn't tell herself that she hadn't wanted it, because she had—still did, in fact—but that didn't mean it had been wise, not that it made any difference now. What had been done couldn't be undone. What she really had to think about was what she was going to do now.

It hadn't seemed to matter last night that he hadn't said anything about love. Nothing had seemed to matter last night but what was happening. Now she wasn't so sure. Had anything changed really? Did he want, expect, her to stay? She didn't know what to think, but it seemed to her that she had no particular reason to hope. It wasn't as if the sex act itself had ever before represented any kind of commitment to Parker.

But he wasn't married to any of those other women, said a desperate voice inside her head. On the other hand, she reminded herself sternly, these days, marriage could be as temporary as any one-night stand. She looked her mirror image in the eye and admitted the truth. She had been irresponsible and foolish. She had no one to blame for what had happened but herself, and whatever happened next would be up to Parker. She had no choice but to follow his lead unless she wanted to look like the ninny she was. It was horribly simple really. If he wanted her to stay, she would stay and without the slightest hesitation, but if he didn't want her... Well, pride was a cold comfort, but it was better than no comfort at all.

Chapter Twelve

The omelet was dry as a brick, but it could have been perfect and still tasted like dust to Kendra. She seemed to have no immediate sensory perception. It was as if her body were intent upon reliving every moment of last night's lovemaking, despite the fact that she sat at the kitchen table calmly eating breakfast while Parker grinned at her. He leaned against the counter, Darla perched on one hip, and simply watched, his every look loaded with sexual innuendo. She wished desperately that she had taken time to dress. She felt naked sitting there in his bathrobe, and the way he moved his eyes over her told her that he, too, was very aware of her nudity. She tried desperately not to remember how it had felt to be touched by him, to be wanted by him, to be *filled* by him. Tried, and failed. And he knew it, damn his hide, he knew it.

She pushed away her plate, afraid that she'd gag if she put even one more bite into her mouth. Parker's brows lifted in silent question. Smiling tremulously, she smoothed the robe over her abdomen in a gesture of fullness. "Guess I'm not very hungry."

"Okay," he said. "No problem. It wasn't one of my best efforts anyway." He smoothed down Darla's hair and smiled at Kendra over the top of her head. "Ms. Hatcher would be *so* disappointed."

Kendra laughed, and Darla instantly mimicked her, which made for fresh laughter all around. Then the laughter dwindled into silence, and with the silence came an awkwardness that Kendra had been dreading since the moment he had awakened her. She opened her mouth to excuse herself, intending to make a quick escape, but he suddenly leapt into the breach with speech.

"What do you want to do today? The princess and I are at your disposal, so you just name it, sweetheart. What'll it be? Christmas shopping, a movie? Maybe you'd like a back rub and a long, hot soak in the tub, hmm?"

A back rub. She took a deep breath, her body betraying her again as sensations she had not even experienced consumed her. She managed to shake her head. "Uh, the bath, or... or a shower, probably."

He nodded. "All right, first a shower. Then what? You must have a dozen errands you need to run."

"N-no."

"Maybe you just want to curl up with a good book," he suggested. "I could make us some hot cocoa and build a fire, and the three of us could—"

"Uh, no, no, I don't think so. I... I'm not in the mood for... reading."

Darla's hair was standing up again. He smoothed it down thoughtfully. "Then what *are* you in the mood for?"

She tried for nonchalance, hitching up one shoulder in a weak shrug. "I don't know."

He slid her a brooding look that said he recognized her reluctance and the reason for it. Then suddenly he brightened, shifting the baby up into his arms. "Why don't you think about it a moment while I put the baby down? It's past time for her nap, but I knew you'd want to see her."

"Yes, of course, but I haven't even gotten to hold her," she said, getting to her feet. "Why not let me put her down?"

His smile was soft and warm as he placed the baby in her arms. "I've been putting her down in the family room," he said. "Her room is just too far from my work area for my comfort. I've been meaning to speak to you about the possibility of having an intercom system installed, but there just hasn't been time lately."

"You don't need my permission," she said lightly. "It's your house."

He stiffened, an odd reaction, but one she chose not to question. Instead, she carried Darla out of the kitchen and down across the gallery to the large multipurpose area they called the family room. Her playpen, several toys and a colorful, slowly drifting mobile had been arranged on an area of tiled floor near the corner that Parker had appropriated as his work space. Kendra saw that a fluffy down comforter had been folded to fit the playpen and covered with a cotton sheet secured to the playpen foundation with special ring-type clips. Speaking softly to the child, Kendra bent and laid her on this soft cushion. Instantly Darla sat up, one tiny hand rubbing her eyes. Kendra picked her up and kissed her, whispering that it was naptime, then gently put her down again. This time the little one merely rolled over onto her side and lifted her leg to pull at the ruffled cuff of her sock. Kendra removed both soft shoes and socks from the baby's feet, then covered her with a blanket that had been left draped over one end of the playpen. Winding the music box on the mobile, she sat down on the floor and reached through the narrowly spaced wood bars to gently stroke Darla's back and arm.

The baby fretted and kicked one foot up and down beneath the blanket, but Kendra hummed softly and patted her back. Soon Darla's thumb crept into her mouth, and then her lashes drooped down to lay dark and wispy-thick against chubby, porcelain cheeks. Before the music box had played out its tune, she was breathing deeply and evenly, adrift in her own little dreamworld. Kendra watched her for some moments, enthralled by the infantile beauty in the small, round face with its delicately pointed chin and cap of dark, glossy hair.

Wistfully, she rose and padded silently from the room, wanting to be gone when Parker came in to work or read or whatever he had in mind. To her surprise he was waiting for her, leaning against the gallery wall, his hands buried in the pockets of pleated corduroy pants. She bowed her head and started past him, muttering that she was off to shower, but he stepped into her path, his hands coming up to trap her shoulders. Instinctively, she recoiled. His hands curled on air and dropped to his sides.

"We have to talk," he said quietly, urgently, but her heart was already pounding like a jackhammer.

She shook her head. "I really ought to get dressed. The . . . the day's half g-gone, and I—"

"Stop it!" he hissed.

Seizing her arm, he marched her farther from the family room door, across the gallery and down onto the living room floor. He steered her toward a chair and released her, but the expression on his face quelled any idea she might have had of escaping him. Reluctantly she sat down and tucked the bathrobe tightly around her, refusing to look up at him. After a tense moment, he crouched before her, his hands going to the arms of the chair.

"Kendra, we can't just pretend it didn't happen."

She turned her head away, at a loss for words. On one hand, she wanted desperately to throw her arms around him and declare that their lovemaking had been the most moving experience of her life. On the other, she wanted, needed, to pretend that it had never happened. It could not possibly have meant to him what it had to her. For him, it could be nothing more than another in a very lengthy string of similar encounters, and that knowledge was a deep, reverberating pain inside her. She did not need to be told that while last night had been pleasant, it meant nothing for the two of them. Indeed, she could not bear to hear him say it. "I—I don't know what to say to you," she finally managed, "and I don't think I want to hear what you have to say to me."

From the corner of her eye, she saw his fingers tighten on the arm of the chair. "I hope you don't mean that," he said roughly.

She bit her lip. "Please..."

His hands left the arms of the chair and slipped beneath the hem of the robe, skimming her shins as they moved upward. "Kendra," he said softly, seductively, "I'm not sorry. I very much wanted last night to happen. You must know that."

"Yes." She gasped and pressed her legs together as his hands slid over her knees.

"I won't apologize for wanting you," he went on, stroking the fronts of her thighs, "and you can't deny wanting me." He pushed his hands higher.

She clamped her legs together convulsively, her head falling back as every treasured and unwelcome memory of the night before rushed over her. "Please!" she said raggedly. "Oh, please!"

He spread his fingers, hands pushing to the very tops of her legs, thumbs delving between them. "Let it happen!" he urged, his voice silky and pleading. "Just let it happen, Kendra. Whatever happens between us is meant to be, can't you see that?"

She shook her head, trembling so violently that the gesture seemed stifled, aborted. "I have to protect myself!" she cried.

He went onto his knees, straddling her feet and pressing himself against her. "Not from me!" he declared huskily, pushing his hands up to span her belly. "Never from me!" He slid his hands higher, forcing them beneath the belt at her waist and loosening it.

"Stop!" She clamped her hands over his forearms near the elbow. "I want you to stop!"

"No, you don't," he said, opening the robe and effortlessly lifting his hands to cup her breasts.

She jerked as if electrocuted. Her nipples hardened instantly, peaking as her flesh swelled beneath his palms. Her hands tightened on his arms, but to no effect. She wasn't impeding him, merely hanging on while her senses reeled.

"Make love to me, Kendra. Now! You want me as badly as I want you, as badly as you wanted me last night. Don't deny it. Don't cheat us of this chance to—"

"Take your hands off her!"

The familiar voice wrenched them both from the swirling fog of sensation and emotion, but it was Kendra who gasped his name.

"Edward!"

He stood in the center of the room, his tan twill overcoat hanging open over his rumpled business suit, hands balled into fists the size of sledgehammers, his handsome face set like angry stone. What struck Kendra most, though, with painful, damning clarity, was the hurt that glittered in his light blue eyes. It was the first time she had ever seen Edward White as frightening, and she knew with chilling certainty that he was much more dangerous than she'd ever suspected. Suddenly he was not the great big, cuddly teddy bear she had always known, but a grizzly ready to unleash his claws. She yanked the robe together protectively, glancing up at Parker, who had rocked back onto his feet and risen in one fluid movement. He stepped squarely into Edward's line of vision, shielding her as much as possible as she stood and knotted the belt securely at her waist.

"You selfish son of a bitch!" Edward snarled. "I knew you'd try to take advantage of her!"

Parker's reply was strangely casual and somehow all the more intimidating because of it. "You know, Ed, I'm getting pretty sick and tired of looking up to find you standing in *my* house glowering like some demented guardian angel. I'm not going to tell you again. You knock, and you wait, before you walk in my door."

Edward's smile was thin and contemptuous. "It's hell getting caught at being a slime ball, isn't it, *old buddy?*

"I wouldn't know," Parker said calmly. "I was just having a very private conversation with *my wife* when you came butting in where you're not wanted!"

"You may not want me here just now," Edward retorted, "but *your wife* will undoubtedly thank me for this interruption. In case it's escaped your notice, she's not some slut you can buy for the price of a good dinner and a bottle of wine!"

Parker stiffened, his own hands fisting now. "You self-righteous, high-handed bastard! What makes you think—"

Kendra grabbed his forearm and stepped in front of him, hoping to derail what could quickly become a very ugly physical confrontation, one she feared Parker would get the worst of. "Stop it!" she demanded. "Both of you stop it right now!" She faced Edward squarely, lifted her chin and lied through her teeth. "I don't need rescuing, Edward. You needn't be concerned. Parker and I have an understanding. Nothing important was happening here, nothing that—" she swallowed "—mattered to either one of us."

If he looked stricken at that, it was no more than she felt. She couldn't seem to catch her breath, though the air was pumping in and out of her lungs with hasty regularity. She folded her arms across her middle and stiffened her spine, feeling Parker at her back.

"I'm only human, Edward," she said as evenly as she could manage. "I have my own needs, and as an adult I'm fully capable of deciding how and with whom I want to fill them. Now, I'll thank you not to meddle again in what is not your concern."

He seemed incredulous. "Do you know what you're saying?"

"Of course I do," she snapped, but he would never know how it was tearing her up inside. She saw her own folly only too clearly, but it was too late for anything except regret. All she could do now was live with it and try to salvage some shred of her pride. She made herself look him squarely in the eye and delivered the death blow. "Look at it this way," she said, reaching for a light tone and managing only a crude tremor. "Now that your worst fears have been confirmed, you can stop worrying about it."

His face literally paled. "I can't believe I'm hearing this from you."

She flinched and wrenched her chin up another notch. "I want you to go now, Edward." He stared at her as if seeing her for the first time. She closed her eyes, unable to bear it. "Just go!" After a long moment of silence, she opened them again.

His back was to her. He was standing with one foot on the step leading to the entry foyer. He turned his head slightly, speaking over his shoulder. "The court date is late January," he said dully, "but I'll ask for a continuance, give you time to find another lawyer."

Kendra covered her mouth with her hand and struggled to master the tears burning her eyes and the back of her throat. He walked up the steps and disappeared. A moment later, she heard the door close behind him. Every particle of resentment she had ever felt for Parker Sugarman came screaming together into one loathsome, churning ball of rage. She whirled on him, ready to blame him for this, but the look on his face was clearly that of a man who had just lost his best friend. He looked sick, angry, cut to the very core, and she recognized in him everything she was feeling herself, which was only fitting. They were both to blame. They had made something meant to be noble and kind into something ugly and hateful. It wouldn't help either of them to indulge in invective now. She swallowed the recriminations and dropped her gaze.

"I'm going to take a shower," she mumbled, but suddenly he was the one striding away.

"You go wherever you want," he told her bitterly. "See whoever you want, *do* whatever you want!" He swung around to point a finger at her. "But don't you ever come to me with your *needs*, Kendra. *Never* again."

Her mouth dropped open. Unfair! "You're one to talk!" she cried defensively. "I wasn't exactly alone in that bed last night!"

"Neither of us were," he said caustically, "but obviously *I* might as well have been." He turned down the hall, making for the back door.

She just stared, shocked beyond words. How could he say that? *Why* would he say that? Had Edward meant so much to him then? Was that friendship more important than anything they might have had together? Dear God, what a mistake this had been, what a travesty! But she knew, deep down, that it was no more than she deserved. And no less.

Nothing important...nothing that mattered to either one of us. The words simply would not leave his head. He had tried to drink them away. He had tried to think them away. He had tried to pretend them away. He had even prayed over them, and God knew he had never been a praying sort of man, but somehow leaving home that day for his favorite bar, he had wound up in the cemetery, looking down at his brother's headstone, talking aloud to God. It had calmed him, and yet he couldn't get her words out of his mind. Nothing that mattered to either one of them. Wrong. Wrong. Wrong. It mattered to him. Oh, how it mattered to him. And that told him how stupid he had been all those years, how foolish, how selfish.

All those women. All those women had been looking for love. His object had been pleasure, and the fact that he'd never made any secret of it didn't seem to absolve him anymore. He knew suddenly how it felt to hope for love even when the odds were against it. She had promised him six months, but he had not been able to keep himself from hoping that she would come to want more. Much more. He had not been able to stop himself from hoping that the physical pleasure they shared would come to mean more to her than merely that. It hadn't, but that didn't change what he wanted from his heart, and he knew that too many times he had been on the other side of the equation. He thought of Jeanna Crowe and so many others like her who had hoped he would be the one even while he had told them he would not, and for the first time he was sorry. He was sorry and he was heartsick, and he couldn't help it. He just couldn't help it. He couldn't get those words out of his mind. *Nothing important... nothing that mattered.*

"Well, I think it matters."

"What?" Parker blinked up at his father-in-law, realizing suddenly that he'd spoken aloud those awful words. "I—I'm sorry, Dan, what were you saying?"

Dan Ballard set a cup of coffee on the table in front of Parker and eased himself down into his favorite chair. "I said, I think it matters a lot that you find another lawyer right away. Don't wait until after the first of the year to start looking around again. The Pendletons will use it against you, if you do—I guarantee."

Parker picked up his coffee and sipped it. "Yeah, I'm sure you're right. I just don't know where to start. Ed's always been my attorney. It feels funny to start over with someone else. I keep hoping he'll come around, you know?"

"Don't hope," Dan advised sagely. "You can patch it up with Ed White later. Right now you've got to think of Darla. Can't lose my almost-grandchild before she's even old enough to know me."

"I agree completely," Kate said, coming into the room with a tray of appetizers which she slid onto the coffee table before moving to perch on the arm of Dan's chair. Dan slid his arm around her waist and pulled her onto his lap. Kendra, who had come into the room behind Kate, shifted Darla from one shoulder to another, her face set like stone. She sat down on the sofa with Parker, as far away from him as she could get.

To be polite and to distract his thoughts from Kendra's obvious displeasure, Parker leaned forward and helped himself to one of Kate's appetizers. He chose one that looked like a small, peeled potato with a piece of crisp bacon wrapped around it. He lifted it to his mouth, fixed his teeth in it, and pulled the toothpick out. Interesting. The "potato" was a water chestnut. He dropped the toothpick onto a napkin and reached for another.

"These are good, Kate. You'll have to tell me how to make them."

"Thanks. Nothing to it. I specialize in simple."

He chuckled. "Right up my alley."

"Guess you two have more in common than we realized," Kendra remarked petulantly.

He glared at her. Dan shifted uncomfortably in his chair. Only Kate remained unruffled. Her long, slender legs crossed between ankle and knee, she leaned back against Dan's arm and steered the conversation back to the original topic.

"Dan is right, Parker. You need to bring another attorney in right away. These custody cases can get complicated. You don't want to take any chances with that sweetheart there."

Parker smiled at Darla, who immediately became a flirt, teeny teeth bared in a slobbering grin, eyebrows wiggling. She clapped her hands together and reached out for him. He lifted her under the arms and swung her over onto his lap, kissing her forehead. She loved him. He never ceased to wonder at that, and it never failed to bring him a certain peace. He couldn't lose her, too. "I know," he said to Kate, sighing. "Maybe you can recommend someone, a colleague, someone you trust."

She gave him a couple of names, but he shook his head at each. "No, I've already talked to both of them. I'm sure they're competent, but...I just didn't feel comfortable with either of them." He couldn't tell anyone else about his so-called marriage. He couldn't trust that knowledge to anyone but a very close friend, and he happened to be fresh out of those at the moment. It seemed so utterly hopeless suddenly. But it couldn't be. He just couldn't give in to the hopelessness. He looked down at Darla and smiled grimly. "Ed was just so close to the situation," he said. "I guess

I'm looking for a similar feeling with someone else, I don't know.''

Kate nodded with understanding. ''Well, you've got to find counsel. I'll keep my ear to the ground.''

Dan cleared his throat, causing everyone to look at him. ''Use your heads, folks. If it's someone close to the situation that you want, you couldn't get any closer than Kate.''

Kate. Of course. Parker uncrossed his legs and sat up straight, one arm protectively about Darla. ''Hey, that's right. You've been in this thing almost as long as Ed.'' *And I've already told you my lies,* he added mentally.

Kate sat up, too, looking over her shoulder at Dan. ''But I'm not really connected,'' she protested calmly.

''You will be soon enough,'' Dan said, winking.

The significance of that went right over Parker's head. He was focused on Kate, who looked at him and said, ''Family law is not my specialty.''

''It's not Ed's, either,'' he argued. ''If he can handle it, you can, too.''

''Oh, I can handle it,'' she said with her usual confidence, ''but are you sure you want me to?'' For the first time, her gaze strayed to Kendra. Parker's followed it.

He was surprised at what he saw. All the color had drained from Kendra's face, and she was sitting bolt upright, rigid as a board. Surely if Kate could help him keep Darla, Kendra wouldn't object. Or would she? He didn't pretend to understand this animosity Kendra had for her father's girlfriend, but he wasn't about to let it get in the way of what was best for Darla. And he had to believe that being with him was best for his little niece. He cupped her small head with his hand, uncaring that she was busy tasting his tie, and looked at Kate. ''I'm sure,'' he said flatly. ''I can't think of anyone I'd rather have.''

Apparently that wasn't enough for Kate. She looked to Kendra again. ''Do you agree, Kendra?''

Parker watched her stiffen, saw her chin rise a notch. ''It's Parker's decision,'' she said tersely. Then her gaze went to her father, transfixing him relentlessly. "Why didn't you tell me you were getting married?"

Married? Parker glanced at the pair in the chair, and suddenly it all clicked into place. His first reaction was exactly what Dan's had been to his and Kendra's announcement. "Holy cow! That's great! Congratulations, you guys."

"Congratulations?" Kendra snapped, and when he looked at her, he saw that her eyes were brimming with tears. "If any of you think she can replace my mother..." she began.

"No, Kendra," Dan Ballard said.

"Not at all," Kate said at the same time.

"Kendra," Parker coaxed softly, "don't you see that they're in love?"

"But he isn't," she said with conviction. "It's loneliness, nothing more than loneliness."

"Kendra—"

"I was there, Parker! I saw him with my mother. I watched him love my mother all those years. It just isn't the same."

"No, it isn't," Dan said, "and I wouldn't want it to be. Kendra, you have to understand how it was with your mother and me. Your mother—"

Kate stopped him with a hand placed on his chest and stood. Staring down at Kendra, she deftly took control. "You had to know it was coming. Would you prefer that we go on living together? We are, you know. Maybe I haven't officially moved in, but we've been sleeping together for months now."

Kendra shot up to her feet, all indignation. "How dare you speak to me about sleeping with my father!"

Kate folded her arms. "We're all adults here, Kendra. It's time you acknowledged that *Daddy* is a human being like the rest of us. Surely you don't expect him to sleep alone the rest of his life. He's as entitled as anybody else."

"You make it sound so casual!" Kendra scolded.

Parker was dumbfounded. This from the woman who had said sleeping with him didn't mean anything!

"Not casual," Kate said, "but common. Men and women have been sleeping together since Adam and Eve, Kendra. Your mother's dead. Let her go, and let your father have some happiness in his life."

Kendra's chin wobbled. "You make it sound like he wasn't happy with her."

Kate shifted her gaze her way. "I only meant that he has as much right to happiness now as he ever did."

But Parker was looking at Dan Ballard, and he saw the truth on his face. It came as a shock to him, but not to Kendra. One glance at her face told him that. For her, it was only the confirmation of what she had already suspected. This then was what lay beneath Kendra's dislike for Kate Ridley: Kate made her father happy; her beloved mother had not. It was a revelation of sorts, not that it answered all of his questions, by any means, but it did have a strange irony to it. His own parents hadn't been happy together, either, but they had busted up because of it, while Kendra's had stayed together. Life was downright weird sometimes.

He saw regret in Dan Ballard's eyes, but was it regret for the pain Kendra was feeling now or regret for the years spent in an unhappy marriage? He hoped suddenly that wherever his own father was, whatever he had done with his life, he was at least happy. Someone ought to be. Someone somewhere ought to be happy.

Darla, tired of trying to eat his tie, toppled over in his lap and lifted her legs up in the air, a sure sign that she expected a diaper change. Kendra stepped closer and bent to pick her up. "I'll do it," she said tonelessly.

Her expression was so sad that he reached out for her before he could stop himself, fastening his hand upon her wrist. Their eyes met. *I love you,* he tried to tell her. *For what it's worth, I love you.*

She lifted Darla against her shoulder. His hand fell away, and she carried the baby out of the room, leaving silence and regret behind her.

Kate sighed. "If anybody's still interested, dinner will be ready in ten minutes." She strode away in the direction of the kitchen.

Dan Ballard crossed his legs and tapped a finger against the edge of his shoe sole. He glanced at Parker with guilty apology in his eyes, opened his mouth as if to say something, then seemed to change his mind. He picked up his coffee cup from the table beside his chair and lifted it in salute. "Merry Christmas, son."

Parker picked up his own cup. "Merry Christmas, sir."

It was a poor toast, but it was the best they could do.

Chapter Thirteen

Sandra Pendleton shifted Darla on her lap and adjusted the tiny headphones strapped over the baby's ears. Darla's eyes were big with confusion, but after a bit she began to ignore the Spanish pouring into her ears and played with the buttons on the front of her aunt's dress. Sandra patiently moved the baby's hand. Darla just as patiently and twice as doggedly pulled free of her aunt's grasp and went back to picking at the button. They repeated this silent tussle several times before Darla pitched herself backward with a howl of frustration. Sandra caught her before she toppled over her knees onto the floor, but the headphones were knocked askew, and Darla took advantage of that to sweep them to the back of her head. It was Sandra's turn to feel frustration, for as she tried to return the headphones to the proper position, Darla began to shake her head and hunch her shoulders, screaming with rage.

Kendra had had all she could take. She snatched Darla up into her arms, yanked the headphones from her head and dropped them into Dr. Pendleton's lap. Sandra came instantly to her feet, ripely indignant.

"You want her to remain ignorant," she accused.

"Darla couldn't remain ignorant if we locked her in a windowless cell for the rest of her life," she said drolly. "I just don't like to see her irritated needlessly."

"If you would put the headphones on her while she sleeps as I instructed—" Sandra began.

"She would never sleep," Kendra finished. "Honestly, Sandra, don't you think we ought to wait until she can speak *English* before we start her on a second language?"

Sandra rolled her eyes. "You've already waited too late. Instruction should have begun before she was born."

"Well, I didn't have anything to do with that, now did I?"

"No, but if you have your way," the doctor told her ponderously, "she'll grow up as a normal child."

"Good grief!" Kendra mocked. "Not that, please! Let's do all we can to make her an *abnormal* child, shall we?"

Sandra Pendleton was smart enough to know when she'd been insulted. She drew herself up tall and pursed her lips. "You think you're very clever, don't you, marrying Parker, insinuating yourself into all this? I don't know what you hope to gain, but I promise you—"

"I don't hope to gain anything," Kendra said tiredly.

Sandra ignored her. "But I promise you that you'll be disappointed," she continued. "You've done a very foolish thing."

Kendra sighed. "Such as?"

Sandra narrowed her eyes. "He'll never remain faithful to you. He married you to keep me from getting Darla. He doesn't love you. He's never loved any woman. He uses them and he dumps them. A man like him has no business raising a baby."

"That's enough," Kendra said, the softness of her voice emphasizing the unspoken threat behind it. Her palm itched to slap Sandra Pendleton's face, but she wouldn't do it. She wouldn't do it. She wouldn't do it if she could help it. Chest heaving, she stepped back to remove the temptation. "Parker is a fine, decent man," she said, keeping her tone low. "He loves this child with his whole heart. He's changed his entire life for her. He's given up a partnership in one of the country's finest firms. He's left behind his wild friends and his partying ways. He's built on to his house. He's become active in church. He's learned how to care for her, and yes, he's married me to help him, and that's what I'm going to do, whether you like it or not."

"But she would be so much better off with me and my family," Sandra argued. "If Darla is your primary concern, you're doing the opposite of what's best for her."

"I don't believe that. Besides, Darla isn't the only consideration. Parker needs her. She's his only link to his brother."

"I could say the same about my sister," Sandra pointed out.

"But you already have a family of your own, and we both know you and Candace were not nearly so close as Parker and Nathan."

"That wasn't my fault," Sandra said sharply. "Candace was a fool."

"What you really mean is that she didn't appreciate your work," Kendra scoffed, "and you're right. Candace always said that you wanted so desperately to be good at something, to be known for something, that you were in danger of losing sight of what common sense you had." Sandra stiffened as if she'd been struck, but Kendra went on stubbornly. "Maybe that's why she named my husband as her daughter's guardian in the event of her own death, and maybe, just maybe, that's why you're so determined to fight him for her."

Sandra made an obvious attempt to relax. "I only have the child's best interests at heart," she said, shifting her gaze away.

Kendra shook her head. "I feel sorry for you, Sandra. I know Candace's opinion must have hurt you very deeply, but taking Darla from Parker won't help you heal. It can only hurt two innocent people who love each other."

"I see that you don't include yourself," Sandra commented slyly. "Trouble in paradise already?"

She would never know how close to the mark she had hit, but Kendra had had a great deal of practice at hiding her pain, and she wasn't about to let the likes of Sandra Pendleton unmask it now. She lifted her chin and leveled her gaze. "*You* have instigated every problem that we have, Sandra, and you can rest assured that we're going to fight you together until they disappear."

"He doesn't love you!" Sandra hissed, striking back.

"It doesn't matter whether he does or not," Kendra told her truthfully. "What matters is that I love him—and this little girl," she added, lifting Darla to kiss the tip of her nose then hug her close. Darla put her arms around Kendra's neck and attempted to bite her collar bone through the fabric of her shirt.

Sandra huffed, then turned without a word and strode toward the multipurpose room, which her children had been noisily trying to dismantle since their arrival. The moment she disappeared through the door, Parker stepped out onto the gallery from the hall. He was still wearing his coat and carried a small brown paper bag filled with the various grocery items that had been his excuse for being away from the house while Sandra was there. He leaned a shoulder against the corner of the wall and surveyed her thoughtfully.

"What?" Kendra asked, wondering how long he had been standing there and what he had heard.

He shook his head, eyes narrowing speculatively. Kendra felt her heart fluttering nervously and looked away. "I, um, have to change the baby," she lied, hurrying off. He didn't say a word, but his gaze followed her out of the room, and still he stood there, lost in thought.

It was a New Year's Eve tradition. The gang always got together, always, and common sense decreed that the logical place for this year's celebration was the Sugarman house. It had everything going for it: adequate space, a central location, sufficient parking and familiarity. Everyone was well acquainted with Parker Sugarman's address. This year, however, there were added and unexpected bonuses. Once the gang made their preferences known, via Dennis Scherer and Walt Lyons, Parker pointed out to a reluctant Kendra that having the get-together at their house would relieve them of the necessity of finding a sitter for Darla. It would also make amends for the fact that they had never, due to the understandable circumstances, celebrated their marriage with their closest friends. He did not have to say that such an event would help solidify them in the minds of the public and the court as a genuine couple; Kendra was astute enough to see that benefit for herself. When he vowed that she could leave all the details of planning and preparation to him, she ran out of reasons to object, and the party was on.

To her surprise, Parker decided to make it a family affair by informing the Randles that their two youngsters were welcome to bring along their sleeping bags and bed down in the family room for the evening, if they so desired. Cheryl and Bill were delighted to take them up on that offer, saying that they'd bring several of the kids' favorite videos to keep them entertained. Cheryl suggested that Dennis might like to include his six-year-old son from his first marriage, too. Parker called up Dennis and issued the invitation, so the guest list stood at eight adults and three children, not counting Parker, Kendra or Darla. When Walt called the very day of New Year's Eve to ask if he could bring along one of his assistant coaches, his date and *her* two children—for whom she had been unable to locate a sitter—Parker surprised Kendra yet again by responding that as far as he was concerned, the more the merrier.

It was a party unlike any other Kendra had ever attended, let alone hostessed.

The Randles were the first to arrive with their two little towheads, a boy and a girl, ages five and three respectively. Cheryl came bearing buckets of fried chicken and popcorn for the microwave. Dennis and his date, the same Mandy whom Kendra and Parker had met on the night of the movie, contributed soft drinks and packaged dinner rolls. Walt Lyons and his group brought a sack of potatoes, all the condiments, several bags of chips and various dips. Jeanna Crowe and her escort, a widowed banker who wouldn't see fifty again, brought an enormous casserole of mixed vegetables with cheese and a bowl of the traditional black-eyed peas. Parker also contributed. In addition to appetizers—Kate's whole water chestnuts wrapped with bacon strips and crackers with an assortment of toppings—he provided a dessert of chocolate marble cheesecake purchased from a local bakery—and just enough champagne to give the adults two glasses each. He also bought several types of party games. They totaled eleven adults and six children, the Sugarmans included.

While the potatoes were baking and the rest of dinner was warming, the group fractured, splitting between the kitchen and the multipurpose room, the main pasttime being the simple conversation of those becoming acquainted for the first time and those catching up on what was happening in the lives of good friends. Much was said of Kendra and Parker's hasty marriage, and many exclamations were made about how much Darla had grown and how well she seemed. When mention of Nathan and Candace and their deaths was made as the Sugarmans and their guests gathered to eat, there was more than one clogged throat and tearful eye, but as those who had not been privileged to know the missing friends asked questions, the reminiscences turned to pleasant, even funny, times. Soon the conversation was cheerful, despite the ache of loss, and Kendra began to see that Parker deserved more credit than she'd realized for the way he'd handled this party.

How awful it would have been had they come together as the old group had in the past. Without newcomers or children, the absence of dear but departed friends would have been unbearable. This way, they were together—even a piece of Candace and Nathan was with them in the form of Darla—but the experience was new and fresh and thoroughly enjoyable. Kendra could tell that as Parker reigned over the benevolent chaos, he was satisfied, and she thought about telling him how well she thought he'd done, but the emotional distance between them and the general hubbub kept her silent. She would regret that later when, after exuberant hours of games, Darla was put to bed and the older children were left in the family room to enjoy their videos while the adults adjourned to the living area to exhaust additional topics of conversation then, on a whim, to dance.

The dancing had not been on Parker's agenda, but he made no protest when it was suggested. It wasn't the first time, by any means, that his furniture had been moved aside and his rugs rolled up for the purpose. In fact, the sound system in that room had been specially designed with dancing—and parties—in mind. Moreover, Parker had an impressive collection of compact discs and records.

It was all fun and games at first. They started with the lights up all the way and a series of fast rock-and-roll numbers that led to lots of cutting up and silly antics. Then, as the evening progressed and the kids bedded down, the lights got lower and the music got slower. Conversation muted. People started breaking off into couples. There was less kidding and cutting up. Kendra had danced a couple of fast ones with Parker and several others with Dennis, Walt, Bill and Jeanna's banker, including two slow numbers, but during one particularly dreamy song, she felt a distinct longing to be on the floor with her husband.

A careful glance around the now dimly lit area showed her Parker with Jeanna Crowe in his arms. Jeanna and Parker. An alarm went off inside Kendra's head. Jeanna and Parker had had an affair, one Jeanna apparently had not wished to end. With one glaring exception, Parker had been living a life of celibacy for some months now. It did not help that Jeanna's portly, slightly balding banker suffered greatly in comparison with Parker's tall, dark, lithe, sexy handsomeness. Kendra felt a sharp prick of jealousy, even though logic told her that Parker would not risk a liaison at this point. He had too much to lose, namely Darla, if Kendra should dare to walk out on him before the hearing or if word of his misconduct should reach the Pendletons. Nevertheless, when she saw Parker whisper to Jeanna, then take her arm and lead her into the darkened dining room, away from the others, Kendra felt close to tears and physically nauseated.

The moments they were away seemed like years to Kendra. She could not keep her gaze from straying back to the spot where she had last seen them, despite the fact that Jeanna's banker was attempting to carry on a conversation with her about his two college-age sons and his ex-wife. When at last they appeared again, Kendra was wounded and appalled to see that their arms were linked and that Jeanna turned her cheek up for Parker's kiss before parting from him. It helped some that he immediately caught her eye with an uplifted hand, pointed at the impromptu dance floor, and made a circular motion with his finger, clearly asking her to dance. She nodded, but just as he stepped down from the steps to the dining area, the doorbell rang. With a shrug, he hurried across the floor, gracefully dodging dancing couples, and climbed the steps to the foyer.

Kendra wondered who could be calling on them at this hour of the evening. A glance at her watch told her that it was thirty-four minutes past eleven. Jeanna appeared to claim her banker for a dance. Kendra waited, but ten minutes later Parker still had not returned with their mysterious caller. She thought about going out into the foyer to see for herself whom the caller was, but she was afraid she'd find one of Parker's old girlfriends expecting to be admitted to a party of the sort for which Parker Sugarman was famous. After the episode with Jeanna, Kendra didn't think she could take that, especially if Parker was finding it difficult to send away an old flame.

She got up and started gathering used glasses to be returned to the kitchen. She had placed them on a tray when he suddenly reappeared at the top of the steps, Edward White at his side.

Kendra caught her breath. She hoped this meant the two men had patched things up between them. That would go a long way toward reconciling her with Parker, and she was hatefully tired of the estrangement between her husband and herself. She started toward them, but she lacked Parker's adroitness and quickly found herself in the midst of apologies as she bumped into Jeanna Crowe and her plump escort. When she would have slipped away at last, she was halted by Jeanna's hand on her arm. Excusing herself from her date, Jeanna pulled her aside. Kendra squared her shoulders, expecting unpleasantness. She was nearly speechless when Jeanna squeezed her hand, smiled and said, "You've been so good for him, Kendra. I wouldn't have believed it if I hadn't seen it with my own eyes. I just wanted to tell you that."

It took Kendra a moment to formulate a reply. "You think Parker's changed for the better?"

Jeanna chuckled. "I *know* he's changed for the better. Look, when we had that *fling* last year, it didn't mean anything. That's what upset me. Like all the others, I guess I thought I could change him, make him want to stay with me, but only you could do that. I know that now."

"He told you that?"

"More or less." She smiled self-deprecatingly. "Actually, he apologized. Can you imagine it? Parker Sugarman apologizing for doing what he's always done best, lovin' 'em and leavin' 'em."

For an instant, fear swamped Kendra. All she could think was that Parker regretted not asking Jeanna to be his temporary wife instead of her, but then reason slowly returned, and she began putting together everything Jeanna had said. When the truth dawned, it was almost too spectacular to accept. She literally seized Jeanna by the shoulders and demanded, "Are you telling me that Parker was apologizing to you for sedu...uh...misleading you?"

Jeanna shook her head. "He didn't mislead me, Kendra. He told me up front that it couldn't go anywhere, but he knew I wanted it to, and he apologized for letting it happen anyway, for taking my feelings and my disappointment so lightly. He said he was a selfish, unfeeling cad who had let his sex drive overrule his head and his heart for far too long, but never again." She grinned. "Amazing, isn't it? Our Parker settling down and in love."

Settling down, maybe, Kendra thought, *but in love?* She closed her eyes against the pain of hope, then popped them open again and smiled at her old friend. "Thanks for telling me this, Jeanna."

"My pleasure, and if you ever want to tell me how you managed it, I could sure use the tip."

Kendra squeezed her friend's shoulders. "There's nothing to tell, I'm afraid. So much has happened. Darla mostly."

Jeanna sighed. "Yeah, well, I want a man of my own, but not badly enough to wish anything fatal on *my* brother."

"No," Kendra said, "you wouldn't want that." She looked up to see Parker bearing down on them, a determined expression on his face. Ed was nowhere to be seen. "Didn't Edward want to stay?" she asked as soon as Parker drew near.

"Ah, no. He had other plans. He just wanted to talk about Kate."

"He doesn't think she'll do a good job, does he?"

Parker chuckled. "He thinks she'll do an excellent job, and so do I. He just wanted to discuss a little matter of attorney/client privilege."

"Oh." That was easy to decipher. Edward wanted to know just how much he should tell Kate about the circumstances and status of this marriage. "And what did you tell him?"

He looked at her very steadily. "I told him that Kate already knows everything she needs to know. Don't you agree?"

"I suppose."

"Good. Now, if you'll pardon us, Jeanna," he said smoothly, reaching for Kendra's hand, "I'd like to see in the new year with my wife on my arm, and the moment is almost here."

Kendra glanced at her watch as Jeanna winked and slipped away. Four minutes to midnight. Parker tilted her head back with a finger under her chin and smiled down into her eyes.

"Our dance, I believe. Finally."

"Finally," Kendra echoed, loving him so much in that instant that she was sure he must see it on her face.

Perhaps he did, for he turned his hand so that his palm lay against her throat in an odd, life-affirming caress. She wondered if he could feel the surge of blood through her veins and the thump of her heart against his palm. He leaned forward and kissed the top of her head, his hand slipping around to her nape before sliding down and across to her shoulder. Gently, he turned her and escorted her out onto the floor. As he wrapped his arms around her, the music faded to its closing notes, but he merely smiled and linked his hands in the small of her back, waiting. As the next song—a soft, dreamy instrumental—began Dennis Scherer hailed them from across the room.

"Hey, time to break out the champagne, guys!"

Parker stepped into the music, bringing his leg between hers, and looked briefly at Dennis. "Help yourself," he called. Then he turned his smile down on Kendra. "I'm going to dance with my wife."

For show, she thought. *Remember this is all for show.* But it didn't feel that way, not for her. She lifted her arms and curled them about his neck, matching the sway of her body to his. He bowed his head and laid his cheek against hers, his nose lightly nudging her ear as they danced. They were sweet, sweet minutes.

Held close to him, her body in perfect tune with his, she floated on a cloud of emotion, playing out a dream she hadn't even known she'd had until she'd married it. And yet, she could look back now and recall so many moments fraught with love for this man. She hadn't understood that the disgust and pain she'd felt at each new conquest of his had been rooted in her own love for him. She hadn't realized that one reason she and Nathan had been drawn so close was because they both loved his wayward brother. She had always understood why Nathan didn't just abandon Parker, but she had never had the presence of mind to wonder the same about herself, and she knew now that every time he had come around again after some romantic exploit, she had extended the hand of friendship because love had prompted her to keep the connection whole. And it was love that had prompted her to marry him when every sensible argument had been against it. She closed her eyes, hurting from the sheer intensity of that love.

She opened her eyes again when the cheer went up. "Happy New Year!" was called by a dozen voices. She and Parker swayed to a halt. He lifted his head, and for a long moment he did nothing more than stare down at her; then a smile curved his lips and his hands moved up to cup her face.

"Happy New Year," he whispered, and his mouth descended to hers.

Gentle at first, he brushed his lips across hers, then brought them back for a siege, parting them to draw the very heart from her. It was as if he took her love into himself, as if he drank it in, water for a thirsting man. She gave it up willingly, tears welling behind her closed eyelids as she hoped, prayed, it would be enough for him, enough to hold him, for suddenly she knew that she couldn't possibly let him go. Whatever bargain they'd made when they'd married, she knew she could never really let go now, not of him, not of Darla. They were her family now. They were everything now.

She turned her palms against the back of his head, fingers riffling his hair as she sought from him what she gave. What she got was passion, hot enough to send them both up in flames. He dropped his hands, encircling her with his arms and crushing her to him. She forgot that they had an audience, forgot that they weren't lovers in every sense of the word, forgot that he wasn't really hers, until a tap on her shoulder brought her back to reality.

Reluctantly she allowed Parker to break the kiss and turned to see who was trying to claim her attention. Mandy giggled as she lifted two glasses sloshing with champagne. A glance in Parker's direction showed Dennis at Parker's side, thrusting a glass into Parker's hand. Kendra recognized the irritation that Parker tamped down as he accepted the glass and shifted his gaze to her. He inclined his head and shrugged almost imperceptively, regret dimming the desire in his eyes. What did he regret, she wondered, that reality had intruded or that the dream had overtaken them in the first place?

The clamor at midnight had awakened the Randles' little girl, and she came trailing into the living room in her footed pajamas, a bedraggled stuffed rabbit held by one ear. Cheryl hurriedly put her down again to sleep while the others drank champagne and teased Parker and Kendra about that kiss. Parker kept her close by his side, offering silent comfort, but Kendra surprised herself by feeling little embarrassment, if any. Somehow it seemed natural to have publicly kissed her husband, the man she loved. She stayed by his side for the remainder of the evening and vice versa. He even went with her when she checked on Darla after Cheryl returned and several toasts were made to the new year. Darla was sleeping peacefully, her little mouth open and her thumb glistening wet from a recent sucking. They stood and looked at her for some time, marveling, then went out, leaving the door ajar, to play host and hostess.

It was a late evening. The gang didn't begin to disperse until nearly two in the morning. Walt Lyons and his group were the first to go. Cheryl was asleep in a chair by then, and after much pulling and prodding, Bill gave up and lifted his wife into his arms to carry her to the car. "Do you mind if I leave the kids until the morning?" he asked. "Just call me the minute they get up and I'll come right over."

Kendra was impressed by how graciously Parker agreed. When he turned back to her, he shrugged. "I wouldn't want to drag Darla out in the cold at this time of night."

Kendra smiled and said, "We have plenty of room."

That was when Mandy sauntered up and said, "Well, good. You won't mind two more, then. Dennis has crashed on the couch in the family room. I think he drank more than his fair share of the champagne. All I know is that I can't get him up, and if I can't get him up, then I might as well let the kid sleep, too. Jeanna and her guy are going to give me a ride home. Great party. Thanks. I guess I'll see you again sometime."

Parker and Kendra made all the appropriate noises and gestures, even kissing Mandy's cheeks as she took her leave of them. Jeanna gave them each a hug, her banker settled for a handshake, and then they were alone with the aftermath. Champagne glasses and soda cans were scattered across every table. The furniture sat at odd angles. Plates of chips with dip congealing on them were tucked into corners. Parker groaned and draped an arm across her shoulders.

"Tomorrow," he said. "We can clean it up tomorrow."

She wrinkled her nose. "We'll make Dennis help."

He grimaced. "We'll have to give him breakfast if we do."

"I'll make breakfast if you and he will get this room back together."

"Deal," he said.

She laughed. "Why do I suddenly think I've been taken?"

He tweaked her nose. "Maybe because I'm having visions of waffles and sausage and eggs scrambled with onion, coffee and freshly squeezed orange juice and cold milk. Oh, and toast. Don't forget the toast. Or better yet, biscuits. Mmm, yeah, definitely biscuits."

She rolled her eyes. "Why don't I just skip bed and start cooking now?"

He shook his head. "Nah, I won't have worked up a really good appetite for another four or five hours. You've got time for a nap, anyway."

"Oh, you." She pushed at him playfully, and they laughed together. When the laughter receded, there was nothing left to do but go to bed, separately. It was his night with Darla, so she went to the master suite, stripped off her clothes and tugged on a sleep shirt striped like a baseball uniform, thinking all the while how it had felt to be held in his arms and to be kissed by him. She washed her face and brushed her teeth, then let down her hair and ran her fingers through it, aching for him to come and hold her again, wishing she'd had the courage to ask him to stay with her.

She didn't want to sleep alone. She didn't want to live alone. She didn't want to get a divorce. She didn't want to go to Africa. She only wanted him and Darla and home. She wanted the dream to be true, the marriage to be real, the love to grow. It could happen. He had changed, she told herself, or maybe he had only found what he had been looking for. Or maybe it was only the circumstances in which they found themselves, and when Darla was legally his he would again become the old Parker with his roving eye and exploding hormones. Maybe he really wouldn't want her anymore and it would have to end.

She couldn't bear to think of it. She didn't dare think of it. Instead, she wrapped herself in the memory of the dance, his arms about her, the music playing, the heat of his breath on her cheek, in her ear, the sway of their bodies, the rub of their legs as they moved. She promised herself she would dream of those moments. She would lose this ache in memory.

She turned off the light, opening the door to the outer room at the same time. The soft, flickering light of flames greeted her. She stepped into the room, her gaze going to the fireplace built into the wall between the closet and the bath. He stood as she entered and turned to face her, backlit by the cheery fire he'd built upon the grate. Hope burst into bloom inside of her. She walked toward him, her heart hammering in her chest. She stopped before him and looked up into his eyes. His gaze skittered over her, coming to rest on her face. "I don't want to sleep alone," he said.

She closed her eyes to stop the tears of joy. The dream was real after all. The dream was real.

Chapter Fourteen

"I don't want to sleep alone...on the living room couch with Dennis just in the other room," he said. "If he got up before me, he'd surely wonder why we weren't together. So...so maybe I could make a pallet in here, unless..." He let it hang there, feeling the fool for having come to her like this. She didn't want him. It wouldn't mean anything to her, and he didn't think he could bear that, but neither could he bear to pass this night without her.

He cleared his throat and tried again, wondering when he'd gotten so bad at this, when he'd lost his touch. Seduction used to be his thing, his gift, but that was before Darla, before Kendra. "The little Randle girl is in the bed in Darla's room. I guess she slipped in there sometime after midnight. I—I remember we left the door open, and... I guess she couldn't sleep with Dennis snoring on the couch in the family room."

He couldn't tell what she was thinking. She was so beautiful with her hair down and her face scrubbed clean that it hurt to look at her, but he couldn't look away; neither could he look into those big green-gold eyes for fear of identifying some killing emotion there—pity or scorn or, worse yet, indifference. He closed his eyes, trying to dredge up his courage. It didn't help.

"I—I'll make a pallet in the guest room," he said roughly, then tried to lighten his tone. "We really ought to get some furniture in there. We might want to have the gang over again sometime, and..." Suddenly it came tumbling out of him. "I don't want to sleep on the floor, Kendra. I want you. God, how I want you!"

When she stepped up, slid her arms around him and laid her cheek in the hollow of his shoulder, he thought he might cry with relief, but one part of his mind was busy inventing disasters. He started trying to banish them, holding her tightly to him.

"I didn't mean what I said last time, Kendra, I swear I didn't."

"I didn't either," she whispered.

He hurried on. "I was hurt. No man wants to hear that his lovemaking means nothing, that it's unimportant."

"I didn't mean it like it sounded," she said.

"I lashed out. I said stupid things that hurt me as much as you, more probably, because I've wanted you every moment since."

She lifted her head and impaled him with those large, glowing eyes. "I didn't know what I was supposed to say, Parker. I don't know what you want me to say now. We're married, but we never intended to stay married. We agreed. We both agreed."

God help him, she was going to hold him to it. It hurt even worse than he had imagined. He felt broken inside, literally broken, but he had her now and that was something. It would have to do. He would make it memorable. He pulled her to him and covered her face with kisses from her forehead to her chin, speaking softly between them.

"I don't want to think about that now. I can't think about that now. Just let me love you. Please, Kendra, no more nights alone. Don't make me sleep alone anymore. Let me love you while I can."

"Yes."

She barely breathed the word, but it was enough for Parker. He took her mouth, pulling on it and thrusting his tongue inside to stroke her, fill her. From that point onward, he never took his hands off her. Even as he lowered her to the rug before the fire and stripped them both of their clothing, he loved her with his hands and mouth, kneading and caressing, pressing and tasting, lathing her with his tongue and filling her with his fingers until she writhed beneath him and begged him to come into her. But even then he held back, bringing her to the peak with his hands, glorying in her tremors and soft, gasping cries.

He wanted her to think of no one and nothing but him. He wanted to engage her every sense, to provoke her every reaction, to consume her, to possess her. He wanted her to love him, wanted it more than he had ever wanted anything in his life, and he hadn't the vaguest notion how to go about making it happen. In the past, he had avoided love and all its complications. Now he prayed for them, ached for them, and in his desperation he could do nothing other than pour his own love out on her. It was a unique experience, to actively love another, to desire another with love, to touch another with love. Oh, he had loved Nathan and Candace and, yes, he loved Darla, had done so from the moment of her birth but never more so than now. He had even imagined himself in love with other women for certain periods of time. But this love was unlike any other.

He came to know in that moment before he joined his body with hers that he was incomplete without this woman. He could never be what he ought to be without her. When he lifted her legs and positioned her to accept him, he knew with the heaviest certainty that this was the only moment of pure joy that he had ever experienced— and it might never be his again. He might never again see that look of rapture on her face. He might never again feel the welcome in her arms, the wet, warm acceptance of her body. For that reason alone, he wanted to make it last, wanted it to go on and on and on, but too soon he lost control of his own body. He spilled his love into her with tears in his eyes, his face buried in the cloud of her hair so that she wouldn't see.

He didn't lift his head again until he had mastered himself. She was lying beneath him with her eyes closed, her face serene, her lips curved into a delicate, dreamy smile. He wanted to weep, and he wanted to love her all over again. He levered his weight up onto his forearms and chose the words he could say.

"You're very beautiful."

Her smile grew. "You make me feel that way."

"Do I? I'm so very glad. Shall I tell you how you make me feel?"

"Yes." She opened her eyes. They were lustrous and gold in the firelight.

"Lucky," he said. "Blessed. Complete."

She looked at him, stared at him a long, silent time. Then she lifted her arms and twined them about his neck, pulling him down to her. "No more nights alone," she whispered. "No more nights alone."

No more nights alone—for now. His chest felt as if it would burst with the swell of gratitude he felt as he rolled her gently to her side and turned his face into the curve of her neck. *I love you.* The words burned his throat and tortured his tongue, but he couldn't say them. He didn't dare say them. He had too much to lose now: all those nights between this one and the end, all those nights to love her, to make her want to stay, all those days to take care of her, to share with her, to be her friend and her lover and her husband. If he told her, she might pull away, and even now she wasn't close enough. She was only close enough when he was inside her. She was only close enough when their bodies were joined, and he set out once more to prove it to her in the only way he knew how. Once more. *Please,* he thought, *always let there be once more.*

* * *

Golden days. They were golden days. She woke in his arms and went to sleep in them again at night. They laughed together and loved together and made plans together, but never beyond the next day or the weekend or just the end of her shift. They took care of the baby together and went out to dinner with their friends and danced in the dark to the music on the radio. They fed each other popcorn and stood beneath the spray in the shower, soaping their bodies and tasting clean skin and making love. They sat on opposite ends of the couch and traded sections of the newspaper, their legs intertwined, Darla trapped between them and periodically shredding the newsprint as it passed over her head so that they had to tell each other what it had said. They dressed up on Sunday and went to church, hands clasped at their sides as they prayed. They teased, and they tickled, chasing each other through the house like children until they collapsed in a heap and made love like adults. It was wonderful, and it was awful, for every day was one day less to come.

The new court date was set for the first week in February. Kate said it would provide adequate time for her to plan their strategy, but Kendra was as worried as Parker was confident, especially when Kate said she would be conferring closely with Edward.

Parker missed him. It was obvious in the number of times he mentioned his name, in the many ways he proposed to mend the rift. Finally, at her urging, he called Edward on the phone and asked if they could talk. After some negotiating, they made a date for lunch. Kendra traded shifts with another nurse so that she could stay home with the baby. Parker left agitated and anxious for the meeting. He returned the same way and would say only that they had made a beginning, that they understood one another a little better, and that it would take time.

Time. Time was the enemy. She could hardly bear to spend it in sleep. Workdays were eternal, off days but moments. It did not help that Darla was changing and growing by leaps and bounds, becoming more and more verbal and finding other ways to express herself with almost perfect understanding. Kendra wanted time to stand still. She wanted to freeze them all just as they were and lock out the rest of the world, but reality would intrude into the idyll, primarily in the guise of two particular persons, Sandra Pendleton and Kate Ridley.

Sandra continued to show up with her headphones and flash cards. In general, Darla ignored Sandra as soon as she realized that she could not charm Sandra into doing whatever she wanted her to do. Sandra, however, was determined to capture Darla's attention and direct it as she saw fit. Kendra had to hand it to her. The good doctor was nothing if not inventive. She employed in her campaign everything from hand puppets to colored lights, but if she occasionally won a battle, no one could doubt that she was, nevertheless, losing the war.

As often as not, her sessions with Darla ended with screams of protest, which was not to say that Darla was learning nothing from Sandra. Quite the contrary. In fact, little Darla had perfected several techniques for displaying a rather formidable temper. First she would go limp as a dishrag and become sixteen pounds of dead weight, drool and crocodile tears. Later she would stiffen up like a poker and stubbornly refuse to be bent, holding her breath until her face turned red as a beet and and then she'd explode in a scream of sheer rage. Next she would buck and flail her tiny fists, sobbing with genuine frustration. Finally she would display total rejection by reaching for another person, pushing Sandra's face away as she tried to speak, and turning her own face away, eyes closed, and wailing.

Sandra's own frustration was palpable. It was obvious, she said, that her theories concerning beginning a child's education *pre*birth were right on the money. Darla, she insisted, was not accustomed to learning. Consequently, *post*birth confusion was overwhelming her. She had no sense, poor little thing, of her own intellectual power.

"I wouldn't be too sure of that," Parker argued pleasantly, pointing out that Darla was the one to most often get her way.

"That," declared Sandra, "is because you've spoiled her shamelessly."

Parker just grinned. "I have, haven't I?"

"One day," Kendra told him later, "that woman is going to smack you."

"Not," he said, taking her in his arms, "with you to protect me. And you would protect me, wouldn't you?"

"I would," she admitted, nuzzling the curve of his jaw. But would he do the same for her? She tried very hard to believe he would. If only he would speak of love, if only once in the height of passion he would declare that he loved her, she could relax and simply be happy, happier than she had ever dreamed possible, not that life wasn't sweet just as it was.

These were good times. On the days that Parker kept the car, he would come early to pick her up and bring the baby into the hospital so the other nurses could tell them how beautiful she was and how bright and how charming. Later, they would tell Kendra how lucky she was, and she didn't dispute that assessment at all. But how long could her luck hold? Sometimes it seemed that these happy days would go on forever, but then Kate would call or stop by to discuss some aspect of the custody case.

Kendra couldn't help the depression that descended on her when Kate Ridley was around. She didn't completely understand it herself, but whenever Kate showed up, she brought a serious case of the dismals with her. There seemed to be several reasons for it. One, even with things so greatly improved between herself and Parker, they were still playing a game and calling it marriage, and Kendra was never more aware of it than when in the savvy lawyer's presence. Worse yet, something in the way Kate looked at them made Kendra wonder if she didn't know the truth or at least suspect it. When she tried to talk to

Parker about it, though, he first scoffed and then got angry.

"Why do you have to keep bringing this up?" he demanded one evening after Kate had left them.

"I just can't help feeling that she's on to us."

"In what way is she 'on to us,' Kendra?"

"She knows we're pretending."

The look he gave her was one she couldn't completely fathom. It was anger, yes, but something else, too. If she hadn't known better, she would have thought she had hurt him.

"Is that all this is to you, Kendra?" he asked roughly. "Is it just some silly little scam we're pulling on the world?"

"No, of course not," she said, at once repentant and defensive. "I know this is important to Darla and to you."

"And what about you, Kendra? Isn't this important to you in any way?"

"You know it is," she told him hesitantly, "for a lot of reasons. Mainly I just want what's best for you and Darla."

"Why, Kendra?" he asked, his hands seizing her shoulders, his tone urgent. "Why do you want what's best for me... and Darla?"

She blinked at him. It was right on the tip of her tongue, and for a moment she wondered if he didn't want her to say it, but then she reminded herself that Parker, though he had changed a great deal, was still—at bottom—Parker. He would never want the complications of a real marriage. For Parker, love was almost surely relegated to the bedroom and what happened between the sheets, and while that was undoubtedly incredible for the two of them, it was not enough for Kendra. She wanted all of it. She wanted everything love could be, though she wasn't even sure what that was. Strangely, though, she had known instinctively that she could not have it with Edward, but she had to keep reminding herself that the same was true of Parker.

She lifted her chin and put the best possible face on it. "If for no other reason," she said, "because it's what Nathan would have wanted."

His hands slid from her shoulders. "Nathan," he said. "Yes, of course." He turned away then, and a little while later he went out, saying he had errands to run. She didn't ask what errands he could get done after ten at night, and he didn't volunteer such information. The golden days, even the good days, it seemed, were on the wane.

Parker stood in the doorway of the dimly lit club and searched the room for a familiar face. One presented itself almost immediately.

"Why, Mr. Sugarman," said the manager, his hand outstretched, "we haven't seen you in some time."

"Hello, Patrick. It has been quite a while."

"We heard about your brother—a terrible loss."

Parker nodded. "Yes, terrible."

"Our condolences."

"Thank you."

"We have heard, too, about your marriage. Allow me to congratulate you, and please, the drinks this evening are on the house."

"That's very kind of you." Parker's gaze again skimmed the room. "Ah, you wouldn't know if Mr. White is here tonight, would you?"

Patrick clapped him on the back. "I'm sure you know that I keep track of all our best customers. He's in the back, Cathy's station. If you'd like a bit of privacy, just send her to me."

"Thanks again."

"My pleasure."

Parker shrugged out of his overcoat and scarf as he wound his way through the candlelit tables. The young women serving drinks wore costumes consisting of black tuxedo coats with tails, silver gray vests, bow ties, short shorts, sheer black stockings and high heels. One of them, her blond hair twisted into a pile of frothy curls atop her head, waved at Parker and blew him a kiss as she carried a tray of drinks to a table surrounded by men obviously engaged in an informal business meeting. Briefcases were open, papers were strewn across the table, pens were scribbling, but the conversation was punctuated with relaxed laughter. Parker nodded at the woman, trying to remember her name, and slipped on by. As he drew near the rear of the building, the muted sounds of billiard balls being racked and knocked around a table could be heard, as well as the murmur of voices. Hopefully Edward would be sitting on a stool at a bar that wrapped around two walls of the room, eyeing a television suspended from the ceiling and waiting for an open table, a small rectangular case containing a collapsible cue stick at his feet. If Edward was already engaged in a game of pool, Parker knew his chances of having a meaningful conversation with him were nil.

Parker turned a corner and stepped down into the large room. The only lights were those hanging low over the pool tables, the one behind the bar and those that emanated from the video games. The place wasn't particularly busy tonight, but Edward was at the bar tossing back peanuts and nursing a beer. He didn't look around until Cathy slapped down her bar towel and called out a greeting to Parker.

"Hey, handsome! Long time no see."

"Hi, Cath." He dumped his coat and scarf on the bar and straddled the stool next to Edward, leaning forward to accept Cathy's kiss on his cheek.

"Well, if it isn't the happy husband," Edward quipped dryly. "Stepping out already, I see."

Parker ran his hands through his hair. "Shut up, Ed."

Cathy popped her gum and cocked her pretty head. "Hey, d'you really get married like they say?"

Parker made an attempt to smile. "I really got married."

"God, I wouldn't have believed it!" she gushed, then brought her hand to her hip. "What can I getcha?"

"Bourbon—make it a double. Oh, and Patrick wants to see you."

"No prob. So how's married life?" she asked, pouring the drink.

Parker accepted the drink, swallowed a mouthful, grimaced and said, "Tricky."

"Seems like it would be," she allowed. "Heard you got a kid, too."

"Uh-huh. Sweetest little girl you ever saw. She's got a face that's all eyes and pink mouth, dark hair and a temper like a volcano. I predict she'll be running the world by the time she's two."

Cathy giggled. "Aw, that's sweet. Bet she's a beauty."

"She is that."

"Bet her mom is, too."

Parker opened his mouth to explain, thought better of it and said simply, "Yes."

Edward made a disgusted sound in the back of his throat and jerked a thumb over his shoulder. "Hadn't you better see what Patrick wants, Cathy?"

"Oh, yeah. No prob. Be back in a minute. Have some more peanuts."

"Thanks." He tossed peanuts into his mouth and waited, chewing, while Parker swallowed more bourbon. "So, you going to tell me why you're here, or shall I guess?"

Parker sighed and rubbed his temples with the thumb and forefinger of one hand. "She's going to leave me, Ed."

Edward snorted. "I thought that was the idea."

"It was, for maybe ten minutes."

Edward moved his beer glass in circles on the polished bar surface. "So it has really happened. The great Sugarman is in love."

"I don't know who 'the great Sugarman' is anymore," Parker said. "All I know is that I am very much in love with his wife and I don't want to lose her."

"Have you told her so?"

Parker shook his head, drained his glass and set it down again, aware that Edward was staring at him.

Ed swiveled sideways, never taking his eyes off Parker. "You're scared," he said, clearly shocked.

Parker braced his elbows against the edge of the bar and put his head in his hands. "I'm not scared, Ed. I'm terrified."

Ed turned back to the bar and lifted his glass, saying nothing for a long time. Finally he asked, "She really sleeping with you?"

Parker nodded. "Yeah." It was just a whisper. "And you know something, Ed? It isn't enough." He sighed and rubbed his hands over his face. "For the first time in my miserable life, it just isn't enough."

Edward bounced a knee in agitation and turned his head away. Parker knew he was struggling to control his temper. "Look," he said, "I'd take this to someone else if there was someone else to take it to, but..."

"Yeah, yeah, I know," Ed retorted. "You've about run out of friends and family."

Parker closed his eyes and took the jab. It was, after all, only too true. After a long while, he reached for his scarf and draped it around his neck. Ed grimaced and told him what he wanted to hear.

"I don't care what she said. She wouldn't be sleeping with you if she wasn't in love with you."

"You don't know what I'd give just to believe that, let alone to make it true."

"I know her," Ed said. "She's not the kind who can separate sex from love. I tell you something, I wasn't even sure love would do it. She told me once that sex was the least important part of marriage, and she used her own parents' marriage as an example."

Parker's head snapped around, brows drawn together. "She said that? I mean, did she actually say that sex was the least important part of her parents' marriage?"

Edward shrugged. "Pretty much. I even mentioned it to her father in a roundabout way once."

"And what did Dan say?"

Ed pushed out a heavy breath. "He said that he had protected both Kendra and her mother from certain realities, that he regretted it, and that...well, hell. He said that Kendra needed a man who understood but wouldn't let her off the hook. Huh." He thoughtfully brushed his mustache with his fingertips. "I thought at the time that he meant I should just hang in there and not give up, but maybe..."

Parker picked up where Ed left off. "Maybe he meant that Kendra needs a man who won't let her set the priorities," he said, a note of optimism in his voice for the first time that evening, "and maybe I need to have a talk with my father-in-law."

Edward canted his head. "I played the understanding gentleman and did myself right out of an engagement, didn't I?"

Parker clapped him on the shoulder. "I hope so," he said, "because God knows I've played the son of a bitch all my life, and now it's the only thing I can see that I might have going for me."

Edward shook his head. "Isn't that a hell of a thing."

"Just the opposite," Parker said quietly. "If it works out, it'll be the most heavenly thing ever to come my way."

Edward actually chuckled. "Talk about a lucky son of a bitch."

Parker managed a smile. "That remains to be seen. I could lose everything, Ed—Kendra and Darla, too."

Ed combed his mustache again. "Aw, she'll stay with you until the custody case is settled anyway."

"Yeah, but then what? And what if the court doesn't see it my way where Darla's concerned?"

"Don't worry about it," Edward said confidently. "Kate will do a good job for you."

"Kendra doesn't think so."

"Kendra always did underestimate Kate."

"Kendra doesn't like Kate, that's true," Parker said. "She'd rather have you representing us."

Edward met his gaze flatly. "You're better off with Kate. I know too much, Parker."

"I've put you in an awkward position right from the beginning, haven't I, Ed?"

"It *was* my dumb idea." He snorted. "It sounded so simple at first. Just get married. Maybe you won't like it, but hell, who stays married anymore? I thought you'd dupe one of those bimbos you decorated the place with. I didn't expect you to get into collusion with the one decent woman either one of us has really ever known."

"If it's any comfort to you," Parker said, "I regret the way I did it. I'm not sorry I married her. I'm just sorry I didn't have sense enough to do it right, and now if I can't make it right, I'm going to pay a hell of a price. I already have in some ways."

"Maybe so," Edward said, "but you've still got a shot at it, and that's more than the rest of us can say."

Parker looked down at his hands, picking his words. "I'm sorry, Ed," he said. "I didn't understand how it felt to love someone. I never dreamed . . . Well, I just had no idea what you must have been feeling. Maybe if I had, I wouldn't have—"

"Shut up, Parker," Ed said, lifting his glass, "and go home to your wife."

Good advice. Parker decided he'd better take it. He backed off the stool and picked up his coat, slung it on and buttoned it up. He turned away, then turned back again.

"Ed, I just wanted to say thanks. I mean it. Thanks for everything. You've been a good friend. I want to be a good friend, too, but first I think I have to figure out how to be a good husband. Then . . . maybe . . ."

Ed slid him a glance over his shoulder. "Get out of here," he said, but there was a smile in his eyes, a welcome smile that warmed Parker as the coat could not.

"I'll see you around."

"Yeah. See you around." Ed turned back to his drink, his gaze going to the television high in the corner.

Parker smiled and left him. Friends and family. Why hadn't he ever known before what hell life could be without them? Why hadn't he been better at either one? *Just give me a chance,* he prayed silently. *Just one more chance.*

He wound his way through the tables in the outer room again, spying Cathy at the small bar with Patrick. "Thanks, Pat."

"Anytime. Hey, bring the wife in. We'll buy her a drink."

Parker grinned. "She's too good for this place, man."

Patrick pretended insult. "Huh! She's too good for you, then."

"No doubt about it," Parker agreed. The barkeep waved him off with a laugh, and he pushed through the glass door to the small foyer that fronted the street. "But I'm working on it," he added softly. "I'm working on it." And God willing, he'd be worthy of her one day. God willing.

Chapter Fifteen

"Kendra."

Dan kissed her cheek and swept past her, unusually brusque. Kendra felt a tingle of alarm, a prickling of skin on the nape of her neck.

"It's awfully early for a visit." Her hand went to her wet hair. "I'm still getting ready for work."

"We need to talk," he said, his gaze elsewhere.

She followed his line of sight and saw Parker standing on the dining room steps. He leaned a shoulder draped with a dishcloth against the decorative column flanking the entrance and folded his arms. Recalling their last argument, she knew instinctively that he had had something to do with this, and she knew what it was about: Kate. Anger flared up in her. What right did they have, either of them, to tell her who to like and who not to like? And what made Kate Ridley so wonderful, anyway? She was a tall, blond, aggressive female who'd spent her life cultivating a law practice instead of a family of her own. Kendra knew with righteous certainty that Kate Ridley's interest in her father was purely sexual, not really love at all. *The same,* the hateful thought occurred, *as Parker's interest in you. But there's Darla, too!* her heart cried. Oh, yes, he needed her to secure his hold on Darla, but that wasn't any closer to real love than sex for Parker. She glared that silent accusation at him but felt no satisfaction at all when he shifted his eyes away guiltily. Angry all over again, she jerked away her gaze and pointed it at her father.

Dan had slipped off his coat and was in the process of draping it over the back of the couch. He halted suddenly, his hand filled with corduroy coat collar, and flashed another look at Parker before carefully completing the motion. He turned fully to Kendra, his hands smoothing the bottom of the dark green V-neck sweater he wore over a white T-shirt. "Let's sit down for a few minutes. This is important."

Her first impulse was to tell him that it would have to wait, but she knew that would only delay the conversation, not eliminate it. Grudgingly, she wrapped her quilted robe tighter about her and dropped into a chair. "I don't have much time."

"Yes, I know," her father said, sinking down onto the sofa next to his coat, "but I've been thinking about this a long time, and I want to get it off my chest."

"Sounds ominous," she quipped, crossing her legs.

"No, no, not that," Dan said. "It's just that I should have done it long ago, even before your mother died. Afterward, there didn't seem any reason to rehash it all. I guess I just wanted it left between her and me. Then Kate..."

"Then Kate," Kendra echoed cryptically.

Dan wove his fingers together and let them fall to his lap. "Why don't you like her?" he asked.

Why didn't she like her? She shrugged, pretending that it didn't matter. "She's...cold."

Dan's eyebrows rose. "Cold? Funny, I'd have said she was, well, hot."

Hot. Kendra came to her feet, suddenly agitated. "I guess we just see her differently."

"Let me tell you just how I see her, then," he said. "She's smart. She's successful. She's beautiful. She's passionate, about everything and everyone she values. She's tough. She'll fight fiercely for anything she believes in, and she believes in me. I don't know why, but she loves me. She loves me like I never expected to be loved . . . as I haven't expected to be loved since I married your mother."

Kendra cut him a sharp glance. "Are you implying my mother didn't love you?"

He leaned forward and braced his elbows on his knees, his movements almost painfully slow. "Your mother loved me as well as she was able to, Kendra. I always knew that. It was one of the reasons I stayed."

Stayed? She advanced a step toward him, her heart pounding with the weight of a terrible truth so long suspected, so long denied. "You're telling me that you wanted to leave her?" she asked in a small voice.

He tilted his head back, fixing her with sad eyes. "I wanted to live with her as husbands and wives ought to live together," he said. "I think you know what I'm talking about, Kendra. Maybe when you were small you thought it was normal that we didn't share a bedroom together. By now you ought to know better."

She thought of Parker standing behind her on the steps and deeply resented that he was hearing this. Of course she had known her parents' marriage was not like that of her friends' parents, but they had seemed happy. They hadn't fought. They hadn't divorced. They had, in fact, been unfailingly polite to one another. *Too polite,* came the thought. She tried to push it away, but experience was suddenly lending it credence. Two people couldn't live together without occasionally rubbing each other the wrong way. Look at her and Parker. Look at... No, they weren't like her parents. None of the people she knew were like her parents. Desperately, she fought to right her thoughts.

"M-Mother was a light sleeper. You...you used to snore." He was shaking his head. "S-someone had to stay by me when I was small! Someone..."

"No, Kendra."

"It got to be a habit. Mother told me once. She couldn't..." He got up and came toward her. Kendra watched him come closer and closer. "She couldn't... Mother couldn't get used to sleeping with someone... else."

He put his hands upon her shoulders, looked down into her face, solemn, sad. So sad. "She didn't want me, Kendra. She never wanted me. After she got pregnant with you, she said there was no reason, no need, for me to *bother* her ever again."

Kendra's eyes filled with tears. She saw his anguish, saw his grief. But she couldn't have said that to him, not her sweet, kind, soft-spoken mother, not to him. And yet... She closed her eyes.

"I know that she loved you."

"Yes. In her way. But not *that* way, and it wasn't enough, Kendra. I want you to understand that it just wasn't enough."

She looked up at him in confusion. "But you stayed."

He sighed and nodded. "I thought at first that she would change her mind. Then later I hoped counseling..." He smiled lamely. "Then there was you. She was a good mother. I couldn't take you away from her. I couldn't give you up. She was a good wife in every other way."

"Oh, Daddy," she said. "It didn't matter then, did it? It stopped being important to you."

"No," he said. "It never stopped being important to me, Kendra. It doesn't work like that. I gave up, yes. I resigned myself to living without...real love. But it *never* stopped being important to me." He dropped his hands, sliding them down her arms. "Then...then she died, and I looked in the mirror and I saw an old man whose life had passed him by while he'd waited and he'd hoped and finally given up." He stepped back, hands moving to his hip pockets as if looking for something. "You were grown, off at college. There was the business, a few friends. I got a dog. You remember that old cur I adopted?"

Kendra smiled, blinking back tears. "That crazy old thing? He was scared of his own shadow, that dog. Couldn't even pet him."

"Useless," he said. "Stupid. He ran right out in front of that car. Didn't have the heart to get another after that." He looked at her. "Do you know what it's like to be alone, sugar, so alone that even a dumb old scaredy-cat dog is company?"

"Oh, Daddy," she whispered, stepping up to put her arms around him. She laid her cheek against his shoulder.

"I know," he said, stroking her shoulder blades. "But you had your own life to live."

"Daddy, I'm sorry."

"Not your fault. It was just over, that's all. My life was over, Kendra." He pushed a hand under her chin and lifted it, tilting her head back. "Then I met Kate, and Kate changed everything."

She pulled back. "You make it sound like you were dying before Kate came along."

"I was," he said flatly. "Slowly but surely I was dying. I'd just quit, Ken. I'd given up. I even retired from the business. I just couldn't seem to care about it anymore. Then this beautiful, intelligent, sexy woman brought me back to life. That's the God's honest truth, Ken. She made me alive again, and not just that, young again. She made me *young* again. And she's willing to do anything to make me happy, even put up with your crap."

Her mouth fell open. "Dad!"

He adopted that same stern air that he'd taken with her a thousand times before, starting at about age three. "You've been rude, Kendra. Worse than rude. You've been downright unkind. You've turned up your nose at every overture she's ever made. And all along she's tried to understand. More than that, she's kept the peace, stopped me from saying anything to you, even refused to marry me until you were settled with Parker. My God, Kendra, the night of Nathan's funeral you wanted to come home, so the woman moved into a hotel!''

"I—I didn't know," Kendra choked out. "I thought she still had her apartment."

"And she wanted you to think that, Kendra. She didn't want you to hate *me* because we were together."

Kendra looked down in shame. How unfair she'd been! And all because she hadn't wanted to understand! She hadn't wanted to admit that the woman who had been such a wonderful mother to her had been such a poor wife to her father. But hadn't she known, really? Hadn't she seen her mother in herself at one point? Wasn't that why she'd broken up with Edward? Because she could see that she and Edward would have had no more than her mother and father had had together. And to think that she had blamed her father for that! Not consciously perhaps, but she'd told herself how like her father Edward was, rather than how like her mother she was! But Parker had changed that. Parker, Parker and Kate. Only Parker didn't love her. He simply wanted her. But maybe being wanted wasn't such a small thing, after all. She fought the urge to turn her gaze on him and blinked away tears.

"I—I'm sorry, Dad."

"Hell, Kendra," he said, "I don't want apologies."

She looked up. "What, then?"

He glanced at Parker and back again. "She's trying to help," he said. Just that, nothing more.

Shamed to her core, Kendra nodded. "Yes. Yes, I see. I understand. I'll...I'll..." She lifted her hands beseechingly. "I'll change. I promise."

Dan shook his head and reached out a long arm to hug her to him. "Aw, honey, I'm not asking for that much. Just give her a chance, for my sake."

"All—all right. Sure. Anything you say, Daddy, because...because I love you."

He chuckled deep in his throat. "I know. I know, baby. And everything's going to be fine. You'll see. Kate won't let you lose Darla. I know she won't."

Kendra nodded and swallowed the lump in her throat. "Th-thank you, Daddy."

He kissed the top of her head. "Thank Kate," he said, "and your husband."

So he *had* prompted this. She mulled it over as her father took his leave of her, acutely aware of Parker's silent presence. The moment the door closed behind Dan Ballard, she turned to him.

"Why?" she asked. "Because we argued over Kate?"

His face was utterly inscrutable. "Is that what you think the argument was over?"

She didn't know what to say to that, and it was damned unfair of him to keep turning the tables on her this way. "Why can't you just answer my question?" she demanded.

"Why can't you answer mine?" he retorted.

She glared at him, when what she really wanted to do was throw herself at him and *beg* him to love her, *really* love her. Damn him, bringing her father into their argument, forcing her hand like this. "You'll do anything to get what you want, won't you?" she grumbled.

He seemed to actually think it over before answering; then he said exactly what she expected him to. "Yes. This time I'll do anything to get what I want."

And that's Darla, she thought bitterly, *just Darla.* The saddest part of it was that she'd do anything to help him, anything at all. She loved him that much, and he couldn't even see it. "I have to go to work," she said sharply and left him there, staring at nothing like the blind man he was. It never occurred to her that her own eyesight was as poor as his.

The letter came the morning before the hearing. "Dear Kendra," it read. "The time is now. I offer you a final chance to minister to your fellow man as few are privileged to do. I promise you that this experience will teach you what life is all about. You will never again be the same for your work here. You'll change all those shallow middle-class ideas. Never again will you be content with a small job and a small house and a small life. Instead of being one of those who people the world, you'll be one who changes it. Think of that, my dear, and let me know your decision. I'll be in town for a few days soon, and look forward to seeing you again. I feel sure we can set you on the right course at that time. I only want what is best for you, one more thing we undoubtedly hold in common."

Kendra folded the letter and stuck it in her purse, then went on to work. It was odd how Devon's eloquent words failed to move her. "One of those who people the world," he had said, as if those who made up the world did not matter as much as those whose lofty purposes and high-flown ideas moved them to accomplish "greater" things. What was the difference between a man who tried to save a single child and one who couldn't be content with saving millions? Oh, she knew that Parker's motives were not completely selfless. He needed Darla as much as she needed him, but at least he knew that. Devon Hoyt seemed to consider himself above such mundane emotions; yet, he was apparently lonely—one more thing they might well have in common. It was that that made her keep the letter. Devon might be someone to go to when it was all over with Parker, and the end was coming so quickly.

She didn't think that he'd want her to go immediately after the hearing. That would raise questions better left unasked. Her own self-imposed period of six months might not even put them in the clear. She could probably stretch that to nine or ten months, maybe even a year, but the hearing was the beginning of the end, and she knew it. And the hearing was suddenly upon them.

She stood looking at Parker, Darla in her arms. They were all dressed in their Sunday best, Darla in strawberry pink velvet with lace edging and delicately embroidered roses, matching bonnet, white tights with a ruffled seat and white patent-leather shoes. Kendra wore a gold knit suit with a slender skirt and a collarless jacket cropped at the hips and trimmed in black braid. Black stockings and black shoes with relatively thick soles and high, flanged heels completed the outfit. She had left her hair down, pulling the front and sides back in a soft roll atop her head. With large black-and-gold earrings resembling small targets, she had a definite forties' look about her, elegant but simple, unique without being absurd. She looked, in fact, like a woman capable of doing anything, a woman who knew her own power—mother, wife, warrior—in a well-fitted suit.

Parker was another matter entirely. In double-breasted black with a bloodred shirt and a wide, extravagantly flowered black-and-white tie, he was devastatingly handsome and utterly individual. Clearly, the only fashion he cared about was his own, and he dared the world by his demeanor to tell him that his taste and sense of things were wrong. If Kendra was a warrior woman, he was the male icon she fought to protect and validate, and Darla was the being chosen for his love and blessing, the one individual who could do no wrong, provoke no wrath. Darla was the treasure, and everyone knew it when they walked into family court.

It was a small room, almost cozy with its oak paneling, floors, tables, chairs and small but pretentious judicial bench. There were no spectator seats, only a row of sturdy chairs placed on either side of the door on the back wall. Wanda Hatcher, the social worker, was seated there, along with the Pendletons' oldest boy, Dan Ballard, an unidentified man and, unexpectedly, Edward White. Edward and Wanda Hatcher smiled circumspectly in greeting, while the Pendleton boy stared at them with open curiosity and the unidentified man ignored them completely. Dan Ballard got up and wrapped them each in a bear hug before kissing Darla and tickling her under the chin until she giggled and swiped his hand away, knocking her cap askew in the process. Parker straightened it, meticulously arranging her dark hair into waiflike wisps beneath the shallow front brim. Darla reached for him, and he swept her easily into his arms. Kendra fished a bottle from the small diaper bag on her shoulder and handed it to him, but he didn't offer it to the baby. Instead, he slid it into his left lower coat pocket, and Darla busied herself with trying to kick the cap off the nipple with one swinging toe.

They walked across the floor to the table where Kate stood waiting for them. She looked fiercely competent in a navy blue suit nipped in at the waist. Beneath her jacket, she wore a cream-colored blouse with a wedding ring collar and pleated front. Her blond hair had been twisted into a neat French roll, the top and sides waving softly about her face. She wore a slim gold pocket watch with fob pinned to one lapel and simple pearl earrings. It was the "power look with a feminine touch" that Kate did so well. For once, Kendra was grateful for it. No one had ever looked more competent that Kate Ridley. The rumpled, tweedy aura of the Pendletons' grandfatherly lawyer and the "earth friendly" style of the Pendletons themselves seemed woefully out of place in comparison. But Kendra put no faith in her own powers of observation at the moment. She claimed no objectivity in the matter. How could she? She stood for Parker and Parker alone, no longer even making any pretense to herself that it was Darla's best interests that motivated her, though she still believed, conveniently, that Parker would be better for Darla than the Pendletons.

Kate ignored the baby, targeting first Kendra then Parker with her discerning gaze. "Nervous?"

"A little," Kendra admitted.

Parker only jerked his head toward the rear of the room and asked, "What's Ed doing here? I thought he was out of it."

Kate laid down the ink pen she held in one hand and confronted him squarely. "Do you trust me?"

"What's that got—"

"I said, do you trust me?"

Kendra watched as Parker subdued his irritation, came to a decision and nodded. Kate turned to her next.

"What about you, Kendra?"

She took a deep breath, searching for a truthful answer. Did she trust this woman? She thought of her father and knew that she must. "Yes."

"All right, then. Just accept that I've planned for every contingency and let it go at that."

"But..."

Kate glared at Parker, displaying the ability that regularly reduced witnesses to babbling oracles. "*Every* contingency," she repeated flatly.

He shut his mouth, lips thinning. He didn't like it, but he wouldn't argue. Kate Ridley was clearly in charge—for now.

The door behind the bench opened and the judge swept unceremoniously into the room, his black robe barely clinging to the shoulders of a natty, gray pin striped suit. He nodded to the clerk to call the court to order and collapsed onto his chair, sprawling back with his hands clasped across his middle. They all took their seats. For a moment, the room was filled with rustling and scraping as papers were shuffled and chair legs moved over the polished wood floor. Then suddenly the judge lurched forward and collapsed upon the bench top, elbows splayed, shoulders skewed.

"Ms. Ridley," he said, a caress in his voice, "what a pleasure to see you in my court again."

Kate smiled and inclined her head coyly. "Your Honor." Her voice was husky, sensual, utterly feminine. "It's good to see you again, and please allow me to say what a privilege it is to represent the defendant in this particular case in this particular court."

The judge smiled. "Eloquent—and lovely—as ever." He abruptly turned to the plaintiff's lawyer and said in a loud voice, "Mr. Brower, nice to see you, too. Now let's get to it. I've read the particulars—the briefs submitted by attorneys, the reports submitted by the state's representative and the petition of probate for the willed estates of Nathan and Candace Sugarman, both deceased. At issue here is the assignment and implementation of custodial care for the minor, Darla Gayle Sugarman, aged eight months. I will now hear argument in the case. Mr. Brower.''

During this monologue, Parker and Kendra huddled close and raised eyebrows at Kate, who shrugged and whispered from the corner of her mouth. ''He always flirts like mad with the female attorneys, but he rules against them more than half the time.''

They just looked at each other, both skeptical and wondering whether this boded ill or good for their case. Kendra felt a spurt of I-told-you-so-itis, but she squelched it immediately. No one could say whether or not Kate would prejudice this judge or any other, and Kendra was big enough to admit that she still had lingering resentment against Kate Ridley, as well as her father and her husband. It didn't seem to matter that she knew perfectly well that such resentment was beneath her. All she could do was ignore it until it went away of its own accord. She tried to do that now by listening to the very dull intonations of the Pendletons' attorney.

He went on and on about the ''equality of connection'' between his clients and the defendants, the remarkably similar wording of the welfare worker's reports on both households, even the ''coincidence'' of one partner in each marriage being involved in the pediatric health profession. But there, he claimed, the similarities ended and the true superiority of his clients as caretakers came into play.

He went through a long list of the supposedly superior attributes of his clients. Heath Pendleton was a horticulturist whose natural, pesticide-free growing methods yielded the healthiest possible produce for his family. Why, the Pendleton children were virtually in perfect health. He talked about their large, comfortable home, calling it a ''haven for children.'' He discussed finances, submitting copies of the Pendletons' tax returns and Sandra's royalty statements charting the progress of her "respected" book. He even listed the playground equipment the Pendletons owned and pointed out the safety features of their family vehicles! It was apparent, he argued, that the Pendleton offspring were cared for better than any other children in the whole city. According to him, they were also far superior intellectually to the average child due to their mother's "proven" child-rearing methods. That's when Kate weighed in with her objections, saying that any number of factors could account for the intellect of any given child, beginning with genetics. She stated, too, that Dr. Pendleton's "theories" were not proven effective, that no studies had been done to support her methods, and the quality of child care was far too subjective a matter for anyone, let alone an attorney, to decide what was best and what was not. The judge allowed Brower to attack only the contention that Dr. Pendleton's methods were not proven, and thereby the first witness was called.

The unidentified man at the back of the room came forward and revealed himself to be one of the city's top child psychiatrists. He enthusiastically endorsed Sandra's methods. Kate countered him by submitting *twenty-six* sworn depositions by other professionals, some of them even more distinguished than the witness, saying that Dr. Pendleton's methods were unsupported by scientific methodology, limited mainly to her own children, controversial, spurious and even "kooky," the one contention that Brower managed to get struck from the record.

The next hour passed in like manner, with Brower setting up his arguments and Kate knocking them down either partially or fully. The unprepossessing Brower turned into an oratorical tiger, but Kate matched him snarl for snarl and sometimes outdid him. Darla grew fretful but eventually settled down to sleep in Parker's arms. The judge did not even seem to notice, but all appeared to Kendra to be going well until Brower unleashed his claws.

"And finally, Your Honor," he said, striking a pose at once apologetic and defensive, "one must contrast the

length and stability of my clients' marriage to the Sugarmans', shall we say, surprisingly *convenient* and *impulsive* marriage of only four months' duration.''

Kate was on her feet before the words were out of his
mouth. A regular shouting match ensued, at the end of
which Kendra could not be certain who had won! It
seemed, however, that Brower had won the right to bring
forward a ''surprise'' witness. The surprise could not have
been greater when Devon Hoyt strode into the room. Tall,
slender and fit, his sleek blond hair streaked with silver at
the temples and flowing over his collar in the back, he was
the picture of a charming, erudite academic. His very demeanor spoke of well-formulated ideals far above those of
mere mortals. He smiled warmly at Kendra, even stopped
to kiss her hand at the defense table, an action she was too
shocked to prevent, so that Parker finally had to snatch her
hand from Devon's.

The next twenty minutes were sheer hell. At Brower's
direction, Devon pulled Kendra's letters from his pocket
and read selected passages that made it obvious she had
failed to mention her marriage, referring to it only as ''a
duty to a dearly departed friend.'' The most damaging evidence, however, was Kendra's written intention to reap-
ply for the mission in Africa in six months. Kendra covered
her hand with her mouth and turned tearfully apologetic
eyes to Parker, who looked positively stricken, his face
pale, eyes haunted, as he clutched the sleeping Darla to his
chest.

When it was all over, Kate rose calmly and stated that
the best rebuttal to such obviously prejudicial testimony
could come only from another ''friend'' of the maligned
couple. She called Edward White to the stand. To Kendra's surprise, Parker actually brightened a bit, straightening in his seat, looping an arm about her shoulders and
pulling her tight against his side.

''I'm sorry,'' she whispered, laying her forehead against
his temple.

He turned and dipped his head, kissing her gently upon the mouth. "Hang in there, babe. We'll make it."

She nodded and reached up to curl her arms about his neck, holding on for dear life, while Darla slept peacefully in the crook of Parker's arm, her thumb buried in her mouth up to the second knuckle, and Kate walked around the table to lean against it, arms folded.

"Mr. White," she said crisply, "will you tell this court what you know about the Sugarmans' marriage?"

Edward grimaced and shifted uncomfortably in his seat. "Well, like I told you, Ms. Ridley, the whole thing was my idea in a way. After Nathan Sugarman died and it became obvious that Dr. Pendleton was going to challenge your client, Parker Sugarman, for custody of Nathan's daughter, I was answering his questions about waging such a legal battle—being a lawyer myself and Mr. Sugarman, that is, Parker's best friend. Anyway, among other things, I mentioned that it wouldn't do his, er, Parker's case any harm if he were married instead of single, which he was at the time, single, I mean.

"To my surprise, Parker seemed to take my suggestion seriously. He was absolutely committed to retaining custody of his niece, just as his brother and sister-in-law stated in their last will and testament." Edward shifted position again, crossing his legs and leaning back a little in the chair. "I figured he'd do something stupid like hoodwink one of his bim... ah, more gullible lady friends into marrying him, then dump her once he didn't need her anymore."

Parker swore under his breath at that and tightened his hold on Kendra. Kate sent him a warning glance over her shoulder and turned back to Edward.

"And did he fulfill your expectations, Mr. White?"

"No way. He went right out and found himself the best wife he could."

"Kendra Ballard Sugarman?"

"Right. Kendra."

"And what do you base this assessment of Mrs. Sugarman on?"

Edward renegotiated his position again, uncrossing his legs and leaning forward. "I was engaged to her. We broke up some months prior to her marriage to Parker."

"And what precipitated that breakup, Mr. White?"

"I don't know," Edward growled, then seemed to think better and glanced at the judge. "Yes, I do. Kendra wasn't in love with me. She was in love with Parker Sugarman."

Kendra felt Parker stiffen and loosened her death grip on his neck, eyes downcast. He slid his arm up around her neck and curled his hand under her chin, forcing her gaze up to meet his. She tried to tell him with her eyes everything she felt at that moment, and it seemed to work, because he smiled and kissed her again, rolling his face into the softness of her hair afterward as he hugged her close. She barely heard what was said next.

"So when the Sugarmans married, at least Mrs. Sugarman was very much in love."

"Yes."

"And what do you base that judgment on?"

"Well, for one thing, she's sleeping with him, and I know for a fact that she wouldn't be unless she loved him."

Somebody gasped, but it wasn't Kendra. Her eyes were closed and her head was laying on Parker's shoulder, her face turned into the curve of his neck. Parker splayed his fingers in her hair, holding her there. The Pendletons' attorney objected to something or other—Kendra wasn't sure what—and Kate conceded whatever it was, then went on with her questions.

"Of your personal knowledge, Mr. White, how long has Mrs. Sugarman known her husband?"

"Most of her life."

"And in your opinion, she was very much in love with her husband when she married him. Correct?"

"Absolutely."

"That sort of rules out an impulsive decision on her part, doesn't it?"

"Yes, ma'am."

Brower objected again, but the judge told him to shut up and sit down and took over the questioning himself.

"So tell me, Mr. White, in your opinion, how does Mr. Sugarman feel about his wife?"

"Opinion doesn't have anything to do with it," Edward said. "He's told me himself on more than one occasion how much he loves her, how lucky he and Darla are to have her and how desperately he wants the marriage to continue."

Kendra closed her hand in the fabric of Parker's coat and sobbed audibly onto his shirt collar. Darla woke up then and sat upright, demanding attention. Kendra jerked back, wiped the tears from her eyes and reached for her.

"Hush, baby. It's okay. Everything's okay. Here now, let Mommy rock you."

Darla settled against her shoulder, stuck her thumb in her mouth and closed her eyes while Kendra rocked her gently back and forth. Parker draped his arm around the back of her chair and laid a hand comfortingly on Darla's back, his eyes speaking volumes to his wife.

"Mommy," he whispered, "I love you."

Kendra bit her lip to keep from laughing aloud.

The judge was talking, but she didn't catch a word of it. It didn't matter. It couldn't possibly matter. Everybody stood. Parker's arms came around her, closing the baby between them.

When court adjourned, Mr. Sugarman was kissing Mrs. Sugarman, Mr. Ballard was hugging the future Mrs. Ballard, the Pendletons were looking stunned and attorney Edward White was standing with his hands in his pockets, a certain longing mingled with the affection in his eye, while Darla slept on, content, safe, secure, oblivious. In other words, everything was just as it should have been.

Epilogue

Darla toddled across the grass, careening from Dan to Kate to Parker, who scooped her up, swung her about and lifted her onto his shoulders. She playfully kicked him in the side of the head, prompting a comic rendition of a stumbling collapse that left them both sprawled upon the Ballards' carefully manicured lawn, Darla giggling and Parking moaning until he convinced her that he was truly hurt. Darla scrambled up and pounced on him, landing astride his chest. She grasped his dark hair in her fists and attempted to lift his head, calling, "Daddy! Daddy!"

"Ow!" Parker bolted up into a sitting position, catching her in his arms as she toppled backward. His hair stuck out in all directions. Her own was gradually sliding out of the two tiny ponytails perched on the sides of her head. "Girl, you're brutal," Parker told her as she held her at her arm's length. She laughed, stuck her thumb in her mouth and swung out with both feet. "Cut it out, or Daddy's going to snatch your nose right off your face!"

She kicked at him again, and he made a grab for her nose then showed "it" to her, the tip of his thumb thrust through the coiled fingers of his fist. Darla snatched at it, but Parker scrambled up and was off, Darla running after him and squealing, "No! No!" Seeing she couldn't catch him, she ran straight to her grandfather. "No, Papa, no!"

Dan swept her up onto his hip and called out to Parker. Parker pretended to throw it to him. Dan pretended to catch it and press it back onto her face. "Let me see," he said as she turned her face this way and that. "Beautiful!" he told her. "But you're beautiful even without a nose."

Darla flung her arms about his neck and covered his face with tightly puckered kisses, while Parker jogged over to Kendra and dropped down onto the lawn chair next to her.

"Give me a drink, good-lookin', and I'll slobber all over your face."

She let the papers fall to her lap and eyed him censoriously. "Is that your erudite way of offering to trade kisses for my iced tea?"

"Yes, ma'am."

"In that case," she said, picking up the glass from the wrought-iron table at her elbow and passing it to him, "be my guest."

He took a long, cooling drink, wiped his mouth on the back of his hand and reached across her to return the glass to the table, purposefully brushing the tips of her breasts as he did so. She smiled secretively into his eyes, making silent promises as he leaned forward and fixed his mouth over hers. He kissed her leisurely, his hand slipping into her hair, his tongue making a lazy circuit of the inside of her mouth. When he pulled back, his eyes were smoky with desire. "You don't suppose Dan and Kate would want to baby-sit tonight, do you?"

"Maybe," she said. "I'll ask Kate."

"Naw, I'll ask Dan. He's a softer touch."

Kendra laughed. "True."

Parker settled back and mingled his fingers with hers. "What's that you're reading?"

She picked up the letter with her free hand. "It's Devon's answer."

"To what?" Parker asked, lifting his head.

"Oh, after he slunk away from the courthouse without speaking to me that day, I wrote him and demanded some answers. It seems he was out in the field until recently."

"Yeah, right," Parker scoffed. "It probably took him all these months to think up a good excuse for what he did that day."

"Well, it's pretty much what we figured," she said. "The Pendletons knew about my commitment to the medical field team and deduced that I'd had to beg off. They asked some questions of the right people and wound up in touch with Devon. He put two and two together and came up with fourteen."

"Thanks to Sandra Pendleton," Parker said. "I swear if she wasn't Darla's aunt, I'd tell her to kiss my—"

"But she is," Kendra cut in, "and so you won't. Besides, there's enough blame to go around. I did write that letter Devon read from in court, and you have to admit that Sandra's assumption that you'd duped me into marriage is understandable, given your reputation."

"What gets me," Parker said, "is how badly everyone underestimated you."

She was surprised and pleased. "Oh? How so?"

Parker smiled and leaned close again. "You know what they say, it takes a *hot* woman to change a scoundrel like me."

Kendra rolled her eyes. "I believe that's a *good* woman."

"Same thing," Parker claimed, grinning wickedly.

She laughed and crossed her legs as nonchalantly as possible in an effort to counter the melting desire building at their apex. "Well, now we know," she said primly, folding Devon's letter and cramming it back into the envelope with one hand.

"Yes, ma'am, we sure do," he agreed, wagging his eyebrows.

Kendra spurted laughter and laid her head back, closing her eyes. Parker followed suit, his thumb making lazy circles against her wrist. Kendra smiled, loving the tiny ways he constantly seduced her, proof that his ardor had grown rather than waned. She sighed, content with her world, but then a question that had long nagged her wormed its way into her mind. She lifted her head and looked at her husband.

"Parker, why do you suppose my mother didn't like sex? It had to be that. It couldn't have been my father."

He turned his head and opened his eyes. "I don't know, honey. Could've been any number of things, I guess. Something in her childhood, some trauma, even a simple misunderstanding. One thing I do know for sure, though, she could've passed that hang-up on to you, but she didn't. That says a lot about the kind of woman and mother she was."

"I guess it does at that," Kendra mused, squeezing his hand.

The screen door squeaked as Kate came out onto the patio. She slid a tray of salads and sandwiches onto the table and straightened, shielding her eyes from the glare of the late-summer sun with her hand. "Dan!" she called.

He stopped pushing Darla in the swing he'd hung from the same limb where he'd hung Kendra's twenty years earlier. "What is it, hon?"

"Lunch!"

"Coming." He lifted the safety bar and plucked Darla out of the seat, then started toward the house with her on his shoulder.

Kate looked down at Parker and Kendra. "Take my word for it," she said, her smile just a bit smug, "whatever it was, it wasn't Dan." Kendra's mouth fell open. Parker just chuckled. Kate grimaced. "I know, I know, but I couldn't help it."

Parker hitched up an eyebrow at her. "What else couldn't you help overhearing?"

Kate glared down at him. "For your information, I'd be delighted to baby-sit tonight. That child's just as dear to me as she is to Dan."

Parker laughed aloud and bounced up to his feet. He kissed Kate on the cheek and started across the yard to meet Dan and Darla. "Thanks, *Mom,*" he tossed over his shoulder.

She drilled a hole into his back with her eyes, then dropped onto the chair he'd just vacated and slid a look at Kendra. "I didn't mean to eavesdrop," she said.

Kendra shrugged. "No secret about it. I'm sure you knew before I did really."

Kate nodded and said softly, "I can't help feeling sorry for her."

Kendra sighed. "I don't know, Kate. I'm convinced that she was happy in lots of ways. She missed something special, yes, but I think she had what she most wanted."

Kate looked out across the yard at her husband. "You can thank him for that, you know. He's one of a kind, Dan Ballard."

"Oh, I don't know," Kendra said, her smile private and sweet. Kate lifted an eyebrow and they both burst out laughing.

Dan and Parker trotted up then, Darla spread-eagled between them. "Man, I'm hungry," Dan said.

Kate grinned up at him. "You always are."

"Me, too," Parker echoed, setting Darla onto her feet. Kate and Kendra looked at one another and burst into fresh laughter. "What?" Parker asked, but nobody answered.

The men traded looks over the heads of their wives, shrugged and reached for what they wanted most. It wasn't salad.

*   *   *   *   *

Take 4 bestselling love stories FREE

Plus get a FREE surprise gift!

CONVINCING ALEX

Those Wild Ukrainians

Look who Detective Alex Stanislaski has picked up....

When soap opera writer Bess McNee hit the streets in spandex pants and a clinging tube-top in order to research the role of a prostitute, she was looking for trouble—but not too much trouble.

Then she got busted by straight-laced Detective Alex Stanislaski and found a lot more than she'd bargained for. This man wasn't buying anything she said, and Bess realized she was going to have to be a *lot* more convincing....

If you enjoyed TAMING NATASHA (SE #583), LURING A LADY (SE #709) and FALLING FOR RACHEL (SE #810), then be sure to read CONVINCING ALEX, the delightful tale of another one of THOSE WILD UKRAINIANS finding love where it's least expected.

SSENR

As seen on TV!
Free Gift Offer

With a Free Gift proof-of-purchase from any Silhouette® book,
you can receive a beautiful cubic zirconia pendant.

This gorgeous marquise-shaped stone is a genuine cubic
zirconia—accented by an 18" gold tone necklace.

(Approximate retail value $19.95)

Send for yours today...
compliments of *Silhouette*®

To receive your free gift, a cubic zirconia pendant, send us one original proof-of-
purchase, photocopies not accepted, from the back of any Silhouette Romance™,
Silhouette Desire®, Silhouette Special Edition®, Silhouette Intimate Moments® or
Silhouette Shadows™ title for January, February or March 1994 at your favorite retail
outlet, together with the Free Gift Certificate, plus a check or money order for $2.50
(do not send cash) to cover postage and handling, payable to Silhouette Free Gift Offer.
We will send you the specified gift. Allow 6 to 8 weeks for delivery. Offer good until
March 31st, 1994 or while quantities last. Offer valid in the U.S. and Canada only.

Free Gift Certificate

Name: _____

Address: _____

City: _____ State/Province: _____ Zip/Postal Code: _____

Mail this certificate, one proof-of-purchase and a check or money order for postage
and handling to: SILHOUETTE FREE GIFT OFFER 1994. In the U.S.: 3010 Walden
Avenue, P.O. Box 9057, Buffalo NY 14269-9057. In Canada: P.O. Box 622, Fort Erie,
Ontario L2Z 5X3

FREE GIFT OFFER   079-KBZ
ONE PROOF-OF-PURCHASE
To collect your fabulous FREE GIFT, a cubic zirconia pendant, you must include this
original proof-of-purchase for each gift with the properly completed Free Gift Certificate.

079-KBZ